Praise for the novels of Bella Andre

"Don't miss a single one of Bella Andre's titles."
—*Affaire de Coeur*

"Bella Andre has a knack for creating likable characters."
—*Book Junkies*

"*From This Moment On* is full of lovable characters, sizzling chemistry, and poignant emotion."
—Christie Ridgway, *USA TODAY* bestselling author

"If you are looking for something sweet and sexy, the Sullivan series by Bella Andre is absolutely perfect for you. Each novel in the series is unique, just like the siblings. However, there is one thing that all of the novels have in common: they are all amazing!"
—*Reading, Eating and Dreaming* blog

"I can't say how much I love this series without coming across as a gushing, babbling fool. This family rocks my world with awesome men and sisters, but also a closeness that only comes when a family truly cares for each other."
—*DelightedReader.com*

"*From This Moment On* is a stunning, poignant romance. I just absolutely fell in love with Nicola and Marcus. They are so sinfully sweet together… Bella Andre has penned a remarkable contemporary romance that will leave you craving more of this exhilarating family."
—*JoyfullyReviewed.com*

"Wow… This is something to make us sigh and believe in love."
—*Mrs. Condit's Book Reviews* on *From This Moment On*

"[Bella Andre] has a way of tugging the heartstrings with memorable characters, interesting plots as well as steamy love scenes… I laughed, I cried and I couldn't put the book down until I reached the end. I'm looking forward to reading more about the Sullivan family."
—*Romancing-the-Book.com* on *From This Moment On*

"I loved this book and I love this family. I love family series books, and this is setting up to be one of the best."
—*Smitten with Reading* blog on *From*

P9-DEK-954

Also by Bella Andre

The Sullivans

THE LOOK OF LOVE

Look for the next novel in The Sullivans series
CAN'T HELP FALLING IN LOVE
available from Harlequin MIRA August 2013

BELLA
ANDRE

From This Moment On

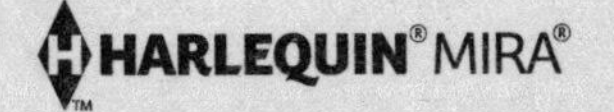

If you purchased this book without a cover you should be aware that this book is stolen property. It was reported as "unsold and destroyed" to the publisher, and neither the author nor the publisher has received any payment for this "stripped book."

Recycling programs
for this product may
not exist in your area.

ISBN-13: 978-0-7783-1557-5

FROM THIS MOMENT ON

Copyright © 2012 by Oak Press, LLC

All rights reserved. Except for use in any review, the reproduction or utilization of this work in whole or in part in any form by any electronic, mechanical or other means, now known or hereafter invented, including xerography, photocopying and recording, or in any information storage or retrieval system, is forbidden without the written permission of the publisher, Harlequin MIRA, 225 Duncan Mill Road, Don Mills, Ontario M3B 3K9, Canada.

This is a work of fiction. Names, characters, places and incidents are either the product of the author's imagination or are used fictitiously, and any resemblance to actual persons, living or dead, business establishments, events or locales is entirely coincidental.

® and TM are trademarks of Harlequin Enterprises Limited or its corporate affiliates. Trademarks indicated with ® are registered in the United States Patent and Trademark Office, the Canadian Trade Marks Office and in other countries.

For questions and comments about the quality of this book, please contact us at CustomerService@Harlequin.com.

HARLEQUIN®
www.Harlequin.com

Printed in U.S.A.

Dear Reader,

Every day when I sit down behind my computer to write about the Sullivan family, I get to laugh with my heroes and heroines, cry with them…and, best of all, fall in love with them.

While I couldn't possibly pick a favorite Sullivan, I have to confess that I'm head over heels for Marcus. As the oldest, he has always been mature, responsible and deeply concerned with the happiness of each member of his family. In fact, he's so intent on taking care of his brothers and sisters that he hasn't always remembered to pay attention to his own happiness. Writing about this strong, giving, wonderful hero was a joy from start to finish. It didn't hurt that he was also one of the sexiest heroes I've ever had the pleasure of writing, too.

In *From This Moment On,* one night is all Marcus and Nicola agree to share with each other. But growing emotions—and sizzling attraction—keep drawing them closer. But is it close enough for them to wonder if stealing one more secret moment together can ever be enough?

I hope you can steal a long, lazy day in the sun to spend with the Sullivans!

Happy reading,

Bella Andre

One

Marcus Sullivan was a man on a mission.

Twenty minutes ago he'd left his brother's engagement party and had headed straight for the belly of San Francisco's Mission District. Dance music pounded out into the streets, loud enough that the crowds waiting in line were already dancing.

Leather and piercings, tattoos and fluorescent hair, weren't part of the look of Marcus's usual crowd. Despite their wild appearances, the men and women in line looked happy, at least.

Marcus was planning on being a hell of a lot happier himself in a couple of hours.

Not, he thought, that he had any chance of being as happy as his brother Chase, who was now engaged to the woman of his dreams. One month ago, Chase had met Chloe in Napa Valley when her car had skidded off the road into a muddy ditch. Unfortunately, as soon as Chase got Chloe out of the rainstorm, he saw the bruise on her cheek and realized that she had much bigger problems than just a busted-up car in a ditch. It had taken Chase several days to gain her trust, and when she'd finally confessed what her ex-husband had done to her, Chase had given her the support she'd needed to report her abuser to the police.

The first time Marcus met Chloe he'd immediately been able to see that his brother was smitten. He also thought his brother had made a good choice in falling for Chloe. She was beautiful, but she was also a very sweet, intelligent, brave and loving person. She clearly loved his brother with the same passion and equal devotion.

Their whole family had been at his brother's engagement party this evening—even Smith, who was one of the biggest, and busiest, movie stars in the world. Chase was the first Sullivan to get engaged, and it was a big deal to all of them. Especially for their mother, who had been both pleased—and more than a little relieved—that one of her eight children had finally decided to take the plunge into "forever."

Marcus had enjoyed celebrating with his brother,

with his siblings and his mother. But throughout the party, he'd felt as if everyone had been looking at him, and wondering why he and his girlfriend, Jill, weren't yet engaged. After all, they'd been together for two years. And he'd settled down with her during those twenty-four months. Way down.

None of his family knew the reason why Jill hadn't come to the engagement party…and he hadn't wanted to ruin Chase and Chloe's party by filling them in on what had happened. Besides, he could still hardly believe it himself.

Even though he'd seen what Jill had done with his very own eyes.

The music from inside the club was getting louder as Marcus walked past the long line of people waiting to get inside. It seemed to him that everyone was at least a decade younger than he was, and even though that age difference should have made him feel out of place, he was even more certain that he'd chosen the right destination tonight.

He needed a complete break from reality, and a club full of twentysomethings in the Mission was as good a place to start as any.

Despite the fact that he was wearing a suit and tie, the bouncer took one look at him and opened up the latch on the rope to let him in. Marcus was a large man, with broad shoulders, and big hands that were capable of doing damage if ever his brothers and sisters had needed him to defend them when they were kids. Although he didn't often use his size to intimidate people, he wasn't averse to using whatever tools he had at his disposal when he needed them.

The dark, heavy beat of the music throbbed through him as he stepped through the black doorway into the crowded club, but neither it nor the strobe lights came close to obliterating his thoughts.

But that wasn't why he was here. He wasn't here to forget what he'd seen.

No, Marcus thought, his gut twisting at the sight of a couple holding each other close as they danced slowly together despite the fast-paced song. He didn't want to forget and he wouldn't let himself make that mistake again. He would never be that stupid, that blind, ever again.

Marcus was here tonight to make up for two wasted years. Twenty-four months ago, he'd met Jill in San Francisco on a hot August night. He was a guest at a charity event her firm was hosting, and Sullivan Winery had made a very sizable donation to the Children's Fund. As soon as he'd set eyes on her cool blonde beauty, he believed he'd found the missing puzzle piece in his life. He was thirty-four and had started to think about a family of his own, about a wife, and kids.

In Jill, he'd seen his future: marriage, kids, estate dinners at his winery with the perfect wife by his side.

Only, as he'd learned that afternoon, it hadn't been perfect at all…

Marcus could hear moaning even as he turned his key in the lock to Jill's apartment. It could have been a movie turned up too loud for the dirty parts, but Marcus knew better—had known better for months, if he was being honest with himself. Jill had been distracted and moody for a while now. He'd tried to convince himself that it was simply pressure from her job that was making her short with him, not to mention being less and less interested in sex. But when she'd stopped coming to Napa to relax at the winery on weekends, he'd had to admit to himself that their problems went deeper than too much work. They were deep enough that he'd tried to talk to her more than once, even though she kept pushing his questions away.

His hand stilled on the doorknob for a split second before he pushed open the door and moved through his girlfriend's apartment, the moaning growing louder with every step he took.

"Ooh, that's it! Right there! Just like that!"

Jill had always been a screamer in bed, but he'd never realized just how false it sounded until now, when he was getting a taste of her show from the cheap seats. His hands tightened into fists as he turned through her kitchen and headed down the hall to her master bedroom. He didn't really want to see this, but he knew he needed to. He'd been so stubborn about sticking with her…and as he heard her continue to scream her heart out in faux ecstasy with whatever guy she was doing, Marcus suddenly had to ask himself why?

He'd long ago asked her to move up to Napa to live at his winery with him, but she'd always had a reason to put it off. The latest was that her current apartment was a rare find barely a block away from her financial planning company with its frequent 4:40 a.m. wake-up calls. She told him he could stay over at her apartment whenever he wanted.

Only, the truth was that Marcus had never felt at home in her apartment. Everything was a cold shade of white with mirrored and glass surfaces that smudged at the slightest touch. It wasn't a home that children would ever be welcome in.

After growing up as one of eight siblings, he knew exactly what muddy feet and dirty hands could do to furniture like this. It wasn't pretty, but it was life. Real life.

His house in Napa Valley, by contrast, was full of large, comfortable couches, colorful rugs imported from Italy and artwork he loved, whether painted by a famous artist or an up-and-coming local painter.

But he'd wanted a future with her and he'd assumed making good on that future meant bending, compromising.

How many weekends had he come to the city to see Jill when it suited her? How many times had he changed his entire schedule at a moment's notice to be there for her when she needed him?

He knew his brothers and sisters all had an opinion about Jill, of course, but amazingly, they'd been fairly reticent about sticking their noses into his relationship with her. Maybe because they'd figured he would come to his senses eventually. Only Chase had recently tried to talk to him about Jill. But, by then, things were a big enough mess that Marcus hadn't exactly encouraged his brother's questions and concerns.

So, yes, Marcus knew he'd given up what he

wanted to try to make Jill happy too many times to count.

But never, not once, had he ever walked in on a live porn show, much less one starring his girlfriend.

She was riding the guy like he was a bucking bronco and she was the star rodeo rider. The only thing she was missing was the cowboy hat, boots and braided rein.

He saw naked skin and limbs—hell, he couldn't miss them from the bedroom door—but it was as if he was watching them from a clinical distance. Like watching a triple-X cable channel that had accidentally flipped on in a hotel room when he wasn't in the mood to watch strangers have nasty sex on TV.

And then, suddenly, the guy under his girlfriend noticed Marcus standing in the doorway.

"What the fuck?" He looked at Marcus with alarm. Clearly, he hadn't been expecting anyone to walk in.

That was when Jill shifted slightly to look over her shoulder at Marcus. Her eyes widened in what was supposed to be surprise. But he knew her well enough to see through it. For as much as her lover hadn't expected Marcus to appear, Jill had been counting on it.

How long had she been deceiving him with this guy?

And what other aspects of their relationship had been a lie?

Not rushing in the least, Jill moved to pull a sheet over her and her lover. As Marcus watched them slide apart, he could tell she was working on looking as seductive as possible as she covered up part of her nakedness. Her lover, on the other hand, was clearly trying to leave as fast as possible.

"I'll get out of here," the guy said as he reached over the side of her bed and yanked his jeans up off the floor, but Jill put her hand over his so that he'd stay on the bed.

"No, Rocco, you don't need to leave."

Rocco? His classically beautiful girlfriend, the woman he'd been planning to marry and start a family with, the woman he'd planned to share the helm of Sullivan Vineyards with, was screwing a guy named Rocco with a nasty-looking goatee and piercings? He looked to be barely in his twenties.

It had to be some sort of sick joke.

The guy looked between Jill and Marcus, going a little white as his gaze lingered on Marcus's fists and the way his shoulders took up the bulk of the doorway, but he remained right where Jill had him, staying on the bed like a well-trained pet.

Jill got up off the bed and dropped the sheet, then slid on a short, blue silk robe that had been draped over a chair in the corner of her room. She moved toward Marcus and informed him, "We should go talk in the living room."

Thankfully, she slipped past without touching him, but she was close enough for Marcus to smell sex on her. To smell some other guy on her.

He wanted to pound his fist into Rocco's face. But, clearly, Jill had engineered this. Start to finish.

So he'd deal with her instead.

Marcus moved back through the hallway to the living room where Jill was waiting for him.

She didn't look guilty. And, for the first time since that day in August two years ago when he'd seen her across a room and decided she was his future, he didn't think she looked beautiful, either. Yes, she was still classically pretty, tall and slim…but there was an ugliness stamped across her face that he'd never let himself see before.

"I'm falling in love with Rocco."

As apologies went, it sucked.

In his silence, as he simply stared at her in

the living room they'd shared dinners and movies and laughter that suddenly seemed so false, she continued with a defensive, "You and I both know our relationship wasn't going anywhere."

Finally, his response came. "I'm the one who wanted it to go somewhere. You said you needed time. I gave you time, enough time to screw around on me. With Rocco."

Jill's eyes widened at the barely repressed fury in his voice. He'd never spoken to her like that before, had never been the kind of man who raised his voice to make a point, or who opted to be a bully to get his way. He'd gotten where he was by working hard and being smart and reasonable, with some Sullivan charm thrown in when he needed it. Only when he was a kid had he ever used his fists to defend his brothers and sisters, and only when a bully wouldn't give up for any other reason.

"Look," she said with an irritated sigh as if he was entirely to blame for the mess they were in, "this thing between us, it was good for a while, at least at the very start, but if we'd really been in love we would be married by now."

He raised an eyebrow and called her on it. "You know I wanted to get married."

She shook her head. "We were together for two

years, Marcus. If you really wanted to marry me, you would have swept me off my feet so that I wouldn't have been able to resist. But you were always so busy with your brothers and sisters, always going to help your mother with something."

Her expression had finally changed from calculating to honest anger. "I tried to love you, Marcus. I really did. But I want something more. Something bigger. Something exciting. And I want someone who puts me first. All the time. No matter what else is going on in his life, even if his friends and family try to get in the way." Her eyes lit as she said, "I want what I have with Rocco, the way he thinks I'm so sexy and important. Not to sit by your side and wear pearls at your winery events. And not to always be the last priority in your life."

Marcus stared at the woman he'd so stupidly assumed would be his wife, the mother of his children. The pearl necklace he'd given her was still on her neck, the only thing she'd had on while she'd been having sex with another man.

She talked about his being too busy with his brothers and sisters, but what did she expect him to do? Walk away from them for her? He could have never done that—would have never done it—not when he was as much a father figure to his siblings as he was a brother. Because after their father had died unexpectedly when he was only forty-eight, Marcus had immediately stepped in to help his mother, especially with the younger kids who were only two and four at the time. He didn't regret one second of time he'd spent with his family.

Hell would freeze over before he'd apologize to Jill for still loving them now.

Especially when what he was mainly interested in at the moment was ripping the pearls off Jill's neck and watching them scatter all over the floor.

Instead, he said in a calm, cold voice, "I'll send my assistant for my things next week. She'll contact you to arrange a convenient time."

"See?" Jill came at him now, her finger pointed at his chest, her robe gaping open across her breasts.

He'd once loved her small breasts, thought they were just as classically beautiful as the rest of her. Now, they did nothing for him. Less than nothing. He silently swore that the next woman he was with was going to be the polar opposite of her, as wild as Jill was polished.

"This is why I can't be with you," she all but yelled at him. "Where are your emotions? Where is your passion? I swear you care more about your damn grapes than you do for me. And I sure as hell know you care more about your damn brothers and sisters than me."

Her chest was heaving with anger, but it all just seemed like pointless melodrama to him now. Hell, the second he'd opened the door to her apartment and heard her having sex with another man, it had been over.

"This is your chance, Marcus! Don't you see? If you leave now, if you can't tell me that you'll at least try to put me first, you'll lose me forever."

That was when he realized that despite his anger, despite his fury at her cheating, he didn't want to fight for Jill.

It had taken Marcus two years to convince himself that he actually loved her...and five minutes to finally realize he'd been wrong.

He didn't actually love her. He'd simply loved the idea of her.

"Goodbye, Jill."

The song switched from a hard-driving beat to a slower melody and rhythm as Marcus resurfaced from his dark memories. He walked over to the bar and ordered a shot of whiskey, then drank it without even tasting it. It burned like hell in the bottom of his gut and he pushed away from the bar.

He had planned to bring Jill to Chase and Chloe's engagement party earlier that evening, but he'd gone alone. What an idiot he'd been, waiting two years for Jill to make up her mind. Waiting for her to be "ready" to commit all the way to him and the life he envisioned for them.

Marcus knew love existed. He'd seen it between his mother and father. He saw it in every look Chase gave Chloe, in every touch between his brother and his new fiancée.

Still, that didn't mean Marcus was up to trying for it again anytime soon. A good long break from emotion was what he needed, a break from his plans. One day he still hoped he'd find a woman who would make him a good wife, a good partner, a good mother to the children he wanted.

But not right now—or for the foreseeable future.

Tonight, he was only in it for pleasure. He wanted a long night of mindless, emotionless sex with someone who didn't know his hopes, his dreams. A woman who didn't want to know about his family any more than he wanted to know about hers. A woman who simply wanted to go back to a hotel and do him. Hell, if neither of them even learned each other's names, that would be perfectly fine with him.

Couples ground against each other in the dark space where sweat and alcohol and sex were all coming together. Marcus moved deeper into the darkness to stand on a rise overlooking the dance floor and scanned the crowd with a clinical eye. A dozen couples ground together on the dance floor, dozens more single men and women flirted with each other by the bar and against the walls of the club. Everywhere he looked, people were looking at one another with hungry eyes, hoping that tonight would be their lucky night.

Marcus had vowed to find someone completely different from Jill. A wild, untamed woman that he could share a few hot hours with before returning to his real life out in the vines of Napa Valley.

He'd definitely come to the right place.

Nicola Harding stood in the window of her penthouse suite looking down on San Francisco's Union Square and watched the people walking on the street below. On a Friday night, people were heading home from work, getting ready for a night out on the town with friends, or a date with the person they hoped was *the one.* Some rushed, some moved slowly through the crowds;

some laughed with such obvious joy that she swore she could almost hear the sound of their laughter through her closed penthouse window.

She was young and single. She knew she should be out there with them, having fun.

Six months ago, she would have been eating dinner at some glitzy restaurant, surrounded by people who were flattering her and trying to make her laugh, trying to win her favor. But she'd learned the hard way that it wasn't her they were interested in.

Nicola Harding, who liked Monopoly and building sand castles and reading biographies of successful entrepreneurs, was an inconsequential nobody. Everyone wanted a piece of *Nico.* They wanted to say they'd hung out with a pop star. They wanted to take pictures of her on their cell phones to text to their friends.

She stepped away from the window and turned back to the huge penthouse suite.

It was too big for one person, but her record label thought putting her up in a place like this for a video shoot and concert was the way to treat her right. No one would ever know how alone she felt, one small person in an oversize suite that could have housed her entire family with room to spare.

She thought about calling her old best friend

Shelley, from high school, and seeing what she was doing, but she discarded the idea before she'd picked up her phone. Things had started to get a little weird between them when Nicola first became famous. And after those horrible pictures had surfaced of Nicola and her ex-boyfriend Kenny…well, it was clear to Nicola that Shelley didn't have the first clue what to say to her.

They were too different now, she supposed. Shelley was engaged to her boyfriend, a guy she'd met at college. They were planning to buy a house and move ahead with their careers and get a dog. Whereas Nicola was always on the road, flying to exotic locations all over the world to do interviews on TV and pose for photos and play shows for thousands of fans.

And the truth was, if she were a stranger reading her press, she certainly would never come up with the word *alone* to describe herself. *Party girl* would be closer. Because, somehow, thanks to tabloids and blogs that couldn't get enough of celebrity culture, and photographers who lurked around every corner, every single event found her photographed with another famous man, no matter how hard she tried to avoid getting into situations that the press could turn around on her.

Inevitably, she'd wake up in the morning and

turn on her computer to learn—via the popular entertainment blogs—that she was systematically screwing her way through not only the Top 40 charts, but through the rest of Hollywood, as well.

Her record label, PR people and management team had told her that "any press is good press" enough times that she'd stopped protesting her innocence to them. Besides, she knew they didn't believe her, not after seeing the pictures that had leaked over the holidays last year—horrible pictures that still seemed to turn up whenever she thought they were finally buried.

After working for years to try to get people to listen to her music, she'd been overjoyed to see her work pay off with her first number-one hit last summer. Although everyone had warned her that the business would chew her up and spit her out if she wasn't careful, she'd believed it was different for her, that she was smart enough to surround herself with good people.

Until the day she allowed herself to trust the wrong one.

Kenny had been so charming, so sweet, at first that, despite his bad-boy looks, she'd fallen for him hook, line and sinker. He'd been one of the engineers who had worked in the studio she used to record at in Los Angeles, and she'd thought they were the perfect pair: the girl with the guitar and the songs and the guy with sound boards and industry cred.

At first there had been flowers, special nights out at fancy restaurants, even a poem he claimed to have written for her. Her manager, along with several of the musicians who toured with her, had been a little leery of Kenny, and had cautioned Nicola not to move too fast into a relationship with him. But Nicola had been like a million other girls who told themselves their boyfriends were simply "misunderstood." She'd loved that she was the only one who saw how good he really was beneath his rock-and-roll exterior.

It wasn't until she was in too deep that she started to see the way he used emotions as if they were bargaining chips. And soon she found the only way to keep him happy—and to be sure he still "loved" her—was to give in to some of the things he wanted her to try.

Stupid girl.

A thousand times since then—no, more like a million—she'd asked herself how she could have been so naive. Naive enough that when her manipulative boyfriend sold his story of wild nights with the pop star, complete with pictures that he'd secretly been taking of her on his cell phone, she'd actually been shocked.

Well, she'd learned her lesson. Big-time.

She would never again trust that easily. Especially good-looking men who were intent on charming her.

Nicola caught a glimpse of herself in sweatpants and a tank top in the full-length mirror on the living room wall. Some party girl she was. After a grueling day of rehearsing dance moves for the video they would be shooting in a few days, her big plans included watching a *CSI* marathon on cable under the covers of her king-size bed. A bed that she could stretch out in however she wanted to because she was the only one who would be getting into it while here in San Francisco.

Ugh, the thought of sleeping alone shouldn't make her stomach hurt. After all, she'd rather sleep alone than with a snake like Kenny. But just because she knew she was better off alone didn't make the long hours of an empty Friday night any easier to fill.

She knew she was pretty—small and curvy with legs that were longer than they should be for her height. Maybe even beautiful with the right hair and makeup and clothes. But even when she was dressed to the nines—or in an outfit that was just this side of too skimpy—she still felt more like the girl-next-door than she did a pop star.

Because she *was* the girl-next-door, regardless of what anyone else believed to be true about her.

The doorbell rang and she realized she'd forgotten about the ice cream she'd ordered from room service. On a night like this, she simply didn't have the energy to care that a hotel staff member would see her without any makeup on and immediately get on Twitter and tell the world about it.

No question about it, chocolate ice cream was her last hope tonight.

She opened the door. "Hi."

The guy looked at her, then looked over her shoulder for the real Nico. Finally turning back to her, his features twisted in recognition.

"I've got your room service, Nico."

She stepped aside so that he could wheel in the big tray, even though she could easily have just picked up the container on top.

"It's the brand you asked for. A quart of it."

"Thanks." She took the pen he handed her to sign the room tab and felt, like laser beams, the guy's eyes on her hips in the snug sweatpants. She'd been feeling those eyes from one guy or another for the past ten years, ever since she'd woken up one morning as a teenager with breasts and hips.

She didn't even mind the leering. What she minded were the assumptions that came with it, that just because she had a figure that guys drooled over, it meant she was going to hop into bed with them indiscriminately.

She wasn't a slut, no matter what the world thought.

She went to hand him back the pen, but he was too busy staring at her chest to notice.

Nicola always made it a point to be nice to the staff anywhere she was staying. It wasn't that long ago that she'd been waiting tables and cleaning hotel rooms while she waited to be "discovered."

Tonight, she was all out of nice.

"Here." She jammed the pen into the guy's palm, then went to the door and held it open for him.

He moved slowly toward it and she was counting the seconds until he was gone when he asked, "Are you all alone tonight?"

Seriously? She had to deal with this just to get some ice cream? Her record company preferred to send her on the road with an assistant who could keep an eye on her, but Nicola hated feeling like she couldn't just relax and be herself when she was offstage. Tonight, however, she wished she had one of those handlers with her to take care of this jerk.

"I've got plans already, thanks," she said. The guy nodded, but she didn't like what she saw in his eyes. "My boyfriend will be up in a minute," she lied.

"Well, if you're looking for company later..."

Damn it, she was sick and tired of people making these sorts of assumptions about her!

"All I needed you to do was bring me ice cream. That's it. Not to try to hit on me. You don't know me at all," she reminded him, before adding, "and I don't see any reason not to report you to the hotel manager."

She headed over to the nearest phone and was about pick it up when he said, "I didn't mean anything by what I said. It's just that you're all alone and—"

He stopped babbling when he realized he wasn't helping himself at all.

"So what if I'm alone?" she threw back at him, unaccountably defensive over his use of that word. It was almost worse to have her own loneliness pointed out than it was to have her body ogled. "Not everyone needs to go out partying on a Friday night to have a good time."

He was backing up toward the open door now, clearly wishing he'd never opened his mouth at all.

"Seriously, Nico, I'm really sorry about whatever I said to upset you. And I...I really need this job, so if there's a chance that you could forget about this, I'd, uh, really appreciate it."

She sighed and put down the phone, knowing she'd never be able to live with herself if he lost his job because of her. Even if he had been out of line.

"Fine."

He raced across the threshold then, and she didn't hesitate to slam the door on his rapidly retreating heels.

The ice-cream container was starting to sweat on the table where she'd set it, but she wasn't in the mood for it anymore.

It wasn't fair. The whole world thought she slept around indiscriminately when the truth was that she'd had sex with a grand total of two guys. Brad from twelfth grade in the backseat of his dad's car. And then Kenny, because she'd thought they loved each other.

Even worse, neither of her previous lovers had

been all that great. Brad, she could forgive, because it had been the first time for both of them and their location had been terrible. But Kenny, she'd finally realized, simply hadn't cared about making her feel good. He'd been all about himself the entire time and she'd only fed into it by constantly trying to please him so that he'd "love" her more.

If she'd at least ever experienced anything approaching real pleasure, maybe she wouldn't be so bitter about her reputation. Maybe then she could just own it. Maybe then she would actually feel like the sexy woman she portrayed on her album covers and in her music videos, instead of like a girl playing dress up.

And maybe then she wouldn't have made her choreographer, Lori, stay so long with her tonight, long past when she should have let the woman leave for her brother's engagement party. It occurred to Nicola suddenly that Lori had probably agreed to stay because Nicola seemed so lonely to her, too. Heck, if the clueless guy delivering ice cream to her hotel room could see it, everyone must be able to.

All of a sudden, a crazy impulse hit her square in her solar plexus: since she was never going to shake off her reputation, what if she went out to earn it instead?

Nicola had always been impulsive, from the time she was a little girl. Her report cards said the same thing, year after year: "Nicola is a bright girl, but she often acts without thinking."

Okay, she thought as she tossed various articles of clothing onto the bed and tried to figure out just the right look for what she wanted to accomplish tonight, so she'd learned her lesson about trusting jerks. And, of course, one day she wanted love. Real love. True love.

But tonight all she wanted was to feel something besides remorse and loneliness.

She was tired of living like a nun, sick of trying to constantly convince everyone that she wasn't a wild party girl when they all thought she was regardless. For just one night she wanted to know what all the fuss was about. She wanted to find a man to share her passions with, a real man who was experienced enough to take her to a place she'd never been before.

She thought about wearing tight, shiny black pants and a sparkly top that showed several inches of her midsection before tossing them aside. She didn't want to look tough tonight. She wanted to look sexy. Wild. And so dangerously sensual that people would see that nothing, and no one, could ever tame her.

Her heart beat hard as she stripped off her sweatpants and tank top and slipped into a short, strapless leather dress. One wrong move in any direction and the T and A she was so famous for would be popping out for the entire world to see.

But, suddenly, Nicola didn't care anymore. Anything was better than this bone-deep loneliness.

So she'd end up on the cover of another tabloid magazine. At least she'd be in control this time.

She'd been on the cover of lots of magazines, had been front and center on plenty of entertainment blogs with headlines she'd been embarrassed for her parents to read. And she'd survived.

Well, mostly, anyway.

Two

Marcus was known for his patience. After helping to raise his seven siblings, he'd learned to wait out tantrums, fistfights, even tears.

Tonight, he was all out of patience.

He'd been watching the women on the dance floor for long enough to know that he wasn't interested in taking a single one of them to bed. Plenty of women had tried to get his attention during the past thirty minutes, and more than one had walked over to try to engage him in conversation. But he hadn't even had to speak to them to know he wouldn't be spending the night with these woman, not when he could practically smell the desperation on them. He knew what he'd come here for tonight, but there was a big difference between *wild* and *easy.* And none of the women who'd walked in through the thick red curtain—

which separated the front door from the interior of the club—in the past thirty minutes had been contenders for his bed, either.

Then, suddenly, the curtain parted…and *she* walked in.

Marcus felt like a fist had slammed straight into his gut.

The woman was young, mid-twenties probably, and so damn beautiful it almost hurt to look at her. Her black leather dress left nothing to his imagination, fitting her like a second skin with wide cutouts that ran down the sides of her insane curves.

Where Jill was tall, this woman was tiny. Where Jill had been slender and controlled, this woman was luscious and…utterly untamed. There was nothing desperate about her. And despite how revealing her outfit was, and how much of her gorgeous legs were on display between the short leather hem and the sexy straps of her very high heels, there was nothing *easy* about her, either.

A man would have to work to please her…and wouldn't mind begging for his own pleasure if it meant getting to be with her.

She was the one.

As she stood in the doorway and slowly scanned the crowd, every eye in the room was on her. She was magnetic, had that special something that made it impossible to pull your eyes away from her. Lord knew he couldn't pull his eyes from her, didn't ever want to stop drinking her in.

And then her eyes met his, illuminated by a beam of light in the dark room, and although Marcus hadn't drunk nearly enough at the bar to be unsteady on his feet, one look at those clear blue eyes had him fighting for balance.

What was wrong with him?

He needed to remember, at all times, what tonight was about. Sex. Pleasure. Not emotion. Not a relationship. It was okay for certain parts of his body below the waist to react like a match had been lit from nothing more than looking at this woman. But everything else was off-limits. He wasn't looking for a woman to respect. He was looking for sex, pure and simple.

And he sure as hell wasn't going to fall in love.

It was why he'd come to this part of town, to this club. Because there was no way on earth that he could possibly meet a woman here that he would end up falling for.

Marcus let his gaze move down the woman's barely there leather dress. From the look of things, it didn't appear as if respect was going to be much of an issue. There was only one reason why a woman would go out to a club wearing a dress like that…and he knew it had to be the same reason he'd come: for one wild night with a stranger to obliterate real life for a few sinful hours.

And then, the dangerous curves began to shift beneath the thin layer of leather and he realized she was moving. Straight toward him, never once breaking stride, even in impossibly high heels.

The eyes of everyone in the club, both male and female, followed her over the cement floor, but she didn't acknowledge anyone else. Only him.

Marcus lifted his gaze from her made-for-sex body and couldn't miss the challenge in her eyes, a look that asked if he was man enough to handle her, despite the fact that she had to be at least a decade younger than him. He couldn't wait to prove to her that he most definitely was capable of not only handling her, but giving her more pleasure than she'd ever had before.

He'd come here tonight to find a woman, to proposition her, to claim her for one no-holds-barred night. Instead, it looked as if he was the one who was about to be propositioned.

He'd always liked his women tall and slim, not barely coming up to his chest like this one. And he'd never been with a woman who was this much younger than him, had never even been tempted.

And yet, as a voice in his head told him she was way too young for him, young enough that if this were any other night he'd walk away from her now, he couldn't stop thinking that if things had gone as he'd planned for the past two years, he wouldn't even be here.

But he was.

And he wasn't planning on walking away from whatever this incredibly sexy woman offered. Not until first light.

Definitely not until he'd had his fill of those curves.

My God, he was beautiful.

Talk about big and strong—if this guy's broad shoulders and gorgeous face weren't enough, he stood out from the rest of the scummy crowd in his pressed shirt and slacks, clearly not giving a damn that he was different from them all. His dark hair was just slightly too long as it brushed over his collar; his jaw was chiseled and covered with a five-o'clock shadow that made her want so badly to reach up to feel the bristles against the sensitive pads of her fingers, and his mouth was full yet utterly masculine.

But it was his dark, hungry gaze that had held her spellbound from the first glance.

He was the one.

The hassle of getting inside with all of the people in line clamoring to take pictures with her and have her sign autographs for them the second she'd stepped out of the cab had almost been enough to make her hop right back into the taxi and go back to hiding out in her hotel.

What had she been thinking, coming out to a club to find a man? Especially when she knew darn well that pictures of her and the guy would surface on the internet within hours. Not to mention the fact that her label and manager were going to freak out if they found out she'd come to a place like this without at least one bodyguard.

But she was sick of feeling like a prisoner in her gilded penthouse prison. She'd remembered overhearing about this club from some of the dancers working on her video shoot and it had seemed like the perfect place to let loose for one night.

So despite knowing better, she just didn't care about the price of fame tonight, or about the inevitable ramifications of what she was doing. Not when a long, lonely night was all that waited for her in her hotel suite if she turned tail and ran.

And thank God she'd kept her courage up, because she'd barely walked into the club when she saw him. Beyond glad that she hadn't chickened out at the last second, Nicola was practically licking her lips as she approached the man who held every ounce of her attention.

He was the exact opposite of Kenny, broad and muscular where her ex had been thin and narrow. Kenny had frequently worn skintight leather pants and in a club like this would have likely taken his shirt off the second he got inside to show off his tattoos. In contrast, this man looked like he could be in a magazine ad for Hugo Boss wearing the expensive suit that had clearly been tailored to his exact measurements.

This was what a real man looked like, she found herself thinking. Kenny, she suddenly realized, had been nothing more than a kid playing dress up in a rock star's closet.

As she moved closer, it was pure instinct to try to make herself look more attractive. She pushed out her breasts, swayed her hips that extra little bit. Yes, she often silently bemoaned having to use her sexuality to get things out of people, but darn it, when it worked so well, what was a girl to do?

And she really wanted tonight to work out.

Especially now that she'd finally seen a man she absolutely had to have.

She waited for him to say her name, for that flicker of recognition to rise in his eyes. Two years ago, she wouldn't have been sure if he'd know who she was, but after the way she'd been splashed across all kinds of media thanks to Kenny and the secret pictures he'd taken of her, she rarely met anyone who didn't recognize her.

But when he simply stared down at her with gorgeous dark eyes that were full of a desire he wasn't trying to hide, and still hadn't mentioned her name after several long seconds, it finally occurred to her that he might not know who she was.

Or, she thought with the cynicism that had taken deep root within her post-Kenny, maybe he was just faking it because he thought it would pique her interest in him if he seemed aloof.

"Hi, I'm Nicola." Her real name popped out before she realized it. She hadn't gone by anything but Nico for so long with anyone but her parents that the name felt strange on her tongue.

Kind of good, too, though.

She waited for him to correct her, to be surprised that she hadn't introduced herself as Nico. Instead, he simply repeated her name.

"Nicola."

His low, rough voice had her shivering, goose bumps actually rising on her arms despite the swampy heat of the club from all the moving bodies.

In the dim light, with attraction pulsing between them, she made herself pull back enough to carefully study him. She could see that he knew what she was doing, even if he didn't understand her reasons, and she liked the way one corner of his mouth quirked up just the slightest bit while he allowed her the time to make her assessment.

Finally, she decided there truly wasn't a shred of awareness in his brown eyes. Nothing at all that resembled the way the guy at the hotel had looked at her, like he was dying to say he'd hung out with a pop star.

Had she actually run into the one person on earth who had no idea who she was?

It felt too good to be true.

Of course, even if she had just gotten lucky, she knew her luck would only hold out so long in a public place. From the moment she'd walked in, everyone's eyes had been on her—and now everyone was watching the two of them. Normally, she wouldn't care. She was used to people staring, had figured out how to mostly tune it out, even if she still felt like a bug squashed under the lens of a microscope from time to time.

But, suddenly, she wanted more than just a night of hot sex with a gorgeous guy. She wanted to experience it as Nicola. Not Nico.

Which meant she needed to get them out of the club as soon as possible, before any of the strangers staring at her from over by the bar or the dance floor came up and asked for an autograph or a picture with her.

"I'm not in the mood to dance tonight..." she began, before realizing, "Actually, I don't know your name."

She liked the way that didn't stop him from reaching out to brush a lock of hair out of her eyes. She liked it even more when he said, "My name is Marcus." He looked down at her mouth, then back up at her eyes. "And I'm not in the mood to dance, either."

She supposed there were lots of things they could both say to each other. Things like, "Should we get out of here?" or "Why don't we go back to my place?" But, amazingly, Nicola realized those words, those questions and answers, weren't necessary.

Everything they'd needed to say to each other had already been said.

In one look.

In one touch.

Her skin burned where he'd touched her, his fingertips rougher than she'd thought they would be given his clothes, and so much warmer, too. She'd felt calluses and strength in that one brush across her skin. The thought of being touched like that—with those hands—on even more sensitive parts of her body had heat blooming inside of her in places that had very rarely gotten that warm, let alone sizzling hot.

Following the instinct that had brought her this far, Nicola turned without another word and began to move back to the door through which she'd just entered. A moment later, Marcus's large, warm hand was on the small of her back as he followed her. She often traveled to events with her main bodyguard, a man who was even bigger than Marcus. But she'd never felt so safe, so protected.

And never this tingly, head to toe.

The sizzling warmth from the spot on her lower back where he was holding his hand against her quickly spread down her hips and across to her stomach and breasts.

The music was still playing, louder than before,

perhaps, but all she could hear was the beating of her own heart.

And all she knew was that she wanted this night with Marcus more than she'd wanted anything in a very long time.

Still, in the back of her mind she knew that what she was doing was stupid, not just because of the pictures that would surface of her with a "mystery man," but because she shouldn't be leaving a club with a man she knew nothing whatsoever about. For all she knew, he was a sadistic murderer out trolling for his next decapitation victim. But the way he was touching her, so carefully and yet with such assurance—along with the way he'd gently stroked her face—made her want to trust her initial instincts about him.

They stepped out into the cool night air, and while it was such a welcome relief from the swampy heat of the club, it didn't do anything to lessen the heat that had built up inside of her from nothing but a look, a touch.

Marcus kept his hand on the small of her back as he hailed a cab, and even though she had always believed in taking care of herself, she couldn't deny how nice it was to give up the reins for a few moments, even if it was just something small like finding a taxi.

The crowd waiting outside the club was a fairly loud bunch, but she'd noticed the way their chatter had died down when she had come back outside. Now, without having to look, she knew there would be dozens of cell phones trained on her and Marcus and she made sure to keep her hair in front of her face so that it would be harder to identify her. Fortunately, Marcus's back was to the line of hopeful clubbers. Still, she'd been famous for long enough now to know that pictures taken from a distance wouldn't be enough for the crowd.

Normally, she wouldn't mind taking pictures with fans. She adored her fans, who were, after all, the reason she was able to keep making music for a living.

But tonight—for one precious night in Marcus's arms—she wanted to be nothing more than a pretty girl having a one-night stand. If strangers started coming up to talk to her and take pictures, she'd have to explain to Marcus who she was. Something told her that, unlike Kenny, Marcus might be one of the only men on the planet who wouldn't relish the idea of having sex with a pop star.

Fortunately, just as she saw a group of people start to leave the line and head toward her—one of them even calling out, *"Nico!"*—a taxi pulled up. Marcus opened the door for her and she kept her long hair over her face to hide her profile from the driver, just in case he took one look at her and blew her cover as a regular person.

Her gut churned as she slid inside, then tightened down hard as her soon-to-be lover joined her on the ripped leather seat. It was then that she realized just how big he really was. Compared to most of the anorexic singers and actresses she knew, even though she wasn't tall, Nicola had never felt tiny before. But sitting next to Marcus made her feel shockingly small and feminine.

He was so big, had so much presence, she swore there wasn't enough oxygen left in the car for her or the driver.

"Where to?" the driver asked, giving her a blank look in the rearview mirror.

Unexpectedly, the stranger's voice was what finally broke the spell that had pulled her toward Marcus from that first glance.

Oh, God, what she was doing?

Yes, she wanted Marcus. Desperately.

Yes, she was lonely. Terribly lonely.

But neither of those things were good enough reasons to act like an idiot or to put herself in a dangerous position. After all, look what had happened when she'd trusted her instincts with Kenny. What he'd done hadn't only hurt her, it had ended up hurting her family, too.

She could still hardly believe her mother had lost her position on the school board, that the community had dared to accuse her mother of not being a good role model for the other parents because she'd obviously made huge mistakes in teaching her own daughter right from wrong. Nicola couldn't deny she'd been more than a little stupid with Kenny, but wasn't it bad enough that she beat herself up about it every single day? Why did everyone in her hometown also have to take it out on her family? However poorly she might have behaved, it wasn't their fault.

As panic rose higher and higher inside of her, Nicola blindly reached out her hand for the door handle, readying herself to escape out the other side.

"I'm sorry." She suddenly felt like she couldn't breathe right, like everything she'd worked so hard to rebuild for herself since Kenny was about to collapse in around her if she didn't get out of the taxi right that second. "I can't do this. I don't know you."

Marcus didn't try to stop her, didn't put a hand on her to keep her from opening the door. Instead, just as she was pushing open the door, he pulled his cell phone out of his pocket and held it out to her.

"Call anyone in here."

Amazingly, his deep, calm voice managed to cut through her panic. Plus, she was so stunned by his offer, that instead of leaping out onto the street to get away from him, she stilled and turned her gaze back to his beautiful face.

"Seriously?"

"Seriously," he confirmed. "Call them all if you have to, anyone you want. Ask them about me. You can ask them anything."

Surely he was kidding around. Who did something like this? Just handed over their cell phone and said to call any number on it to do a background check on him? It had been a very long time since Nicola had been able trust anyone completely—not since Kenny had hurt her so badly—and it was nearly impossible for her to wrap her head around what he was telling her she could do.

Cynicism dripped from every word as she said, "You really want me to surprise dial someone in your address book and say, 'Hey there, I just met your friend Marcus in a club. Could you tell me all about him, please?'"

He didn't so much as flinch at her tone, or her clear disbelief in him. "I want you to feel safe with me tonight, Nicola."

God, every time he said her name in that deep, rich voice, she got the shivers. What, she couldn't stop herself from wondering again, would it be like to be lying beneath him, naked and filled with him while he said her name?

A hot rush of desire moved over her, through her, at just how badly she wanted to find out.

The taxi driver cleared his throat and looked pointedly at them in his rearview mirror, but Marcus didn't acknowledge the man's irritation with them.

She liked that he clearly had no intention of being rushed, and that it seemed like he was happy for her to take as long as she needed to make up her mind about leaving the club with him.

Before she could reconsider, she took the phone from Marcus and dialed the most recently called person, someone named Mary. It was probably his wife, Nicola thought with a fresh dose of cynicism as the number rang a handful of times.

After several rings, a woman picked up. "Marcus, I wish you hadn't left the party without saying goodbye."

Surprised at a voice that clearly belonged to an older woman rather than a lover waiting for Marcus to come over and do her later tonight, Nicola finally said, "Um...hi. This isn't Marcus. He—"

She felt like a total idiot sitting in the back of a cab trying to find the right words to say to a complete stranger on Marcus's recent calls list. All while Marcus watched her with those dark eyes.

Knowing she had to at least take a stab at explaining to Mary why she was calling, Nicola said, "He just gave me his phone and said I could call you."

There was a brief moment of silence before the woman she'd just dialed said, "Is my son all right?"

His mother? That was the last person he'd called before coming to the club?

Nicola was stunned silent for a moment, before realizing she needed to reassure his mother. After all, a random stranger had just called her late on a Friday night using her son's phone. She was probably picturing a car accident, or worse, at this point.

"Yes, he's fine. Perfectly fine."

Marcus was leaning back against the seat, his arms folded across his chest as he watched her fumble through this unexpected conversation. He wasn't smiling, but the corners of his mouth looked like they might be twitching just the slightest bit. Nicola had the thought that he was too mature, too good-looking, too full of heat and desire for her, to be considered "cute." But right then as he tried not to smile while watching her navigate the conversation with his mother, *cute* was exactly the word that came to mind.

All these years, she'd never met anyone else who spoke with their parents as much as she did. Especially not a man, probably because they thought it made them seem less masculine.

Nicola found herself feeling exactly the opposite. A man who loved his mother won a lot of points in her book and, instead of seeing Marcus as less sexy, or as some kind of mama's boy, a glimmer of respect began to form for the beautiful stranger sitting beside her.

"Good," his mother said with obvious relief. "I'm glad he's fine."

Nicola knew she should simply apologize for bothering the woman and disconnect. Instead, she found herself saying, "Mary, can I ask you a question about your son?"

She could have sworn she heard a smile come across the line from this ridiculously patient woman who, for all Nicola knew, got calls like this every Friday night from the girls Marcus picked up to fool around with.

"Yes, you may, although I'd very much like to know who I'm speaking with."

"Oh. Sorry. My name is Nicola."

For the second time in one night, she was getting to be the girl she used to be, rather than the pop star she'd been playing for the past several years. It felt good to be normal for a night. So much better than she'd ever realized it would be. Nicola was too thankful for her music career to whine to anyone about the burdens of fame…but it didn't mean they weren't big sometimes. Like every time she walked outside, for instance.

"Nicola is a lovely name."

"Thank you." Nicola tried to regain her bearings, but it was really difficult to do with Marcus continuing to stare at her, his eyes never once leaving her face.

"What would you like to know about Marcus, Nicola?"

Oh, God, she shouldn't be asking his mother a question like this, but if she hung up now she'd only be left with doubts. Doubts she didn't want to have if she and Marcus were going to be alone together and naked in a hotel room in a little while.

She looked up into his eyes and held his dark

gaze as she asked his mother, "Will I be safe with him?"

"Oh," his mother said after a moment, "well, that's certainly an unexpected question."

Nicola could feel her hand trembling slightly as she held the phone up against her ear. "Why is that such a strange question?"

"Marcus is my oldest son," his mother gently explained. "He helped me take care of his brothers and sisters when my husband passed away many years ago. I love all of my children and, without a doubt, Marcus is one of the most trustworthy men I've ever known. No one has ever needed to ask me if they'll be safe with him because the answer is so obvious."

"Obvious?" Nicola echoed as all signs of humor left Marcus's eyes and the heat surged between them again.

"Yes," his mother confirmed with perfect confidence, "you will be safe with him. Perfectly safe."

Nicola's heart shouldn't have swelled at his mother's words. She shouldn't have cared that the man sitting next to her was a good son and a good older brother. All that should have mattered was that she was going to be physically safe with him and, also, that he wouldn't dare hurt her now that she'd spoken with his mother and alerted her to what was about to go down.

And yet, she couldn't manage to pull her gaze away from his—or stop herself from feeling any of those things—as she said, "Thank you for telling me that."

"It was my pleasure, Nicola."

"I'm sorry I bothered you so late," she said suddenly, still feeling bad about worrying his mother with her out-of-the-blue call.

"It's no problem at all, although I would love to speak with Marcus for a moment."

"I'll give him the phone right now, Mary. And thank you." Nicola held the phone out, hardly able to believe she was actually telling the guy she was about to have a one-night stand with, "Your mother wants to speak with you."

This night wasn't going at all the way she'd thought it would. Well, meeting a ridiculously gorgeous guy in a club was right on track with her plans, but talking on the phone with his mom to be reassured that she wasn't going to end the night in a body bag…that just didn't happen in her world. In anyone's world, actually.

The conversation she'd just had with his mother made her feel almost as if she'd met him at some family gathering, rather than at a club downtown.

She watched him listen to whatever his mother was saying. A slight frown moved across his face before he said, "Yes, tonight. Before the party," and then, "Don't worry, I will….Yes, she is. Very, very beautiful."

Nicola felt herself flush as she realized he was talking about her to his mother, and that he thought she was pretty. No, not pretty.

Beautiful.

He wished his mother a "Good night," then slipped the phone back into his pocket. "Do you feel better now?"

"Your mom seems really nice," she said, rather than answer the question that suddenly seemed a thousand times more loaded than it had ten minutes ago, especially after the awkward phone call she'd just made to his mother.

She shifted on the seat, but too late, she realized her short leather dress had ridden up nearly high enough to flash Marcus a significant bit of bare thigh.

"She's great," he told her, even as his eyes moved to the inches of exposed skin he couldn't possibly miss, then back up to her face.

His jaw was tight, his expression full of desire…and something else she couldn't quite decipher. It was, she finally decided, almost as if he was warring with himself over wanting her as much as she'd been warring with herself over it a few minutes earlier.

The taxi driver interrupted them again. "Are you going or not?"

Marcus looked at her. "Nicola?"

If he'd said her name differently, if there'd been any pressure, any demands behind it, she might still have said no and gotten the heck out of there.

But his question was gentle enough to have her suddenly making up her mind. "I do feel better. Much better." Yes, her heart was still leaping around inside her chest, but not because she was worried about him being a serial killer anymore. "I'm ready to go with you now."

He reached across her lap to close the door she'd opened an inch before calling his mother, then told the driver, "Take us to the Fairmont."

Nicola's muscles instantly tensed again. Here she'd just convinced herself he wasn't some creepy star-stalker. Had she been wrong? How did he know she was staying at the Fairmont?

Or was it just a coincidence that he'd picked out her hotel as the place to have their tryst?

Obviously sensing her sudden discomfort, he turned to her and said in a low voice, "I don't live in San Francisco. The Fairmont is the best hotel in town."

She nodded. "It is."

He gave her a strange look and she realized she'd almost given herself away. Marcus clearly had no idea who she was, didn't know that no one other than her parents had called her Nicola in half a decade at least. He wouldn't think someone her age could afford to stay at the Fairmont, and if she wasn't a successful pop star, she certainly wouldn't be able to.

But if she let him take her to her hotel, he'd find out the truth about her as soon as they pulled up in front of the building and the staff called her by name…and catered to her every need. After all, she was staying in their most expensive penthouse suite for the week. The too-forward man who had delivered her ice cream earlier that evening had been a strange blip in the middle of the Fairmont Hotel's perfect, cultured luxury.

Trying to think quickly was difficult when sitting this close to Marcus sent her synapses flying off in a billion different directions, but she finally managed to say, "Is there anywhere we could go that isn't a hotel?"

"Your place is off-limits?"

Again, she nodded, hoping he wasn't going to

ask her for an explanation. She didn't want to outright lie to him, didn't want to have to make up some excuse about roommates. She didn't want to tell him she wasn't from San Francisco, either.

It was a heck of a position to be in, she suddenly realized. Here she was on the verge of taking off all her clothes with some total stranger, but she didn't want him to actually learn anything about her apart from how she liked to be kissed.

Sure, she knew he'd find out soon enough. As soon as he went back to his home—wherever it was—he was bound to see her face on some magazine somewhere, probably next to his from whatever pictures had been taken of them at the club.

But for one night she didn't want to have to live up to being Nico.

Instead, she wanted the chance to see what Nicola liked, what Nicola wanted, what Nicola desired. Then again, she supposed she already knew at least one answer to each of those questions.

She liked, wanted and desired Marcus.

And now that she was this close to the promise of real pleasure with him, she couldn't stand the thought of losing that chance.

As soon as she confirmed her place wasn't an option, he pulled his phone back out and texted something to someone. When it beeped in response a few seconds later, he gave the driver a street address. It didn't take a brain surgeon to figure out that he had a friend in the area with a place they could use.

She smiled at him. "Thank you." She'd always been a tactile person and, without thinking, she put her hand on his arm to emphasize her words. His hard—and big!—biceps twitched beneath her fingertips and she jumped. But before she could pull away, he covered her hand with his.

Oh, God, what was she doing? What made her think she could actually do this? What made her think she could go home with a total stranger?

Maybe if she'd had more experience with men she could have rolled with it better. But she couldn't even handle touching his arm, for God's sake! How was she possibly going to deal with seeing him naked?

Or touching him in other, much more intimate places?

Nicola belatedly realized Marcus was lightly stroking her hand with his fingers, as if she was a wild animal that needed to be calmed before it bolted. After the way he had brushed back the hair from her face at the club, and now this gentle caressing, she wasn't sure he could ever touch her in a way that didn't send her cells into Jell-O overdrive. And yet, at the same time, his gentle caresses were incredibly soothing.

Each stroke of his fingers over hers seemed to say, *I understand that you're nervous and that's okay. I'm going to take good care of you tonight. Just as I didn't rush you to make a decision to leave with me in the cab, I'm not going to rush you into anything you're not ready for in bed, either.*

Slowly relaxing again, she let herself scoot a little closer to him, close enough that it was pure instinct to lean her head against his broad shoulder.

This time, she felt *him* tense beneath *her* touch. But before she could freak out about doing the wrong thing, he was wrapping his arm around her shoulders and pulling her in tighter.

Her body wanted to be close to his so badly that without any conscious thought or planning, she found herself turning so that her cheek was laid against his chest, the steady beat of his heart sounding against her ear.

Nicola found herself smiling against his chest at the intimacy inherent in the way he'd pulled her closer on a groan of obvious need.

Intimate. Why did she keep thinking that word?

He was a stranger. This was supposed to be a night full of fun, hot sex. Nothing more.

But her conversation with his mother had whetted her curiosity enough that a part of her wanted to ask him about his family, to find out how many siblings he had.

No, she thought with some regret, she knew better, knew she had to tamp down that desire. Tonight was about a physical hookup. Not an emotional one.

And hopefully, if things went really well, she'd finally experience the hot sex she'd never had before. Besides, if she sat here and quizzed him on his family, wasn't all the sizzle bound to go out of their initial connection? Even if, strangely, talking with his mother about what a good man he was had only made her want him more....

As the driver slowly wound through city traffic toward the address Marcus had given, Nicola silently counseled herself to remember to keep her boundaries in place during the next few hours. Because no matter how good sex with Marcus ended up being—and she could already tell just from the way he held her in his arms that it had the potential to be really great—she couldn't make the mistake of connecting pleasure with love.

She didn't know Marcus. He didn't know her. As long as they made sure to keep things totally on the surface and all about pleasure, one night shouldn't affect their futures.

Only, the truth she didn't want to admit was that she already felt affected, simply by how good, how warm, how safe, she felt in the circle of his arms.

What, she found herself wondering, *would it be like to have a man in my life who would be there to hold me like this every night?*

Three

Nicola slipped into sleep, her breathing going slow and even, her previously tense muscles loosening against his.

Sweet.

God, she was so sweet, from the surprise in her big blue eyes when she realized she'd called his mother, to the fresh scent of strawberries in her hair, to her soft curves in his arms.

And now, she'd—very unexpectedly—fallen asleep in a complete stranger's arms.

Marcus guessed whatever his mother had said to Nicola must have really relaxed her, to the point that she would let down her guard this much. Even though the truth was that he could take her anywhere right now, could have her bound up and gagged before she could wake up enough to fight him.

The thought of that happening to her—the thought of what kind of guy she could have gone home with—had his heart pounding hard in his chest and his hand moving to stroke her hair again. More to soothe himself than her, this time.

She made a soft sound in her sleep, burrowing in closer to him like a kitten in search of warmth.

He couldn't help but be struck by the fact that nothing about his day had gone as planned, including this. They should have been checking into a hotel by now, getting ready to strip off each other's clothes. Instead, they were pulling up in front of his brother Smith's house in San Francisco and he was putting his finger to his lips as he paid the taxi driver, to let him know not to wake Sleeping Beauty.

As gently as he could, he lifted Nicola into his arms and out of the vehicle. He was just putting in the code for the security gate that surrounded his brother's property when her eyelids fluttered as she tried to come awake.

Looking down at her, he finally noticed the dark smudges beneath her long eyelashes. The club had been too dark for him to see the evidence of her exhaustion, but now he couldn't deny that as much as a part of him wanted to wake her up to make good on the implied promise of hot sex they'd made to each other in the club, he could see how desperately she needed this sleep. He didn't know her, but the vulnerability he'd seen on her beautiful face while she'd been talking to his mother had tugged at his heart despite his knowing better.

"Shh." He couldn't resist pressing his lips to her forehead and kissing her lightly. "You're safe with me, Nicola."

Her eyelids opened then, her pretty blue eyes fuzzy with sleep, as she softly said, "I know."

Her full lips, lips he'd been aching to kiss since the moment she'd walked up to him in the club and introduced herself, moved up into a little smile before her eyes closed again.

Just inside the gate, Marcus had to stop and regain his bearings to keep from stumbling with her in his arms. Not because Nicola was the least bit heavy. For all her gorgeous curves, she was a tiny thing.

It was the sudden trust in her eyes that had his knees weakening.

Jesus, the things he'd been planning to do with her tonight...

Guilt knocked straight into his gut as his previous visions of stripping her out of her dress came at him. Hell, he was still having those visions—

visions that were far more explicit now that he was actually holding her and breathing in her scent.

A stranger wasn't supposed to affect him like this.

A stranger wasn't supposed to fall asleep in his arms.

A stranger wasn't supposed to trust him with anything more than her body, her pleasure.

Since the age of fourteen, after his father had died, Marcus had been the one everyone could count on. He'd known his mother couldn't do it on her own and, overnight, he'd assumed the role of man of the house for his seven younger siblings. He'd thought Jill had liked his family and that she understood how much they still needed him. Instead, she'd been threatened by his connection to them.

How had he not seen that before?

In any case, tonight was supposed to be his night to cut loose. To shake off those trappings of responsibility.

Look where he'd ended up instead, with the responsibility of protecting a young beauty for a night from his own dark and dangerous desires. Desires that grew stronger with every second he held her soft curves in his arms, with every breath she took against him, her arms twined gently around his neck.

He stared down at the woman in his arms. Awake, her charisma, her strength of will and purpose, had been breathtaking. Asleep, he could only see the sweet vulnerability she'd shown while speaking with his mother in the taxi.

Damn it, regardless of his original intentions and the fact that she'd clearly walked into the club in her skintight leather dress and high heels with the same sexy intentions, hers was a vulnerability he now had no intention of taking advantage of.

Finally, he headed toward the front door. After climbing the front steps of the large house in the most exclusive part of San Francisco, Marcus unlocked the door and stepped inside Smith Sullivan's house.

Marcus and Smith were barely more than a year apart in age, but their lives were very different. Marcus enjoyed coming into the city from Napa to visit his siblings, or heading down to the peninsula to see his mother at one of the Sunday lunches she often put on for the family, but he spent the bulk of his time at his winery, and was happiest there out among the vines. Smith, on the other hand, had lived the bulk of his adult life "on location." Shooting a movie in Canada, filming a commercial in Hong Kong, attending a premier in Australia. Marcus couldn't imagine how hard it would be to travel that much, or to feel at all grounded while always on the move. It wasn't a life Marcus would want for himself, and he couldn't imagine anything—or anyone—that would ever convince him to make a sacrifice like that.

Smith had a whole host of houses around the world, not because he wanted to show everyone how rich and important he was, but because he liked to feel at home when he was filming his movies. Considering he'd shot several in Los Angeles, New York and London during the past few years, it made sense for him to buy a place in each city. He hadn't shot many films in San Francisco, but this was the home he always returned to in the rare spaces between projects. Smith made the best margaritas Marcus had ever tasted and his blender got quite a workout on those weekends he invited the whole Sullivan crew over to hang out.

Tonight, the house felt empty and unlived in, even though he knew Smith had someone who came in once a week to keep the surfaces dusted and clean.

Marcus had never called in a favor like this from Smith. Not because his brother was stingy with his possessions. The truth was, Smith would love for one—or more—of his siblings to stay in his mansion high on the hill, but all of them had enough pride to want to earn their own way. Even if it meant his little sister Sophie was living in a tiny apartment in a not-so-great part of town on her librarian's salary. Marcus couldn't keep up with the number of times Smith had tried to get their sister to move into his place. But she'd been firm in saying no.

But even though he knew there wouldn't be any payment expected for the favor of using Smith's place, after the text he'd sent his brother a few minutes ago—I need to use your place tonight—Marcus knew he'd be hearing from his brother to get the dirt on why he needed the house.

And who he needed it for.

Stepping past the foyer, Marcus looked over at the stairway leading up to the bedrooms, but somehow it didn't feel right to take Nicola up there.

If they'd stayed on track with ripping each other's clothes off, of course he would have taken her into one of the bedrooms. But considering that wasn't going to happen anymore, a bed would be too intimate. Not only did he not want her to wake up in the middle of the night and assume that something had happened between them, but he didn't want to tempt himself, either.

He had a bad feeling that getting too close to a bed with Nicola in his arms would do crazy things to his brain—possibly even help to convince himself that it would be okay to wake her up so that they could get into it together.

Fortunately, Smith's couches were as plush and comfortable as they came. Moving into the living room, Marcus laid Nicola down on the longest couch. He still wanted her bad enough that he knew the best thing to do would be to walk away now. Instead, he slipped off her high heels and the little purse she had wrapped around her wrist. Even her feet were pretty with painted toenails, and the skin on her calves was so smooth, looked so soft, that he couldn't do anything but stare for a few seconds. Nothing, that is, except to continue wanting her more than he could remember ever wanting a woman before. Especially a virtual stranger like her.

Even in her sleep, she seemed reluctant to let go of him and he found himself kneeling with her so that she could lie down and still have her arms around his shoulders. She sighed with pleasure as she immediately curled up into a ball on her side, her face toward his, her full lips turning up slightly at the corners as she slid one of her hands from his shoulder to slip it into his hand.

What would it be like to kiss that mouth?

Marcus had to work like hell to shove the thought away.

Those plans, those fantasies, were gone now. He was now on tap for a quiet evening watching over a beautiful girl whose scent and soft curves he wouldn't be able to forget for a very long time.

He covered her with a blanket that was thrown over the couch, then looked around for a pillow, but there were none. He could go upstairs to get one off a bed, but considering the way her hand had sought out his when she'd been shifting around getting more comfortable, he had a feeling she might wake up if he moved completely away.

Not letting himself overthink it—clearly, the time for thinking things through had passed the second he'd walked in on Jill and Rocco going at it in her apartment—he moved so that he was sitting on the couch by her head and shifted her so that his thighs became her pillow.

Nicola seemed unsettled again for a moment, her free hand pressing against his leg as if she was wondering why her pillow was so hard.

Without thinking, he captured that other hand with his free one. She immediately settled into him, curling into an even tighter ball on the couch beneath the thick blanket, reminding him again of the wild kittens that he often found sleeping in patches of sun at his winery.

He wanted her so badly that it was difficult to relax at first. Every breath she took moved her curves against him and stoked his libido higher, especially when her head shifted on his lap over his pounding erection. He was glad she was so soundly asleep; otherwise, she'd realize that his thigh muscles weren't the only hard thing she was lying on.

Calling on his steel will that had rarely, if ever, let him down, he forced himself to move his gaze away from her to the huge living room windows that overlooked the lights of San Francisco and the bay.

Marcus had been in other actors' houses over the years and he was always struck by how many pictures—and even paintings—they had of themselves. Almost as if they were afraid to ever let anyone, including themselves, look away from the face that had made them famous, just in case they were forgotten. Smith was the exact opposite. Not only were there no photos of him, there were no personal photos anywhere in the house. Of course, Marcus knew that Smith traveled with his family photos, and that if anyone stepped into a trailer on any one of his sets, they'd be bombarded with countless Sullivan family photos.

Yes, he thought, *thinking about his family was a good way to distract himself from how much he wanted the woman lying across his lap.*

None of the Sullivans spent much time in front of the mirror. Not even his sisters, except Lori when she was working. Her job as a choreographer meant she needed to keep a careful eye on her lines, her movements, her expressions, as she danced. And even though Marcus's mother had been a model when she was younger, he couldn't remember her ever wasting much time with makeup or hair. Raising eight kids would make it pretty damn hard for anyone to find the time to primp and be vain. Regardless, Mary Sullivan was a naturally beautiful, elegant woman.

His mother had asked him during the very brief conversation they'd had on the phone in the taxi if he and Jill had broken up. When he'd told her that it had happened before the party, the very next words out of her mouth hadn't been, "I'm sorry to hear that," but were instead, "Nicola sounds very nice. Take care of her tonight, Marcus."

"Don't worry, I will" was what he'd said before

confirming that Nicola was indeed as beautiful as his mother guessed she was.

Now, looking down at the woman sleeping on his lap, he knew with perfect certainty that his mother would agree with his assessment of Nicola's beauty.

His chest tightened again as he looked down at her pretty profile. Recognition tried to jog in his mind. He'd been so struck by his attraction to her right from that first glance that he hadn't been able to think of anything else.

But now, as he got the chance to simply stare at her, he found himself wondering if he'd seen her somewhere before. She did look vaguely familiar....

No, he decided a moment later. It was impossible.

Nicola wasn't a woman he could ever have forgotten.

He stared down at her for a long while, memorizing the curve of her cheekbones, the sweep of her eyelashes, the way her eyebrows arched and peaked, her slightly pointed chin that fit her so perfectly, the sweet curve of one ear.

The soft hairs at her hairline were several shades lighter than her current hair color and he wondered why she felt she had to change anything about herself when she was already perfect. One day, he found himself thinking, he'd like to see what she looked like with her natural hair color.

What the hell was he thinking? He wasn't going to see her again after tonight.

But he couldn't stop looking at her, not when she had to be one of the most beautiful women he'd ever seen in his life. And not when he still wanted her with a desire that, frankly, shocked him.

Somehow, he managed to drag his gaze up and away from her, to stare out at the city lights beyond Smith's living room window again. The view was spectacular—one of the best in San Francisco—but it had nothing on Nicola. He could see the two of them in the reflection, looking like a couple relaxing together on a Friday night.

His thoughts cycled back to his ex-girlfriend, to how furious he'd been to find Jill with Rocco. Then again, if he was being honest with himself, he'd been angry and frustrated for longer than that. For weeks, even months, as Jill had made more and more excuses about why she wasn't ready to get engaged, as she canceled one weekend together after another, as she committed to seeing his family at various events and then backed out at the last minute.

Earlier this evening, he'd assumed he'd be struggling with his fury toward Jill all night long. But since meeting Nicola, he hadn't thought about Jill once until now. And, amazingly, with Nicola sleeping on his lap and her hands in his, Marcus's anger was on a slow simmer rather than a rolling boil.

Sex was supposed to be his medicine tonight, not the soft, even breathing of a beautiful stranger.

And yet, instead of being even more frustrated by the turn his evening of mindless sex had taken, a smile was on his face as he leaned back against the couch, closed his eyes and fell asleep.

Four

Nicola could tell without even opening her eyes that she wasn't in her childhood bed. For one, her bed didn't smell like leather. Her pillow wasn't made of hard muscle. And there hadn't ever been anyone who had held her hands so gently.

She swallowed hard as she realized what must have happened. She'd propositioned a gorgeous man at a nightclub last night…and then she'd promptly fallen asleep on him.

Oh, God, how stupid had she been? Had she actually thought she was taking control of her life by going to that club to pick up a stranger to sleep with?

In the cold light of day that she hadn't wanted to think about last night, she had to face facts. First, she needed to come up with a game plan to get out of there with the minimum of embarrassment and awkwardness. She almost groaned aloud at the sure knowledge of just how difficult that was going to be. And then, after she left Marcus, she was going to have to deal with the fallout from being hooked up with a strange man in the press.

The irony that, once again, she hadn't actually done a darn thing with him—not even kiss him—wasn't lost on her.

And yet, as she lifted her lashes just enough to look around while trying to keep her breathing shallow and even so he'd still think she was asleep, she saw that he'd laid her down on a soft leather couch and covered her with a thick blanket.

She wiggled her toes beneath the blanket and a surprised smile moved onto her lips as she realized that while he'd left her leather dress on, he'd obviously thought to slip off her heels so that she'd sleep more comfortably. It had been sweet of him to think of that.

As she lay there on his lap, she knew that if they had actually been boyfriend and girlfriend she wouldn't have wanted to move away from him. Not when being with him like this made her feel so warm. And, amazingly, so safe, too. Safer than she'd felt in years, not since she'd still lived in her parents' house rather than in hotels throughout the world.

Despite the way they'd found each other last night, and the sexy things they'd intended to do with each other, Nicola couldn't remember the last time a stranger had taken such good care of her.

Sure, people were always trying to do her favors, but ninety-nine percent of the time it was because they wanted something.

But Marcus hadn't taken a single thing from her. Instead, he'd not only let her keep sleeping when exhaustion had gotten the best of her after countless hours of dance rehearsals for her video shoot, he'd also given her the best night's sleep she'd had in ages.

It had been six months, at least, since she'd slept really well. It didn't matter how soft the sheets were, how expensive the mattress, the bed always felt too big, and she couldn't seem to stop the racing thoughts in her head. She'd written a ton of songs when she should have been sleeping, and practiced dance moves when the songs all started to run together in her head. She supposed her music was getting better than ever, and she was starting to actually look like one of the professional dancers who shared the stage with her, but at the same time she could feel herself edging closer and closer to burnout.

How she'd longed to have a clear head. And how amazing it was that her chance to recharge had come in some stranger's house while lying on a man's lap. A man whom she knew nothing about beyond his first name, the fact that his mother was nice and that he was a good older brother.

That was when she felt his thigh muscles shift beneath her cheek and realized he must have figured out that she was awake. All at once she felt the way her tongue was sticking to the roof of her mouth. No doubt, in addition to having morning breath, she also had tons of mascara and eyeliner stuck to her face.

Nicola badly needed to go to the bathroom to clean up before she let him see her in daylight—before she faced him and apologized for not being the sex goddess she'd pretty much promised she would be the night before—and then she needed to get the heck out of there.

Pushing the soft blanket off, she quickly sat up and found her footing on the plush rug. She didn't say a word to him as she hurried off in the direction of what she desperately hoped was the bathroom.

It would be really embarrassing if she ended up

in a closet. So embarrassing, in fact, she'd already decided that if she guessed wrong, she'd just lock herself into it and die of mortification in private.

Fortunately, luck was on her side as she peeked in an open door between the living room and the kitchen and found a large bathroom.

Oh, God, she thought as she caught a glimpse of herself in the mirror, she looked like a witch. Not one of those pretty ones, either, that could put a love spell on any man she looked at. Nope, in the unflattering bathroom light she was definitely more like one of those evil ones who fed pretty princesses shiny red apples.

Her makeup must have melted against the heat of his legs and her hair was sticking up all over the place. If only she'd thought to bring her small bag into the bathroom with her, then she could have at least fixed her lipstick. As it was, all she could do was wash everything off her face with the bar of really nice-smelling soap.

Nicola hadn't grown up wearing makeup, but once she'd decided to pursue music, it had become a given. She still wasn't crazy about how it felt on her skin—which was sensitive enough that she now had everything custom blended so she didn't get a rash from wearing it during twelve-hour days in photo shoots and while taping videos for her songs—but she knew it made her look older, more mature and sexy. Without her makeup, she could likely pass for eighteen. If that. If her pop music career had ever been a bust, she figured she could have gone undercover in high schools.

Turning on the tap, she closed her eyes and cleaned off her face. Once that was done, she bent down to see if there would be a miracle of a toothbrush and toothpaste under the sink. Thank God, her prayers were answered, and a few minutes later her smile, along with her skin, was sparkling clean. All that remained was her hair, which she was able to finger-comb with a little water.

She looked at herself in the mirror and grimaced at the way her fresh-faced look clashed with her leather dress. Last night the dress had seemed like the perfect fashion choice. And, she supposed, it had been since Marcus had noticed her in it. But in the light of day, short, tight, barely there leather was borderline ridiculous.

What she wouldn't give to be able to change into jeans and a T-shirt right now.

And, oh, what she *really* wouldn't give to be able to sneak out of the bathroom—and the house—without having to face Marcus again. Only, he'd been so nice to her last night, and she just didn't feel right about sneaking out. Even if doing so would likely make the whole morning-after bit easier for both of them.

Nicola's heart was beating way too fast by the time she stepped out of the bathroom. Slowly, she tiptoed out into the hall until she could see the couch if she craned her neck. But it was empty.

Had he snuck out before she could?

The thought had her almost laughing with relief, but ten seconds later when she found him in the kitchen, she wasn't surprised he was still in the house. She barely knew him, but what she had learned about him last night told her he wasn't the kind of man who snuck away from anything. No, she guessed he was more than capable of facing even the most awkward situations head-on.

His back was to her and from the loud sounds coming from the room, she quickly guessed that he was grinding coffee beans. She didn't want to sneak up on him, but there really was no way to announce her presence apart from yelling louder than the grinder, which she wasn't going to do. Moving slowly toward him, far more cautiously than she had the night before in the club, she waited on the other side of the kitchen island for him to turn and notice her.

How, she wondered, was he managing to look as good this morning as he had last night? From the back, his clothes barely looked worn, and his dark hair certainly wasn't sticking up all over the place like hers had been.

Just then he finished grinding the beans and turned to her, looking as if he'd known all along that she was there. She stood there stunned as she looked at him. He was even more gorgeous this morning with a dark layer of stubble across his jaw. No man had ever taken her breath away before.

"Seemed like coffee would be a good idea," he told her with a smile that she could see was deliberately gentle.

She nodded, trying to smile, but she was so nervous her lips felt all wobbly and she was still having trouble catching her breath around him.

"Thanks," she finally got out. "Coffee would be great."

His eyes held hers for a long moment, almost as if he were assessing how she was feeling, and she swore he could see far more than any man ever had before. Even the few she'd actually been intimate with.

"I turned the heat up a bit. I thought you might be cold." He lifted a sweatshirt from the counter. "I know it's too big, but—"

She grabbed the thick cotton before he could

finish his sentence and pulled it down over her head. It was as if he'd heard her silent prayer to cover up her skimpy dress. A few seconds later, she looked down at herself in the ridiculously big sweatshirt. The bottom of it went past her kneecaps and there no point in even trying to roll up the sleeves, they were so long. She had to barely even look eighteen anymore.

"I'll find you something else."

Pushing the excess fabric up her arms, she shook her head and finally found her smile. "No. It's perfect." And it was, because she no longer felt inappropriately naked. She couldn't tear her eyes away from his as she said a very genuine, "Thank you for thinking I might be cold. And for finding me something to wear." She rubbed her cheek against one of the sleeves. "It's very soft."

She couldn't read his expression as he stared back at her, but finally he nodded. "You're welcome."

As he moved back to the expensive coffeemaker on the corner of the granite countertop, she couldn't stop thinking how sweet it was of him to be more concerned about her being cold, rather than taking the opportunity to stare at her boobs in the ridiculous leather dress. Still, just the thought of his dark eyes on her curves had her body heating up all over again.

Knowing she needed to get her brain to focus on something other than how gorgeous and sweet and sexy Marcus was, she turned away from him and made a slow perusal of the house where she'd spent the night.

It was nice. Really, really nice. Although, she quickly noted, there was nothing all that personal about it, either, almost as if it were just an extended version of one of her fancy hotel rooms.

Marcus must have noticed her taking it all in, because he said, "My brother owns the house."

She could feel a new flush of heat move over her skin at his warm, somewhat rough voice. It was a voice at odds with his polished clothes and the fact that he was clearly a successful businessman. She liked that deep, raw edge very much. Too much, given the way her body was responding to a few simple words. And she couldn't help but wonder what it would have sounded like if they'd ended up making it into a bed together the night before, if he'd said her name while levered above her…right before he took her.

The dark shadow on his jaw should have seemed out of place, too, but somehow it didn't. She remembered the calluses on his fingertips, musing that calluses and business suits were a dichotomy she couldn't make sense of. But, oh, how she suddenly wanted to figure him out. Far too much than was wise considering that she'd planned on his remaining a perfect stranger.

"It's very nice," she replied. And then it hit her. What if his brother was about to walk in on their cozy little coffee scene? Odds were pretty darn low that his brother wouldn't recognize her, either.

For the thousandth time since she'd woken up, she wondered what she could possibly have been thinking, going home with Marcus from the club last night. It had seemed okay when it was just the two of them, when she could convince herself that finally finding pleasure—and letting loose, for once—was more important than anything else, but somehow knowing his brother was going to come down the stairs any minute and find her there in her totally inappropriate leather dress and bare feet and too-big sweatshirt made her feel like she'd made the world's biggest mistake leaving her hotel room in the first place. *Why hadn't she just stuck to* CSI *reruns and chocolate ice cream?*

She started backing away from the counter. "I should leave before he—"

"Don't worry, Nicola." Marcus's saying her

name in that sinfully seductive voice of his had her stilling, the rest of her sentence falling away. "He's out of town for work. It's just you and me."

Hearing that should have made her feel better. But it didn't. Because she honestly wasn't sure that being alone with Marcus was such a good idea. Not when she felt so off-kilter around him, not when her tongue was tied up in knots along with her stomach when they hadn't so much as kissed last night.

Just think if they'd actually had the wild and crazy sex she'd been planning on. Yes, she had no doubt it would have been awesome. Beyond awesome. Possibly mind-blowing given how much just one of his dark, hungry gazes affected her. But she knew she'd be dying right now.

Dying.

Clearly, one-night stands weren't her thing. And, suddenly, it seemed imperative that he know that about her. Despite all the evidence to the contrary.

"I've never done something like this before." She made herself look up from the shiny black granite she'd been gripping for dear life. Unclamping her fingers from the edge, she saw the damp imprint of her hand on the surface, a telltale sign of just how nervous she was feeling.

She was surprised when he said, "It's been a while for me, too."

At the same time, unexpected jealousy hit her at the vision of Marcus standing in this kitchen with another woman that he'd picked up for a one-night stand. Nicola had no claim on him, no right to that tightening of her chest.

But she felt it, anyway.

Especially since she could place a million-dollar bet on the fact that she was the only woman who had ever dozed off before they'd even had their first kiss.

"I didn't mean to fall asleep on you last night."

His lips finally moved up into a small smile. He'd been so serious until now that she was beyond surprised to see the corners of his mouth twitch in an upward direction. Those butterflies that had gathered in her belly at her first sight of him in the club, so big and strong-looking, started flying in every direction at his smile.

She still wanted to kiss him, of course, but suddenly, she wanted to see him smile, too. Wanted to see his chocolate-brown eyes look at her with laughter and know that she was responsible for it.

"You were clearly exhausted."

He wasn't smiling anymore, but his gaze was warm. Giving. Exactly the way his mother had told her he was with his siblings. He handed her a cup of coffee.

"I didn't mind being your pillow for the night."

That same sweet feeling that had come over her when she'd learned what a good son and brother he was stole through her again. Nicola was sure any other guy would have been angry with her right now, would have been expecting her to drop to her knees, unzip his pants and make up for what she hadn't given him last night.

But Marcus seemed more concerned about how she was feeling than he was with being left high and dry.

If he'd been coming at her aggressively demanding a do-over, she would have kicked him straight to the curb and been out of there so fast his head would spin. Instead, she was trying to find her footing in this strange new world where she'd finally met someone who didn't seem to want anything from her at all.

Not her fame, which he clearly didn't know about, and not even her body, which she'd outright offered to him less than a dozen hours ago… verbally, at least.

"You were a really great pillow."

This time, the smile he gave her in response had her smiling back. She wasn't a big believer in things she couldn't see, taste, hear or touch, but in that moment she could have sworn an invisible ribbon reached out between them and wrapped itself around them both.

No longer quite as ready to run, she slid onto one of the bar stools. "Please, sit with me."

Last night she hadn't wanted to let herself learn anything about him beyond whether or not he could make her scream with pleasure. But since they hadn't even gotten near first base due to her strangely narcoleptic behavior, she decided to give in to her urge to find out more about the mystery man who'd held her hand while she slept soundly for the first time in ages.

Marcus hesitated for several seconds, and just when she thought he was going to refuse her invitation, he picked up his cup and walked toward her.

"So, I take it you don't live in San Francisco, either?" she asked him.

He shook his head. "No. I live in Napa Valley."

"I've driven through it a couple of times and the area is really beautiful." She left off the fact that she'd been there to play a couple of private gigs for some very high-profile Napa residents. She sipped at her coffee again. "But I'm not much of a wine drinker." She shrugged. "I never know what to order with what."

If she were being straight about who she was and what she did, she would have told him that even a light buzz made it hard for her to keep hold of her control. And with so many people surrounding her all the time asking her to make decisions, coming at her with contracts and offers, she had to work double time to remain fully present and lucid. Which was why she rarely drank anything at all, and certainly didn't do any drugs. Only with Kenny had she made that mistake. And she'd paid for it a million times over.

"Are you in the wine business?"

"I am," he said, then asked her, "You don't live here, either, do you?"

She hadn't missed the fact that while he'd answered her question, he'd quickly changed the subject afterward. Clearly, he didn't want her to know what his job was, or which winery he worked at.

It was a non-too-subtle reminder that this was just small talk between two strangers who were never going to see each other again. She shouldn't be upset that he didn't want to tell her where he worked. He was probably afraid she'd hunt him down and become a big nuisance. No doubt plenty of girls had tried to latch onto him over the years.

Besides, she wasn't exactly gung-ho about sharing a bunch of details about her life with him, was she?

Nearly as vague as he'd been, she said, "I'm from a teeny, tiny little town in upstate New York, but I've always loved the West Coast."

There. That was perfectly impersonal. They were both behaving like two rational adults who had almost made the mistake of having a one-night stand, but had somehow slipped out of the night unscathed.

She should be happy.

But she wasn't.

Because for a few wonderful minutes the previous night, she'd reveled in irrational, unfettered desire and anticipation.

Rationality and levelheadedness sucked by comparison.

She swiveled on her stool to face him more directly. "I'm still really embarrassed about calling your mother like that."

The last thing she expected was for his laughter to rumble through the room.

It was a beautiful sound, rich and deep, if a bit rusty. She had a sudden vision of capturing that sound the same way the sea witch had captured Ariel's voice in *The Little Mermaid* movie. If she could, Nicola would put that sound in a little locket she would wear around her neck to take out to replay whenever she needed a pick-me-up.

"Trust me," he told her, "I'm sure she enjoyed talking with you. A great deal."

"What are you going to tell her?" She quickly clarified, "About me, I mean, and the question I asked her about you."

He paused for a moment before saying, "When you asked her if you were safe with me?"

Her breath left her in a whoosh and it was all she could do just to nod as the sensual tension between them jumped up a notch.

But instead of dropping it, she said, "I was safe with you," barely above a whisper. Almost before she realized it, she was reaching out to touch his hand, only inches away.

She wished she'd been awake for long enough to really appreciate his holding her hand. Instead, she'd slept through some of the most wonderful moments of her life—Marcus's hands holding hers, his warmth cradling her.

Now, as the sunlight streamed in through the large kitchen windows of his brother's house, she pulled her hand back barely an inch before making contact.

She thought she saw his fingers twitch, almost as if he also wanted to reach out and take her hands to hold them again, before he asked, "What do you want me to tell her?"

She lifted her eyes from his large hands, hands she still couldn't stop wishing were holding her, caressing her, and despite the warm sun coming in, a shiver went through her as she looked up at him.

"Maybe," she said slowly, "you could tell her you made a new friend last night."

"A new friend."

As her words came back at her in his deliciously low voice, she thought, *I wish it were actually true. I wish we actually were friends. And more. So much more.*

She licked her lips and his eyes followed the path of her tongue. When his gaze met hers again, the heat from the night before was back in spades.

She knew he had to see it in her gaze, too. A part of her thought she should try to hide it, but nothing had changed between last night and this morning.

She was still powerfully attracted to him.

On the verge of saying something else to try to

break the sensual tension between them, she suddenly wondered why she was so intent on pushing him away.

Marcus was gorgeous, the best-looking man she'd met in forever. Okay, so last night hadn't worked out, but she wasn't leaving San Francisco right away. Between actually shooting her video and putting on a show, she would be in town for several more days. And nights.

Oh, God, she was terrible at this. She honestly didn't have the first clue how to proposition Marcus for the second time in twenty-four hours. Last night, she'd been able to play off the loud music, the dark lighting, her leather dress and heels… and the desperate urge to escape the penthouse walls that had felt more like a prison.

But sitting here in a kitchen drinking coffee in an oversize sweatshirt…she had none of those sexy trappings to help her find her way.

The thing was, she already knew she'd regret it like crazy if she walked away from Marcus without even trying.

One night. She deserved one night with a guy like this, didn't she? Just because she'd blown last night by falling asleep, didn't mean she should give up. If that had been how she'd approached the music business, she never would have gone beyond playing open mikes at coffee shops.

Of course, she knew she'd have to tell him who she was if he agreed to another night with her. Heck, she knew she needed to tell him, anyway. How unfair would it be to him if he walked out of here and got a call from one of his friends or family asking him why he'd been holding out on them about being Nico's newest flame?

Not looking forward to that part of the conversation one bit, she decided to lead with, "I'm going to be in the city for a few more nights." She picked up her cup again and gulped the rest of the delicious coffee he'd made for them.

His expression was unreadable. She didn't have the first clue what he was going to say to her proposition. But she knew she needed to make it, anyway, or forever brand herself a coward.

Her throat felt tight and dry as she spoke into the silence again. "I've got to get going in a few minutes, but I was wondering if maybe you'd like to try to get together tonight?"

She swore she saw heat flare in his eyes, the heat neither of them had been able to bank. *Oh, please, please, please let him say yes!* Because now that she'd put herself out there, now that she'd admitted what she wanted—him!—she couldn't stand the thought of not getting it.

Only, instead of agreeing to meet her again, he asked, "How old are you, Nicola?"

"Twenty-five." She tried not to say it defensively, even though she knew it couldn't be a good thing that he was asking for her age.

"I'm thirty-six." He pushed off his stool and picked up both coffee cups as he headed for the sink. "I shouldn't have been in that club last night." His shoulders were tense as he explained, "I was angry about something and I thought I could get over it by going to a club and taking someone home for sex."

It was the first time either of them had used the word.

Sex.

One syllable, three little letters, sizzled between them. And, oh, it made her want him more than ever, even though he was trying to use the word to back away from her, trying to set up reasons why they couldn't have their night.

Her parents had always said what a stubborn child she'd been, and nothing had changed for her as an adult. If anything, her experiences in the music business, dealing with almost constant rejection and having to bounce back from it, had only made her more stubborn.

"I had my reasons, too," she told him.

Only, those reasons had changed. Last night had been all about getting something everyone already thought she had.

This morning she didn't care about anyone else, didn't give a fig for what a bunch of strangers thought about her. Now her reasons were all about wanting Marcus entirely for herself.

"Even if I weren't too old for you—"

Nicola cut him off. "We're both adults."

He finally turned to look at her again, his gaze skimming her from head to toe, and she knew he was taking in the too-big sweatshirt that went past her knees.

Despite the fact that she knew she looked really, really young with no makeup on, she lifted her chin and said, "You thought I looked plenty old enough last night."

His jaw tightened. "Last night was a mistake. And if you hadn't fallen asleep it would have been a truly huge mistake."

Wow.

That hurt.

She had to turn away from him on the stool as she scooted off it so that he wouldn't see just how bad his words had made her feel. She'd thought her years in the music industry had made her a pro at letting rejection just bounce right off her.

Turned out she had a long way to go, if only a few words from Marcus could make her feel like crumbling inside.

"Nicola."

She didn't turn around to face him when he said her name, didn't stop heading for the couch where she hoped her shoes and purse were. She stripped off the sweatshirt while she walked, not caring how much skin she was showing anymore, or how ridiculously inappropriate her leather dress was in the full light of day.

She wanted nothing more than to just leave, to get the heck out of the house and drown herself in work, the work she'd been drowning in for the past six months.

She was just bending down to pick up her shoes when Marcus beat her to them.

"It's not your fault," he said, his low voice skimming over her skin as if he'd touched her with his big, warm hands instead. "Nothing that did or didn't happen is your fault."

She held out her hand and willed it not to shake. "Can I have my shoes, please?"

For a few seconds she wasn't sure he was going

to give them to her, but then, he finally handed them over.

She made sure their fingertips didn't touch as she took them from him, then sat down on the edge of the coffee table to slip her heels on. Somehow she was going to keep it together long enough to sweep out of the house like a woman who couldn't care less if one man found her attractive or not. There were plenty of other men who wanted her. One day, when she was feeling stupid and reckless again, she would find one of them.

"You're beautiful, Nicola."

She'd been certain nothing he could have said would have stopped her from stomping out of there.

Nothing but that.

"When you were sleeping last night, I couldn't stop thinking how beautiful you are. I can hardly believe you came home with me last night."

She couldn't keep herself from staring up at him as he ran his hand over his face. And she definitely couldn't keep her heart from starting to pound hard and fast again as he said, "I shouldn't be telling you that, but it's so damn true, I can't let you think otherwise. Last night I told myself

I could sleep with a stranger and not worry about her feelings."

His eyes caught hers and held them fast. "I don't know a lot about you, but you don't feel like a stranger anymore, Nicola."

A flicker of hope lit in her chest. "Neither do you," she said softly.

This time, when she instinctively reached out for his hand, she let herself make it all the way there. She slipped her fingers through his and that contentment she'd felt when she'd woken up on his lap, with her hands in his, filled her again.

"You're right," she told him, "we don't know each other very well yet, but I already know you make me feel good. And I also know you were the perfect gentleman last night." She pulled herself up off the coffee table to stand in front of him, her breasts close enough to his chest to almost touch. "If we gave the night one more try, then maybe this time we could see what it's like when you're not the perfect gentleman anymore?"

Desire flared even hotter in his eyes than it had before and she could feel the evidence of it against her lower body when she shifted even closer to him.

"I just got out of a relationship. I'm not looking for another one."

Ah. So that was what had him going to the club last night to pick up some hot thing to screw silly.

"I'm not looking for a relationship, either," she told him firmly. "I swear I'm not." She put his hands on her hips. "Just one night to feel what it's like to be touched by you." She went up on her tippy-toes in her heels to gain an extra inch and be a breath away from his mouth. "Just one night to know what it's like to be kissed by you."

She could almost taste his kiss, and she knew how much he wanted to lean into her and take what she was offering. Her eyes were closing and she was puckering up when suddenly cold air rushed across her as he quickly let go of her and stepped away.

"It would be better for both of us if we didn't go there."

Anger and embarrassment caught her in their grip. It was bad enough to be turned down once.

But twice?

"You don't know enough about me to know what would be better for me!"

And, frankly, she was too pissed off now to want to tell him about who she really was. He'd just have to find out the hard way, by turning on his computer or opening a magazine and seeing the pictures of the two of them leaving the club in full Technicolor. Oh, how she wished she could see his face in that moment he realized who he'd almost slept with.

"You're right." A muscle jumped in his jaw. "All I know is that you're beautiful, and that you're too young, too sweet, for me to even think about doing any of that with you. I made a mistake last night and I won't make it worse now."

Young.

Sweet.

Mistake.

She was going to throw up.

Here she'd thought she was going to regret not getting up the nerve to ask him to be with her for the night. What an idiot she'd been, how stupidly sure she must have been that he'd jump at the chance to be with her again.

Because when was the last time anyone had turned *Nico* down?

Well, she wasn't a famous pop star right now. She was simply a woman who wanted a man.

A man she evidently couldn't have.

Because all she was to him was a way-too-young, far-too-sweet mistake.

Turning from him, she pulled her cell phone out of her bag and called for a cab, giving the driver the address she remembered Marcus saying the night before. After hanging up, she was sorely tempted to storm out of the house like the little girl he thought she was. Lord knew, it would be so much harder to hold her head high like a mature woman and take her lumps.

But that was what she was going to do, damn it.

Turning back to him with a fake smile, she politely said, "Thank you for not taking advantage of me last night."

That muscle jumped in his chiseled jaw again. "You don't have anything to thank me for."

She shrugged and the devil she didn't care about restraining made her say, "Sure I do. I could have woken up in some guy's bed this morning ravished and exhausted from having sex all night long. Instead, I'm still just as pure as the driven snow and perfectly well rested." She lifted the corners of her mouth up even higher into the smile she didn't even begin to feel. "Thanks to you. The perfect gentleman." She held out her hand. "Goodbye, Marcus."

He looked down at her outstretched hand for several drawn-out beats before finally moving toward her to grasp it in his own.

Uh-oh. She should have thought that handshaking thing through, should have remembered that every time they touched her body went up in flames.

Because he had an uncanny knack for reducing her insides to a pile of ashes.

"Holy hell," he said in a low, raw voice. "I shouldn't want you this much."

She'd barely begun to wrap her head around his words when he was pulling her into him and crushing her mouth beneath his.

The kiss—their first kiss—was beyond anything she'd ever experienced. Every ounce of his desire, every ounce of his frustrated need, everything she now realized that he was denying himself by letting her go, poured from his mouth to hers.

He didn't taste her gently, didn't learn the curves and contours of her mouth. Instead, he took what he wanted…and gave her something she'd never really known she needed before.

Nicola liked to be in control of everything, cherished that control, especially in the wake of Kenny's betrayal. But for the first time in a very long time, she gave up that control to a man who knew exactly what to do with it.

His tongue owned hers, his teeth captured her lower lip, and she heard herself gasping and moaning as if through a long, narrow tunnel.

And then, just as quickly as his kiss had taken her over, it was taken away.

"Damn it. I didn't mean to do that." His expression was well beyond frustrated. "You need to go, Nicola. Now."

She blinked at him, trying to clear her vision, about to tell him their first kiss couldn't possibly be the end when it was the most glorious beginning she'd ever known. But then she got a good look at his face, saw the way his eyes were completely shuttered, totally closed off to her.

And she knew there was no point.

He was done with her.

And she needed to be done with him, too.

Fortunately, that was when the taxi driver hit the buzzer to be let in the gate. She and Marcus hadn't exchanged last names or phone numbers. She had no idea how to reach him apart from camping out on his brother's front step.

This was it.

This really was goodbye.

She wouldn't let herself give in to the urge to take one last look at Marcus. She simply turned and walked away.

Five

Marcus couldn't stop thinking about Nicola.

On Monday morning he was sitting in the boardroom of a San Francisco skyscraper, staring at a PowerPoint presentation that someone had taken a lot of time and effort to put together, with a stack of documents and glossy images on the table in front of him...and all he could think about was a twenty-five-year-old woman who had the prettiest eyes he'd ever seen.

From the first moment he'd seen her at the club, he'd thought she was gorgeous. Sexy as hell in that leather dress, her bare legs toned and sleek in her heels.

But Saturday morning, when he'd turned around in his brother's kitchen and seen her with no makeup on, her cheeks pink with what he guessed was embarrassment at having to speak with him in the light of day, his heart may have actually stopped beating for a few moments.

Marcus's father had loved to tell his kids about the first time he'd ever set eyes on their mother. She'd been on a modeling assignment in San Francisco, and when Jack Sullivan had taken one look at Mary, he'd felt as if a lightning bolt had struck him clear through the heart. He'd known from that very first moment that he had to make her his.

Marcus had never felt anything like that before. Not until Friday night, and then again Saturday morning when Nicola had been even more beautiful without makeup, in her bare feet, wearing the enormous sweatshirt.

What a beauty she was…and so young-looking.

Despite the fact that she'd told him she was twenty-five, guilt roiled in his stomach not only at what he'd almost done with her Friday night, but at what he'd *still* wanted to do even after she'd covered up the dress, cleaned off the makeup and told him her age.

"—to get it through production. Marcus," the man sitting directly across from him asked, "how does that sound?"

He looked up at the group of men and women who were waiting for his decision about the new corks they were considering using for his latest vintage. For the first time ever, he didn't have an answer for them. Because he hadn't heard a word they'd said.

Out of the corner of his eye he saw his assistant, Ellen, frowning at him, obviously confused by his unusual lack of focus. Fortunately, she was so good at her job that she quickly covered for him.

"The materials they're using sound quite close to what we've been looking for," she told him. She lifted up her iPad so that he could see her spreadsheet. "Of course, we should review their documents and my notes further before we sign any contracts."

Ellen had started working for him several years back in the tasting room and he'd quickly realized that while she had an excellent touch with the customers who came by to try his wines, she was too bright and quick to be wasted there. Yet again, she was proving her worth to him.

"Yes," Marcus agreed as he quickly read through her clear notes, "the specifications look good."

His phone buzzed and he looked down at it, hoping for a moment that it was Nicola even though he knew that was impossible. He hadn't given her his number. And he didn't have hers.

He'd done that on purpose, knowing even the faintest trail would find him heading straight toward her.

Especially after that kiss.

Jesus. That kiss.

She'd tasted so good. A faint taste of coffee, a hint of toothpaste, but none of that could disguise her own sweet essence.

What, he'd been wondering every single second since then, would her skin taste like? Not just on her face, her shoulders, her breasts, but between her legs, while she was gorgeously naked and—

His sister Lori's face popped up on his phone and he realized he'd been doing it again: losing the thread of everything but Nicola.

"Excuse me, I need to take this phone call," he told the group before pushing away from the table and walking out into the hallway.

Family always came first for Marcus, just as Jill had accused. If one of his brothers or sisters or his mother needed him, he would do anything he could to be there for them. Even before his father had died, as the oldest there'd been an instinctive weight of responsibility on his shoulders. Of course, after his father died that weight had grown infinitely heavier.

"Hi, Naughty," he said, using the nickname Chase had given Lori years ago.

He could almost see her expression, that faintly irritated look she had whenever they called her that, even though she was twenty-four now and not a little girl anymore. But despite her protests that she didn't like it, Marcus knew better. Lori definitely loved people thinking she had a little edge. Especially since she would have hated being called Nice like her twin sister, Sophie.

"Are you still in the city?" She sounded like she was dancing even as she spoke to him, her breath coming a little bit faster than usual at the end of the sentence.

He looked out the window of the skyscraper down to the busy streets below. The energy of San Francisco was so different from Napa Valley where his business, and home, were. He enjoyed both the city and the country, one feeding his need for change and excitement, the other giving him a much appreciated place to relax and appreciate the beauty all around him.

"I'm just about to finish my last meeting," he told his sister.

"Great! I was hoping you'd say that."

Lori's energy was palpable even through the phone. Dancing was the perfect career for her, considering she had more energy than two people combined. If anyone thought she was a lot of work to deal with now, they should have seen her when she was a little girl. She'd been a terror as a toddler and preschooler. A really cute terror who knew just when to turn on the smiles to get what she wanted or the waterworks to get out of trouble. And, of course, she was a master at getting her twin, Sophie, to smooth over any rough patches caused by her impulsive behavior.

"Do you have time to come by and see me at my video shoot before you head back to Napa?"

He'd known that she was working in San Francisco with a pop singer to choreograph a video, and had originally planned to drop by if he had time, but thoughts of Nicola had pushed everything else out of his head.

"I wouldn't miss it. Text me your location and I'll leave now."

Ellen had things well covered here. And considering he couldn't concentrate worth a damn today, the meeting would be better off without him.

Hanging up, he walked back into the conference room. "I need to leave early, but as you already know, Ellen is well versed in what we're looking for and can take it from here. If you could excuse Ellen for a minute while I give her my notes, I'd appreciate it."

Everyone in the boardroom stood up and shook his hand. A minute later, Ellen joined him in the hall. "Is everything okay? You seem, well, not quite like yourself today."

She was right. He had never felt like this before. Had never been able to get a woman out of his head before. It occurred to him that it should have been Jill he was thinking of, but even though he was still angry with her, he honestly hadn't given her a second thought since Friday night. Not when thoughts about Nicola's beauty, her sweetness—and the hottest kiss he'd ever had in his life, bar none—had consumed his every waking thought.

"Everything's fine." It would be, at least, once he got his head back on straight. Going to see Lori dance, focusing his attention on the little sister he adored, would help clear his head. "Lori's working on an exciting project right now, and she'd really like me to be there. Thank you for covering this meeting and the negotiations for me. I know I can count on you."

"No problem, boss," Ellen said with a wide

smile that told him how pleased she was about his faith in her abilities. "Say hi to your sister for me, will you?" He was just about to turn and head out when Ellen put her hand on his arm. "And, about your brother Chase…" She shook her head as she admitted, "Nothing happened when he came to do the photo shoot."

Marcus knew all about the one-night stand Chase and Ellen had been planning to have the night Chase found Chloe standing in the rain by her totaled car. Marcus had been upset with his brother for even thinking about messing around with one of his most valued employees, but if almost hooking up with Nicola on Friday night had taught him anything, it was that people didn't always do things that made sense when sex was involved.

"I know that," he said in a matter-of-fact voice that he hoped would mitigate any of her lingering embarrassment over the situation, "but I didn't see any sense in bringing it up when nothing happened. I hope you haven't been worrying about it, Ellen. Your private life is just that. You don't have to ever feel that you need to explain it to me."

She was flushed with what he guessed was relief as she said, "I work for you, but we're also friends. And I hope as both my boss and my friend you can forgive the rare break in my good sense. Although," she added with a teasing glint in her eyes, "I don't know if it's entirely my fault. After all, you Sullivans are pretty darn hard to resist."

He laughed, glad that everything was smoothed out between them, before saying, "Just as long as you don't let any of my other brothers know you think that. Their heads are big enough already."

Lori texted him just as he was heading out: R u lost?

He grinned at her impatience to see him as he texted back to let her know he was finally leaving the meeting. No question about it, she was just the person he needed to see. Even though their brother Smith was a movie star, Lori hadn't gotten the job working on the pop star's video through her connection to him. She'd worked hard to get this gig all by herself, and Marcus, along with the rest of them, was incredibly proud of not only her talent, but her dedication.

He and Lori had always had a special relationship and he was glad she'd asked him to come watch her work.

It was the perfect way for him to forget all about Nicola.

* * *

Nicola lifted the water bottle to her lips and drained it. They'd all been working hard in preparation for the filming that began tomorrow. Shooting a video was never cheap, and as soon as the cameras started rolling the costs went up exponentially. Nicola and the rest of her dancers needed to be ready to the nth degree by the time the director walked into the room.

On Friday during rehearsal, she'd thought she was good to go.

But today had been a disaster.

She couldn't focus. Not after the call that had come in from her publicist. Nicola always had Sandra inform her of any pictures she saw circulating of her and whatever star of the week she was supposed to be dating so she'd be prepared to deal with questions.

After a long weekend of staying holed up in her hotel room writing song after song—all of them completely unrecordable—Nicola had been beyond glad to get back to the dance studio. But then, Sandra caught her as she was leaving the hotel and told her, "I've just seen pictures of you leaving a club with some guy I don't recognize."

Even though Nicola had expected this, her

heart had pretty much stopped. Especially because she'd been too upset about her battered pride at Marcus turning her down to actually get around to telling him who she was and to mention some unexpected press might be coming his way in the very near future.

She'd screwed up big-time. And it was even worse because she hadn't even gotten the pleasure she wanted to go along with it…just the obliterated pride.

She had to ask, "How bad are they?" even though she really didn't want to know.

"Fortunately," Sandra had said, "they're amateur pics. Both of your faces are too blurry for anyone to bother running them, which is why they didn't surface this weekend, but you might want to be more careful in the future."

No kidding. After narrowly dodging the bullet like that, she vowed to be the most careful person on the planet from now on.

Yet now, as they ran through the complicated choreography again and again, she still couldn't stop flashing back to her night—and morning—with Marcus.

The lyrics to her new song "One Moment" weren't helping at all.

All it took was one moment
One look in your eyes
One taste of your lips
To know that you were the one

The afternoon she'd written the song, she'd been listening to Cole Porter's "From This Moment On." Back then everything had still been sunshine and butterflies in her life and she'd believed true love was just another beautiful gift waiting around the corner. She'd written "One Moment" as an ode to that future love and had even incorporated samples from the classic Cole Porter tune. Her label had loved it, calling it fresh and catchy. It helped that they also owned the license to the song and hoped sales of Porter's songs would take off, as well.

Of course, once everything had busted apart with Kenny, she hadn't wanted to record the song. She'd felt like a fool for ever believing in one moment, in one kiss, in one touch, that could change everything. But her label insisted it should be her first single. And she knew they were right. She couldn't let Kenny and what he'd done remove the joy she got from her music, so she'd recorded the song, putting every ounce of her heart and soul into it.

But even though she'd hurdled that first huge bump months ago, today she found herself hitting a new one.

She couldn't stop thinking of Marcus every time they got to the chorus.

She couldn't stop seeing his face, couldn't stop feeling his hands holding hers.

And she couldn't stop reeling from his kiss.

Her dancers had been given a thirty-minute coffee break before coming back to put in another hour or so to try to pull it together. She knew how frustrated they all were with her. She'd never planned on being a dancer, hadn't trained for it like they had, but she'd always enjoyed moving her body, and had picked up a handful of pretty good moves over the years.

Not that anyone would know it from watching her today.

Even Lori, her fun—and normally extremely positive—choreographer, seemed frustrated.

The sound of Lori's laughter drew Nicola's attention across the room. Earlier in the day, Lori had asked if she could invite her brother to observe for a bit. Nicola had been a public figure for long enough that she wasn't particularly concerned about one more person watching her.

She could see how much Lori adored her

brother by the way she lit up while she was talking to him. Not that Lori was ever anything but sparkling. She had a ready laugh and a wicked glint in her eyes. Apart from being a genius choreographer, Lori had a special warmth about her that drew people in.

"Good news," Lori said as she walked back across the large dance studio with a smile. "My big brother is heading over now."

"Great," Nicola said, trying to sound enthusiastic despite how low she'd been feeling all day.

But Lori was way too perceptive. "Seriously, Nico, you should tell me if you don't want him here. I can see him later."

Nicola shook her head and forced herself to smile wider—and more convincingly. "I really don't mind at all."

Lori frowned. "Is everything okay?"

"I know I've been sucking today. Sorry about that."

Lori reached out and put her hand on Nicola's arm. "No, you're doing great. But you seem kind of—" she paused "—well, sad, I guess."

Nicola knew better than to talk to someone she was working with about her personal life, but Lori seemed different than most of the people Nicola worked with. Nicer. More honest, somehow.

Kind of like Marcus.

Even though she should keep her mouth shut, she found herself saying, "I met a guy Friday night."

Lori's eyes widened. "A hot guy?"

Nicola was glad for another chance to smile. "Yes. Very hot." She felt compelled to explain, "But nothing happened. Except for me falling asleep before we even kissed."

"Oh," Lori said, clearly caught off guard. "How'd he take it?"

"Great, actually. He made me coffee in the morning." And then told her she was way too young and sweet for him.

"Coffee? That's all?"

She sighed. "Actually, he kissed me. Just once."

"And?"

"And it was awesome."

"Awesome is good, right?"

"Not when it was followed immediately by goodbye," Nicola told her.

Lori looked confused. "Wait, so he kissed you and then you were done?"

"Yup. And for some reason the whole thing is messing with my head. I'm really sorry, Lori, I'm not usually like this. Especially over some guy I just met and will never, ever see again."

When Lori didn't say anything for several

long seconds, Nicola began to panic. What had she been thinking, sharing all of her secrets with someone who was still, for all intents and purposes, a stranger? Hadn't she been burned hard enough to know better?

"Look, I shouldn't have said anything."

Before she could finish her sentence, Lori was throwing her arms around her and saying, "I so get it. Guys suck." She looked a little guilty when she pulled back. "There's something I should have told you before now. I'm related to Smith Sullivan."

"Oh. Wow." Nicola had met Smith at a few industry events in the past couple of years. Something jogged in her memory and she asked, "If you're his sister, then don't you have like a dozen siblings?"

Lori laughed. "Not quite. There are eight of us. Although I'm sure it felt more like twelve to my mother."

Nicola didn't understand something. "Why didn't you want me to know that?"

"I'd hate for anyone to hire me because of who he is."

"I would never do that."

"I know that now," Lori told her. "I'm sorry I wasn't more forthright."

After last night, Nicola was the queen of not being forthright. "Don't worry about it, Lori. It's really no big deal who you're related to."

Lori grinned and then said, "If the guy you met last night didn't get how freaking awesome you are—and how lucky he was that you even let him kiss you—then he doesn't deserve to be with you, anyway."

Nicola found herself blinking back tears. People were always nice to her. Because she was a star, because she had power in an industry that thrived on power, because they wanted something that they thought she could give them.

But people were very rarely nice to her *just because*.

The doorbell to the studio rang and Nicola assumed her dancers were back from their break. She stood up and walked over to the barre on the mirrored wall to stretch before they began again.

Her head was down over her kneecap when she heard Lori squeal with joy. "Yay, you're here!"

Nicola smiled and was about to lift her head to take a look at the man Lori clearly idolized when she heard a voice that resonated through every cell in her body. "So this is where the magic happens, huh?"

Oh, God.

Marcus was Lori's big brother?

Six

No.

No way.

Marcus stiffened beneath his sister's hug as he made eye contact with the only other person in the room.

Nicola.

What the hell was she doing here?

He could tell from the way she was dressed in a cutoff tank top and tight short-shorts that she was a dancer. It was just his luck that she'd turned out to be one of Lori's dancers.

Only, what should have been bad luck…wasn't.

Because no matter how many times he'd told himself that walking away from her Saturday morning had been the right thing to do, he hadn't yet been able to make himself believe it. Not when his body was utterly at odds with his brain.

And not when he'd wanted to take their one kiss and turn it into an all-day—and all-night—tangle of naked limbs and heat.

He'd known how beautiful her shape was Friday night in that leather dress, but she was much closer to naked now, with only the thinnest layers of cotton and spandex covering her beautiful curves.

And—*oh, Jesus*—was that a bead of sweat trailing down her chest between her breasts?

Lori pulled back in his arms and he forced himself to drag his gaze away from Nicola. His little sister looked up at him, studying him more carefully than usual.

"Were your meetings okay today? You look a little tense."

He worked to keep his attention on his sister rather than the shockingly beautiful woman by the wall of mirrors. "They were fine."

Lori frowned at his curt response. She'd always been fascinated with the wine industry and he usually shared the details of his business with her. Not just because she was interested, but because she had good ideas. If she hadn't been such a great dancer and choreographer, he'd have hired her straight out of college.

"Something's wrong." She didn't say it as a

question. "Later. I'll make you tell me later." And then she dropped one of his hands and used the other to pull him toward Nicola, who'd been watching them warily. "Come here. I can't wait to introduce you to Nico."

Nico?

Something flashed in his mind, a hint that he should know something he'd been missing since Friday night, but he was so off-kilter from seeing the woman he'd been reluctantly fantasizing about all weekend, that he couldn't make heads or tails of it.

"Nico, this is my brother Marcus."

Nicola—Nico didn't sound quite right to him, even though his sister said it with such confidence—was gripping the wooden barre in front of the mirror so tightly he could see her knuckles turning white. Her face was on the white side, too, and she wasn't doing a damn thing to erase the horror on her face at seeing him again.

Guilt hit him square across the chest. She'd put herself out there by asking him for another night and he'd turned her down cold. Apart from the kiss, which had been anything but cold.

And now, here he was, barging in on her dancing gig for a big pop star.

Seeing him had to be the very last thing she wanted.

Lori was looking between the two of them with an utterly confused expression. Knowing he'd better break the ice—and fast—before his sister clued in to just how wrong things were, he held out his hand and said, "It's nice to meet you."

Nicola stared down at his hand for a long moment, before looking back at him with those big eyes that had been haunting him. Her movements were jerky, almost robotic, as she finally pushed away from the barre and put her hand in his.

"Hi." She cleared her throat as she yanked her hand away. "It's nice to meet you, too."

The silence hung heavy and thick between them before he asked, "So, how long have you two been working together?"

Lori shot him another strange look. "You know I've been working on this video shoot for the past couple of days."

Okay then, Nicola must be one of her new dancers. But before he could ask any other questions or try to make small talk to set Nicola more at ease, a large group started coming in through the doors. He recognized most of them as men and women Lori had worked with in the past and they raised their hands in greeting.

"Got any vino for us, Marcus?"

He smiled, but it didn't feel right on his face, not with Nicola still looking at him as if his appearance in the studio was totally and completely unwelcome.

"I'll make sure there's a case waiting for you guys at the end," he promised. He turned back to Lori. "Looks like you're getting back to it. I'll get out of your way."

She put her hand on his arm. "I wanted you to stay and watch." She looked at Nicola. "It's still okay if he hangs out, isn't it?"

Nicola licked her lips, looking uncertain. And then she smiled, a lifting of her lips that looked about as genuine as the smile he'd just given the dancers.

"Of course." Her lips moved into a wider smile, almost a grimace. "Your brother should see the magic you've created, Lori." Finally, she looked back at him, their gazes locking together and holding for a long moment before she said, "Your sister is amazing."

Nicola was so beautiful—and so incredibly vulnerable as she stood there in front of him—that he had to focus hard just to get out the words "I know."

They stood like that for way too long, staring

at each other without speaking. At last, Lori said, "Come sit over here where no one will accidentally kick you in the face."

Someone turned on the music as he and Lori walked away from Nicola. "Marcus, what's the matter? I didn't think you'd act that way around her," she hissed.

Marcus mirrored back his sister's frown. Had Nicola told his sister about meeting him? About going back to Smith's house and falling asleep on his lap?

No. Lori wasn't capable of holding something like that inside. She would have called him immediately to demand to know what he was doing fooling around with one of her dancers.

"Nico has to deal with people stuttering and acting weird around her all day long, just like Smith does. I asked you to come because I knew you'd roll with her fame and wouldn't make a big deal out of it."

Partway through getting chewed out by his little sister for the way he'd acted, a lightbulb went on in Marcus's head.

"*Nicola* is the pop star you're working for?"

Lori looked at him like he'd left his brains out to fry on the sidewalk. "Her name is Nico. And you know she's the one who hired me to work on her video. Why are you acting so weird?"

Marcus suddenly realized where that hint of familiarity had come from Friday night. Lori must have shown him pictures of Nicola after she was hired to work on the video, but all he could remember was a lot of makeup and a sparkling bodysuit.

Thankfully, Lori didn't have time to wait for his answer because one of the dancers was calling out to her for guidance. Shooting one last disgruntled look at him, his sister moved back onto the dance floor.

Nicola's back was to him, but he could see her face reflected in the mirror. God help him, he couldn't keep from staring at her or drinking in her incredible beauty again. Her hair was pulled up in a ponytail and he could tell how hard she'd been dancing by the damp tendrils that were curling around her face.

All of the dancers had great bodies, but for Marcus, the curvy shape of Nicola's hips and breasts threatened to make him rock-hard right there in the middle of the studio.

Her eyes met his briefly in the mirror and she quickly lowered her head. Lori moved to Nicola and put a hand on her arm, leaning in to say something. Nicola shook her head, then moved into position.

A heartbeat later, Lori turned the song on and Nicola went into action.

Jesus, she was beautiful.

Marcus was mesmerized as she sang along with the surprisingly great song and danced in the center of her troupe. No wonder she'd become a star—he didn't have a prayer of taking his eyes off her.

He remembered the way she'd commanded the attention of everyone in the nightclub simply by walking into the room. Now he knew it was partly because she was famous, but even if she'd just been a regular woman, people would have stopped and stared.

As her curves shifted and grazed the thin spandex barely covering her skin, he couldn't stop himself from wondering what she'd look like naked, her soft skin shiny from exertion as she writhed beneath him on his bed. Would her eyes light up for him the way they did when she was singing? What would those strong, flexible limbs feel like wrapped around his hips as he drove into her? What would she taste like—would the rest of her be as sweet as her mouth had been?

As if she could read his thoughts, Nicola suddenly stumbled, knocking into a male dancer, and Lori quickly shut off the music.

He knew he should leave, that he was throwing her off. But he wasn't going anywhere. Not when he was lucky enough to get this second chance at coming face-to-face with her again.

Marcus Sullivan didn't believe in hiding from his mistakes. Hell, his relationship with Jill was the only time he'd ever tried to convince himself that something wrong was right. He should have trusted his gut, but he'd been so focused on what he wanted to see, instead of what was actually there.

But he knew exactly what was between him and Nicola, sparks that lit and sizzled so bright and hot he was still singed from their one and only kiss.

He'd been a fool to turn her down.

He wasn't going to be an even bigger fool by walking away from her again.

Seven

Somehow Nicola managed to pull things together and they'd actually ended up having a great rehearsal. But all afternoon *Please leave* warred with *Please don't go* inside her head.

From moment to moment she vacillated between wanting Marcus gone and needing him to be so much closer. No wonder she'd barely been able to concentrate on rehearsing, with her brain and body pulled in two totally disparate directions the entire time he was there watching her with those dark, hungry eyes she knew she'd never be able to get out of her head.

When they were finally done for the night, the dancers quickly scattered, leaving her alone with Lori…and Marcus.

Nicola had gotten over her nerves a long time ago. She'd had to, if she ever wanted to get anyone's attention with her music. But Marcus made her incredibly nervous in a way she'd never been nervous before. Clearly there was a big difference between being a performer and being a woman.

Shoving the rest of her things into her big dance bag, she was just saying, "Thanks for working us all so hard today, Lori. I'll see you tomor—" when a knock came at the door and a guy wearing a Mel's Diner shirt walked in carrying several large bags full of food.

"Marcus, this is awesome that you thought to order food for us!" Lori clapped her hands. "These are the best burgers and fries in the world, Nico. I'm starved so you must be dying of hunger since you barely touched your lunch. You can stay to eat something, can't you?"

Nicola looked at Lori in alarm. What was Marcus doing? Had he forgotten that he'd turned her down flat less than two days ago? Couldn't he feel how awkward this was? Why on earth had he ordered dinner for the three of them?

"I'd love to, but I think I'd better just call it a night. Besides, you two probably have some catching up to do, so thanks, but—"

"Stay for dinner, Nicola. Please."

Marcus's low words pulled at Nicola, so hard that she could almost feel herself leaning toward him. It hadn't been a request, not quite a command, either. But whatever it was, it had turned her brain to mush. Just as his one kiss had stolen her control on Saturday morning.

"Well," she finally said, "it does smell really good."

A few moments later she found herself sitting with them at the small table by the window, unwrapping a burger she couldn't possibly eat. Not with Marcus so close that her belly kept clenching.

"So what did you think, Marcus?" Lori asked her brother. "Isn't Nico amazing?"

Nicola felt like she was blushing with her whole body. During rehearsal, she'd tried to keep eye contact with him to a minimum, because every time she accidentally looked at him she lost her footing. As they'd gone over and over the song, she hadn't been able to read his expression, couldn't tell if he was impressed with her or if he thought her song—and dancing—were total crap. She told herself she didn't care if he liked it. Thirty-six-year-old men weren't necessarily her core audience, after all.

"Yes, she is," he said in a voice that had her insides melting right there in front of his sister. He quickly shifted his gaze from his sister to Nicola.

"I never realized how much work went into making a video. You were all working so hard. I'm very, very impressed."

Nicola didn't know what to say, and couldn't have found her voice even if she did. Fortunately, Lori was easily carrying the conversation as she told her brother, "Nicola works harder than the rest of us combined."

"That's not true," she somehow managed to get out, but Lori simply waved away her protest as if it was ridiculous.

"You do, Nico. Seriously, your work ethic puts the rest of the singers I've worked with to shame."

Marcus's eyes hadn't left her face, and she felt the intensity—and heat—of his gaze all the way down to her toes as he asked her, "Did you write that song?"

She tried not to have a chip on her shoulder about being a pop musician as she replied, "I did."

His mouth moved up into a small smile. "You're very talented."

Nicola let out the breath she hadn't realized she'd been holding just as Lori's phone started bouncing around on the tabletop. Whoever was calling had her jumping up and saying, "Sorry, guys, this will just take a sec."

Nicola could see from the look on Marcus's

face that he wasn't happy with the name and face he'd seen flash across his sister's phone. True to her word, Lori was back after barely saying two words to the caller, but she was flushed and clearly flustered.

"I'm really sorry, but I completely forgot about something I promised I'd take care of tonight. Did you need anything else from me tonight, Nico?"

Nicola could tell something was wrong and she didn't want to add any extra pressure to Lori's life. "Not at all. Let me know if there's anything I can do to help."

Looking relieved, Lori turned to her brother and said, "Marcus, could you make sure Nicola gets back to her hotel okay?"

"Of course," he replied at the exact moment that Nicola said, "I'll just get a cab."

But Lori didn't seem to hear either of them as she gave Nicola a quick hug goodbye and apologized again for needing to leave so suddenly. Nicola picked up her burger and dropped it into the trash as Marcus followed his sister to the door.

She didn't mean to eavesdrop on their conversation, but they weren't exactly doing a great job of keeping their voices down, so she couldn't help but overhear.

"I thought you weren't seeing him anymore.

Didn't we agree that he isn't good for you and that you can do so much better?"

"I'm not seeing him anymore...and it's complicated."

Marcus didn't look at all happy with his sister's response. "At least call me when you get back home tonight so I know you're okay."

Now Lori didn't look happy, either. "I'm a big girl, Marcus. I don't have a curfew anymore."

He was the perfect, protective older brother. Nicola could feel herself melting more with every word out of his mouth. Because even though she should be making sure her guard was all the way up, seeing how concerned he was about his sister got to her in a serious way.

When Lori left and he came back over, running his hand through his hair, Nicola had to ask, "Is everything okay?"

He shook his head. "I don't know. She says I worry too much about her, but I can't help it. She'll always be the little girl who needs me."

Oh, God, could he be any sweeter?

Certain that she was bound to do something really stupid if she hung around him any longer, Nicola said, "I'm not hungry, so I'll just catch a cab back to my hotel."

But before she could turn and leave, he asked

her, "Why didn't you tell me who you were?" The hunger in his eyes was still there, but so was a hint of anger that she couldn't possibly miss.

Hating how off-kilter she felt around him, she knew she sounded defensive as she replied, "I didn't lie to you. My name is Nicola."

"You should have told me you were also Nico. That you were a pop star. Why didn't you?"

"You wouldn't understand."

"Try me."

She didn't want to explain herself to him, but she also knew she was being stubborn and unreasonable. He had a point that it hadn't been fair of her to keep her fame a secret from him, especially if the pictures taken of the two of them in the club had been good enough to print. And for some reason she wanted him to understand.

"For one night it seemed exciting just to be normal." *To be myself again.* "I almost never meet someone who doesn't know who I am."

"Nico."

She didn't like the way he said her stage name, didn't like the idea of Marcus treating her like everyone else did.

"My name is Nicola." Her chest hurt again, like it had on Saturday morning when he'd kicked her out of his brother's house. "And I really need to go now."

The last thing she expected him to say as she turned and headed for the door was, "I was wrong, Nicola."

A smart woman wouldn't have stopped. A smart woman would have just kept walking through the door and caught a cab outside to take her back to her big, lonely penthouse suite.

So then, Nicola thought helplessly, what was it about Marcus that always had her doing the foolish thing instead?

Shouldn't she know better than to turn back to him and say, "What were you wrong about?"

Despite the fact that he hadn't moved any closer to her, the way he looked at her, with none of the reserve from Saturday morning, had her feeling like he'd just pulled her into his arms.

"About another night with you."

All of the desires, the hopes, she'd been trying to shove down and away immediately popped up to the surface.

Trying one last time to save herself, she said, "What about all of your reasons from Saturday morning? What about how young I am?" She shot his excuses at him one after the other. "What about the colossal mistake you're so glad you didn't make?"

"I'm sorry for what I said that morning," he said first, and then, "I want one more night with you, if you still want one more with me."

His words were a caress over her skin. He hadn't answered her question, and she knew their age difference must still be an issue for him. But just as she wasn't able to walk away from him, it seemed that he couldn't walk away from her, either.

"Of course I still want you," she said, barely above a whisper.

The words had barely left her lips when he captured her hand and dragged her body tightly up against his. "Thank God. Because I've been dying to kiss you again."

The next thing she knew, his mouth was pressing hard into hers, his tongue suddenly there in her mouth, tasting her, forcing her tongue to taste him, too. No one had ever kissed her like this, like he wanted to possess her, body and soul. She forgot to be nervous, forgot that, until Marcus, it had been six months since she'd kissed anyone, and even before that she'd hardly had much experience with kissing.

She didn't need to worry about any of that with

him, she realized now. He was entirely and completely in charge. All she needed to do was follow his lead.

And if the way his kiss was making her feel was any indication of what his lovemaking would do to her, she was being led straight toward ecstasy.

The tips of her breasts throbbed tight and hard beneath her sports bra and sweatshirt, and although she pressed them against his hard chest, it didn't soothe the ache. She wanted—needed—more.

Way more.

Fortunately, *way more* was just what it looked like she was going to get.

Eight

Hand in hand, they headed down the stairs to the large parking garage beneath the dance studio. Apart from the moment when she got into his car, Marcus didn't let go of Nicola's hand.

Utterly lost in the feel of his thumb rubbing sensuous circles on the inside of her palm, it wasn't until they were almost at the hotel that Nicola remembered to say, "There's a special entrance around the side that I usually use." As they pulled up to the private hotel entrance she reached into her bag for her key cards with her free hand and handed the extra one to Marcus. "Why don't you drop me here and I'll meet you at my room. I'm in the penthouse suite."

His hand stiffened in hers and she realized, too late, that she'd probably just insulted him.

"It isn't because I don't want to be seen with

you," she explained softly, hating what she had to say to make him understand. "If people see us walk in together tonight, if someone takes a picture of you and me together, they might think we're a—"

She paused before she used the word *couple.* Not because she couldn't stand the thought of it. But because she suddenly longed to be a part of a couple with Marcus so badly that the force of that wanting stunned her. Even more than the strength of her desire for him already had.

Her voice was barely above a whisper as she amended what she'd been about to say. "They might think you and I are going to be together for more than one night."

Already, she knew one night wouldn't be enough.

What was wrong with her?

She and Marcus had been totally clear with each other from the outset. Their one-night stand would be about sex, nothing but physical pleasure.

And yet, the reminders made no difference.

Because she'd already learned enough about him via his mother and sister—and the time she'd spent in his arms the other night—to know that her heart was a heck of a lot more involved than was going to be good for her.

"You had no problem walking out of that club with me Friday night."

Wanting him to understand, she said, "You know how you were upset about something that night? Well, so was I and I acted without thinking. I shouldn't have gone to the club like that. And I definitely shouldn't have left with you." It was finally time to come clean. "There were pictures taken of the two of us."

She refused to look away from him, even though his reaction to that was exactly as she'd expected. He was pissed.

Before he could ask questions, she said, "My publicist called and told me. I knew people had to be snapping pictures on their phones, but fortunately the lighting was really bad inside the club and they're too blurry for anyone to want to run." She pulled out her phone and showed him the pictures she'd been emailed earlier that day as proof. "Here they are."

Marcus was dangerously silent, silent enough that she forced herself to say, "I understand if you don't want to do this anymore, if this is all too complicated for you."

His eyes moved from the pictures on the phone back to her face. He didn't look happy about the situation, but the hunger, the desire for her, was still there. He wound his finger through a lock of her hair and pulled her toward him with it.

"It isn't any more complicated than this."

His mouth was so hot and sweet and perfect that with each slow slide of his tongue against hers, she almost forgot her hard-won caution. Even though this was the special VIP entrance, someone could walk by and look through the windshield to see them making out in the car. She shuddered at the thought of what those headlines would look like in the tabloids…or maybe it was the incredible sensuality of Marcus's kiss that had tremors moving through her.

When he finally pulled away and said, "I'll meet you in your room," her hand was shaking as she opened the door. Her legs were shaky, too, and she needed a moment to regain her bearings before walking inside the hotel.

Marcus had never understood how Smith put up with this kind of shit. Private entrances and calls from publicists about pictures that had leaked and entering and exiting buildings under cover just wasn't normal.

As he pulled around to the front entrance and gave his keys to the valet, he couldn't quite believe that he was sneaking around to get it on with a beautiful pop star.

He didn't like how not coming clean to Lori about already having met Nicola had felt like lying. And he didn't like the way Nicola had handed him her hotel room key and told him to meet her in the penthouse suite.

But then, he wasn't exactly calling his sister to come clean or getting back in his car and leaving, was he?

Hell, no. He might have his pride, but he wasn't completely stupid.

And only a total idiot would turn down a second chance to be with Nicola.

He was just heading out of the hotel's large reception area when he saw a crowd of what looked like college football players surrounding someone. They were clearly drunk and even though he wanted to get up to Nicola's room as soon as possible, something told him to go check things out.

Veering off course, he was almost at the group when he heard her voice. Chills ran up his spine as she told them, "Give a girl some room to breathe, guys."

He read right through the playful edge in Nicola's voice and heard the terror that had crept in.

"All of you need to back off," he told them in a hard voice. "Way off."

A couple of guys looked over at him and made the mistake of dismissing him as some old guy in a suit. Several of them had their cameras out and they were putting their hands on Nicola to get her to pose for pictures with them.

Where the hell was hotel security? The Fairmont was the kind of hotel that catered to stars like her. There should have been a half dozen staff members intervening right now. Instead, somehow each and every one of them was busy...and Marcus was beyond angry about it.

Over the years, Marcus had been forced, one too many times, to sit back on the sidelines and watch his brother deal with overly aggressive fans and paparazzi. Smith had repeatedly told his family that while he appreciated how much they wanted to defend him, calm and cool was the best way to deal with them.

Marcus was working to remember Smith's advice when one of Nicola's "fans" said, "Hey, Nico, take off that big sweatshirt so everyone can see how hot you are."

Marcus pushed into the group so hard and fast a couple of the college kids knocked over like bowling pins. "Get your hands off her," he growled. When they didn't move fast enough, he grabbed them by the shoulders and shoved them away.

"What the hell are you, her bodyguard or something?"

Marcus's hand was already in a fist when Nicola grabbed his arm. "Yes, he is. And I'm afraid I'm late for something. Nice to meet all of you!"

She dragged him away from the group. "Good timing," she said under her breath as they made a beeline for the elevators. "They were getting a little annoying."

Annoying? That's all those buffoons were to her?

Forgetting that they were supposed to be going upstairs separately, he said, "They weren't just annoying, they were outright dangerous." He wanted to run his hands over her body, make sure nothing had happened to her. More than that, he wanted to take her someplace safe and make her stay there, out of harm's way.

"They weren't dangerous," she said, dismissing his concerns. "They couldn't have done anything really bad in the middle of the hotel lobby."

But Marcus could think of a dozen different things they could have done to her, including ways they could have kept her from crying out for help.

It suddenly hit him how dangerous it could potentially be for her to do what other people took for granted. "How could you have gone to that club alone on Friday night? What if a bunch of drunks had cornered you on the street? Or by the bar?" And what if he hadn't been the one to take her home?

"Honestly, that kind of stuff doesn't happen all that often. I usually remember to put on sunglasses and a hat so that people can't recognize me that easily. Besides," she added in a supersoft voice, "if I hadn't gone to the club, I wouldn't have met you."

He wanted to make her promise to be more careful in the future, but before he could, a large family got out of the elevator and an earsplitting squeal sounded as soon as the children saw her.

"Oh, my God, it's Nico!"

The boy and his sister, who couldn't have been more than seven or eight, threw themselves at her and she caught them as they impulsively hugged her. At the same time, their mother struggled to get a huge, heavy stroller out of the elevator.

Marcus moved quickly to help her before the

door closed, and with her arms still around the children, Nicola watched him say something soothing to the harried mother that had her mouth curving up into a smile. That soft spot in Nicola's chest grew even bigger for this beautiful man she was about to take upstairs to do very naughty things with.

"Mom! We need your camera to take a picture with Nico!"

Just then the baby in the stroller started crying. Considering their mother already looked like she was at the end of a very frayed rope, it was clear that the last thing she needed was to look for her camera.

"I've got to deal with your sister," their mother told them, already reaching in to unstrap the baby girl.

Nicola had always loved children and her secret hope she'd never shared with anyone was to have a big family of her own. She'd been a heck of a babysitter as a teenager. It was partly why she felt her music translated so well to kids. She genuinely liked them, rather than just putting up with them.

She was about to reach out for the baby girl when Marcus beat her to the punch. "Would you like me to hold her?" he offered to the mother.

Considering the boy and girl were whining now about how horrible it would be to not have their picture taken with Nico, after assessing Marcus in his professional suit and his obvious trustworthiness, the woman said, “Okay, if you wouldn’t mind, it will just be for a second or two. I’m pretty sure my camera is down under everything in the stroller.”

Marcus took the tearful little baby, who stopped crying as soon as he lifted her up to his face. “Well, aren’t you a pretty little thing?”

The mother beamed. “I know, she’s gorgeous, isn’t she?”

He nodded, never once taking his eyes from the baby’s toothless grin. “What’s your name?” he asked the baby as if she could answer, and she happily replied with a gurgling mountain of spit bubbles.

Without missing a beat, he used her bib to wipe off the spit…and Nicola started falling… and feeling…and being overwhelmed again, by this incredible man.

She wasn’t sure how long she stood there staring openmouthed at how good Marcus was with the baby—he was now maneuvering her as if she was a mini diapered airplane, even making the noises to go along with it—until the kid's mother triumphantly declared, "I found the camera!"

Nicola snapped to attention as if from out of a deep fog. The kids were now standing on either side of her, smiling for the camera.

Oh, God. How could this be happening to her? She hardly knew him, didn't know what he did for fun or what his house looked like. She hadn't met the rest of his family, and didn't know if he sang off-key in the shower or had been a choirboy with perfect pitch.

But, a contrary little voice in her head told her, *don't you already know everything that matters? That he loves his family and is good with children and has been kinder—and gentler—to you than anyone else ever has? Not to mention the way you go up in flames when he kisses you....*

"Say cheese!"

Nicola smiled for the camera, the same smile she'd given thousands of times over during the past few years. But when the woman turned the viewer around and said, "Look at how cute you all are," Nicola was shocked to see that she wasn't smiling the same way she normally did with fans.

Because instead of Nico the pop star smiling back at her, it was Nicola, a woman who'd just been flattened by unexpected emotion, looking utterly bewildered by what had just come over her.

Wanting desperately to reset back to normal again, she turned her complete focus on the kids, asking them their names, what grades they were in, if they had a favorite song. She asked their mother if she could have their email to send special concert tickets over for her show on Saturday night.

Finally, Marcus put the baby back in her stroller and gently strapped her in. The family left, calling goodbye. She waved back at them, glad for the movement to hide how unsteady her hands were.

Marcus pushed the elevator button again and followed her in, his hand on the small of her back, just as it had been the night before when they'd walked out of the club. She was immediately enveloped by his heat, along with that sense of safety she'd felt from the first moment she'd met him in the club.

She pressed the button for the penthouse suite and when the elevator doors closed, he said, "You were great with those kids."

"I love kids," she admitted to him. "Babies are so sweet. Elementary school kids are so earnest.

Teenagers are so raw and passionate. And all of them are so honest about their feelings."

"Honesty means a lot to you, doesn't it?"

She thought about Kenny, about how he'd betrayed her trust. "It means everything to me." Realizing how serious a turn their conversation had taken—and that if she wasn't careful she'd be crying on his shoulder about how bad it hurt to be lied to—she smiled and said, "I've never seen a baby take to anyone so fast."

He didn't deflect her compliment, but simply said, "I've spent a lot of time with babies and kids over the years."

She'd wanted to ask him about his family last night in the taxi after speaking with his mother, but she hadn't let herself because she'd been afraid of building anything more than a sexual connection. Well, she was already in over her head on that front, wasn't she? How could it possibly hurt much more to drill the screw in a little deeper?

"Lori adores you. I take it the rest of your brothers and sisters do, too?"

"We watch out for one another."

"It sounds like it's mostly you watching out for them," she pointed out.

"Do you have any siblings?"

"Two younger brothers."

"Let me guess," he said. "They both drive shiny new cars courtesy of their big sister."

She had to laugh at the way he'd turned her comment around on her by pointing out that she did just the same thing with her own family.

"I know I probably shouldn't have, but I just couldn't help myself. My family is really, really great. My parents have always been so supportive of any and everything I've done, and although my brothers can be twerps sometimes, they're mostly pretty cool."

Marcus laughed at that. "I'd be lying if I didn't admit I was thinking of Lori and Sophie when you said that. They're great, but let's put it this way—" he shook his head and gave a little grimace "—they can be a bit of a handful, too."

"Of course you spoil them, anyway," she said with a smile.

"When Lori and Sophie turned sixteen I threw them a hell of a party at a safari place near Napa."

"Complete with elephants and zebras?"

"Alligators and pythons, too."

"No wonder Lori loves you so much," Nicola teased, but then, before she could stop herself, she added, "Although I'm pretty sure you wouldn't need to spend a dime on her and she would love you just as much."

His smile slowly receded at her very personal statement, one that included multiple uses of the word *love*.

Wow. Way to play it cool.

Not.

Thankfully, the door opened to the penthouse just then and she was able to hide her flaming cheeks from him as they walked to her half of the top floor. She pulled her key card out of her bag and opened the door.

She appreciated it when Marcus didn't make a big deal out of how nice the suite was. It always made her uncomfortable when people all but asked what her net worth was.

The thirty minutes since they'd left the dance studio seemed like hours ago now. She felt awkward and unsure of herself again. "I'm all icky from rehearsal. I should probably go take a shower."

Marcus shut the door behind her and locked it. When he looked at her, his eyes held none of their earlier laughter from when they'd been discussing their families.

Now, there was only heat…and so much desire it took her breath away.

"Come here, Nicola."

She didn't move a muscle. She couldn't. "But I should—"

"No showers. Not yet." His gaze heated up even further. "Not without me."

He paused, let his words register, the promise in them, the vision of actually taking a shower together, of being soaped up and all wet with him, doing crazy things to her insides.

She knew he must be able to read her reaction on her face, but he didn't say anything else; he simply stood right where he was by the door and waited for her to come to him.

She could do this. Of course she could. Just put one foot in front of the other and, as long as her heart didn't explode from pounding so fast, she'd be fine.

With her legs as shaky as they'd been that very first time she'd stood up on stage in front of a thousand people to sing her songs, she began the slow walk toward Marcus.

Nine

Marcus was a heartbeat away from picking Nicola up, throwing her on the bed and taking her. It nearly killed him to hold back, to watch her slowly move across the carpeted floor toward him.

She was nervous, the same way she'd been Friday night when they'd gotten in the cab. She had such incredible sex appeal—the video rehearsal confirmed that she clearly knew how to use her sexuality to whip her audience into a frenzy—so her nerves didn't make sense to Marcus. But seconds later, he forgot all about needing things to add up.

Who cared about anything except getting her out of her clothes?

He had to reach for her, had to grab a handful of her sweatshirt in his fist and lean down to take her sinfully seductive mouth with his. She moaned against his mouth and he yanked her sweatshirt up. He pulled back to lift it up and over her head.

Nothing but thin spandex and curves awaited him.

"My God, you're beautiful."

She blinked up at him, her big blue eyes softer now, more aroused than worried. "Thank you."

Hadn't she heard a thousand times over by now how beautiful she was? If not from her fans, then from the men she'd shared her bed with? And yet, the way she'd said "Thank you" was so pure. So honest. As if he were the first lover who had ever told her she was breathtaking.

Again and again, she surprised him. First, when she'd slept like a contented kitten on his lap all night long. And then in the morning, when she'd walked into Smith's kitchen, her pretty face clean of makeup, looking young and fresh and ridiculously innocent, despite the leather dress she still wore. And then again, just a few minutes ago when she'd been genuinely interested in those kids downstairs who'd wanted her autograph.

The least important surprise of all, he realized now, was the fact that she was a famous pop star. He'd been upset that she'd kept it from him, but then again, he hadn't told her he owned Sullivan Winery, either, because it hadn't seemed to matter when they were just planning to have a one-night stand.

He had expected to want her. But he hadn't expected to like her this much. In the wake of breaking up with Jill, he hadn't expected to feel anything for a woman beyond raw desire.

Growing threads of emotion tugged on the tenuous hold he had on his control, threatening to snap it. Marcus knew that he'd better do something, and quick, to get the night back on track.

Back on *his* track.

He'd always been dominant in the bedroom, enjoying taking care of a woman's pleasure at least as much as his own. Jill hadn't liked giving up control to him, though, and during the two years they were together, their sex life had been almost completely vanilla.

He was ready for a different flavor. And based on the sparks that had been between them since the very first moment, he had a good feeling that Nicola was, too.

"For nearly three days I've been imagining you without any clothes on. I've wanted to know how soft and heavy your breasts feel in my hands.

How wet and slick you'll be between your legs as I slide my fingers into you."

She shivered against him as he cupped her stunning face in his hands and kissed her, long and slow, taking the time—finally—to learn the corners and crevices of her sweet mouth. She trembled when he dipped his tongue into the corners where her upper and lower lips came together, then gave a low moan as he nipped her lower lip between his teeth and sucked it inside.

Without giving her any warning, he moved his hands from her face to the bottom of her thin tank top and pulled it up over her head and threw it to the floor. She made a move to cover her breasts and he stopped her hands with his.

"No."

Her eyes were dilated and her breath was coming fast as he slid his fingers through hers.

"I don't want you to hide yourself from me."

From where he was holding her hands between her soft, full breasts, he could feel her swift intake of breath—along with her rapid heartbeat.

"Take a step back so that I can look at you."

He could see how uncertain she was, but it only made him more determined to push past it. He could scent her arousal, knew how much she wanted him. He needed to know how she would respond to his natural sexuality, to the innate dominance he'd controlled for too long.

"Now, kitten."

Her eyes flared with surprise—and heat—at the endearment even as she took a step back.

Not wanting anything to cover up her beautiful breasts—his hands and mouth would have to wait for their chance—Marcus made himself let go of her hands.

Nicola immediately moved to cover herself. He didn't say anything, simply shook his head, once.

Her eyes widened again, and for a moment, he wasn't sure that she would obey his silent command. But then, she took a deep breath and lifted her chin. Her hands shifted down, revealing sweet, soft skin, and his breath caught.

Just before she was about to reveal her nipples, she stopped, blushing furiously.

From what he could recall of seeing flashes of her on TV and pictures on magazine covers, he knew she often wore next to nothing on stage. And yet, if he didn't know better, he would swear she'd never shown another man her naked breasts. She was that shy.

"Show me how beautiful you are, Nicola." He didn't understand why this was so hard for her, but since it obviously was, he instinctively softened his voice. He was gentle, soothing, as he urged her, "Show me how much you want this. How much you want me."

The silence throbbed between them for a long while until—finally—she dropped her hands from her chest.

The hit of lust that knocked into him nearly took him down to his knees on the carpeted floor of her penthouse suite.

Her nipples were erect and a soft pink that made his mouth water at the thought of licking them to see if they tasted as sweet as they looked. Her skin was lightly tanned all over, without a tan line in sight on her shoulders or around her breasts…easily the most beautiful breasts he'd ever been lucky enough to set eyes on.

His erection had already been hard enough to pound nails since their kiss in the dance studio and hadn't much flagged since then. But now, he was worlds beyond hard from nothing more than a couple of hot kisses and the beautiful sight of Nicola's naked breasts.

Full and high on her small frame, they quivered slightly, just enough for him to realize that she was shaking.

At this point he could barely stop himself from jumping her, but he knew he had to hold back at least long enough to ask, "You're not scared of me, are you?"

She shook her head. "No." But the way she dropped her gaze from his and lowered her head gave him an entirely different answer.

"You and I," he said as he moved closer to tip her chin up with his fingertips so that she had to look at him, "we won't ever lie to each other."

Again, it wasn't a question. It was simply a truth that had to be.

When she nodded her agreement, he asked again, "Are you afraid of what's happening between us tonight?"

"I'm not afraid of you. I just—" She made a move to re-cover her breasts with her hands, and when he took them in his to stop her once again, she only shook harder.

"Tell me why you're scared, kitten."

But instead of telling him, she said, "Why do you keep calling me that?"

Despite how badly he wanted her, despite the fact that he was working like hell to rein in the caveman inside, he found himself smiling. "Because that's how you slept on my lap. Like a contented kitten."

Her eyes softened and her trembling stopped.

"I want to rub myself all over you like a kitten," she whispered shyly.

His hard-on jumped behind his zipper as she watched his reaction…and waited for him to tell her if that was what he wanted her to do.

Hell, yes, he wanted it, wanted to feel all those soft, smooth curves sliding against him. But if she did that he'd be a goner. And she hadn't yet told him why she'd been trembling.

"I want you to do that, too," he told her, "but first I want you to tell me what's wrong."

"I haven't—" She stopped, took a deep breath before admitting, "It's been a while for me."

Ah, that explained why she was so nervous. "We'll take it slow," he promised her in a husky voice. "Slow and easy."

"Okay," she said, and the trust in her eyes nearly undid him. "But what if I want fast and hard, too?"

In an instant, the thin threads of his control snapped as he lifted her into his arms.

A bed. He just needed to get her to a bed and then he could stop, think, plan what he was going to do with her…all the ways he was going to make her scream with pleasure.

He quickly walked across the soft carpeting from the entryway to the bedroom and was almost there when she shifted so that her breasts were against his chest and her face was softly pressing into his neck. He could feel her warm breath, and then her lips moving along the tendons that ran down to his shoulders. But it was the soft lick of her tongue against his skin, followed by a nip of her teeth, that broke him.

Barely two feet from the bed, he bent his head and took one of her breasts in his mouth.

She was so sweet, and so responsive, as her nipple tightened even further against his tongue. He felt his hold on sanity loosen as she moaned his name and he had to shift her weight so that her other breast was there for him to suckle on, too.

Knowing he'd never experienced anything as erotic as the way her body responded to his touch, Marcus made himself move those final feet to the bed, and lowered them both so that he was sitting on the edge of the mattress with her on his lap. Her fingers were in his hair now, her neck arched back so that she could give him better access to her breasts. Her hips were cushioning his erection and he knew if he left her there to squirm and wiggle around on his lap, he was going to explode before he was anywhere near getting inside her.

He lifted his mouth from her breasts just long enough to reposition her so that she was standing between his spread thighs. Her legs were unsteady and he held on to her hips, moving her small but curvy frame into just the right place for him to take her breasts back into his mouth, one after the other. Her hands stayed in his hair, and the desperate little sounds she was making as he licked and sucked and nipped at her sensitive flesh had him suddenly wanting the night to be so much longer than just a handful of hours.

Ten

Nicola had never felt this out of control. Her brain, her body, none of it was connected together anymore. Between Marcus's kisses and his hands on her skin—she lost hold of everything that held her down to earth as, in one smooth move, he slid her shorts and thong off so that she was completely naked.

As he dragged her mouth down to his for another soul-changing kiss, her hands automatically went to his pants to start unbuttoning and unzipping so that she could get him naked, too.

One of his big hands covered both of hers. "Not yet. Not until you come for me."

Still holding her hand, she was more than a little shocked when he slid both of their fingers between her thighs.

"Tell me how it feels," he said in a low voice.

"Good." She could barely breathe. "So good."

Her legs were shaking and he held her steady with his free hand as he had them rub their combined fingers over her.

"Marcus."

She gasped out his name as jolts of pleasure zipped through her. His eyes flared with lust a split second before he leaned forward and captured one of her breasts in his mouth again. She whimpered her pleasure as he had them pressing harder and harder circles with their fingers. She was right there, she was so close, she held her breath as—

"Just my hand now."

She barely registered his words before he was letting her hand go so that he could thrust one large finger deep inside of her. She thought she heard him say something about how tight, how small, she was, but it was way off in the distance.

"Come for me. I want to see it. I want to feel your muscles grip me when you explode."

Oh, God, she wanted to, and his naughty words had her clenching on him in a miniorgasm. She was so close, but the closer she got the more her legs shook.

She wanted to relax all the way, to stop being so shy, to fully give in to all the wonderful things

Marcus was making her feel, but one thought kept stopping her.

If she embraced this wildness with Marcus, did that mean she really was the wild slut Kenny had painted her to be?

As if he'd felt her hesitation, Marcus moved his hand from between her legs. She opened her mouth to protest, but before she could, he was lifting her from the floor so that he was lying back on the bed and she was straddling him on her knees.

His hands stroked her back and she realized that he was going to be true to his word.

Slow and easy.

And that was when she realized it didn't matter what the world thought of her. When she was in bed with Marcus all that mattered was what she was feeling. All that mattered was the intense pleasure that he'd already given her.

Bending over to kiss him, her tongue met his wildly, her desperation making the kiss so intense it was on the verge of being rough.

Somewhere in their kiss, she realized he'd slid his hand back between her legs. A low, pleasured moan escaped her as he slid one thick finger back into her. She was beyond pleased to find that this position made it easier for her to rock against his hand.

"More," she begged. "Please, Marcus."

She watched him war with himself, a muscle jumping in his chiseled jaw, and then he finally ground out, "Hold still."

It nearly killed her not to continue rocking up and down on his hand and her breath hitched as she felt the pressure of what had to be more than one finger inside of her.

"Nicola?"

Horribly afraid he would stop, she leaned forward, pressed a kiss to his lips. "Please, don't stop."

But as he worked to slide in farther, her inner muscles tightened on him. He whispered, "Kiss me," a breath before he tangled the fingers of his other hand in her hair and took her mouth with his. Between kisses, he told her, "Just like that."

A hundred wonderful sensations blurred together in those moments as a huge flood of arousal slickened the path of his fingers. And when he moved his free hand to cup her breasts so that he could tease them both at the same time that the thumb of his other hand teased her to perfection, she felt it coming. Pleasure as big as a tidal wave. So big she didn't think she could handle it.

No, she *knew* she couldn't handle it.

She broke their kiss and was putting her hands flat on his chest to try to pull away when his voice broke through her panic. "Nicola. Look at me. I'm right here with you."

She somehow managed to focus on him as wave after wave of pleasure started to break over her, through her, inside of her.

And when he whispered, "Let go for me," the way he was watching her, as if he'd never seen anything as beautiful—or as mesmerizing and magical—in his entire life, was the final key the lock on her body needed to break all the way apart.

Never in his life had Marcus been with a woman this made for pleasure, who came with such wild abandon, who acted like she'd never felt anything as good as his touch before…and whose climax was practically never-ending.

Sweet Lord, he never wanted it to end. He never wanted to forget the way she pulled away from their kiss so that her sweat-slickened body could buck and arch over his as she continued to ride out her release. He never wanted to forget the desperate little sounds she made as she kissed him, gasps that turned into moans. He never wanted to forget the beautiful sounds of her begging for more of his touches, his kisses, for him to take her all the way over the edge.

But he already knew he could never possibly forget those sounds, the incredible sight of the most beautiful girl in the world losing herself to pleasure in his arms.

Finally, she stilled above him, her once-taut muscles now loose, pliant, her head dropping to his chest. She was panting and he could feel her lungs working hard to pull in air as she lay across him. Even though he was still fully clothed—and rock-hard—he loved the way she curled and nuzzled against him, again that soft little kitten from their first night together.

Still, he'd have to let her recover from that orgasm another time. Because he wasn't even close to being finished worshipping her. She'd have the rest of her life to recover from tonight. They both would.

From now until the sun came up, she was his.

Giving her no warning, he flipped her onto her back and rose over her stunningly beautiful naked body.

She blinked up at him, her gaze momentarily

fuzzy. But then she blinked and smiled before saying, "You're wearing too many clothes."

Her hands moved from around his neck to the buttons of his shirt as she worked to undo them. The soft touch of her fingers skimming across his chest had his heart pounding even faster. Her tongue came out to lick her upper lip as she concentrated on undressing him and he couldn't possibly have stopped himself from bending down to lick against it.

As soon as his tongue touched hers, she opened her mouth for him and that simple need to taste her tongue became another soul-destroying kiss.

He could have kissed her like that forever, had the sound of fabric ripping not surprised him into pulling back. She'd ripped his shirt apart, and where the buttons hadn't been able to come undone fast enough, the cotton had actually shredded.

The next thing he knew, she was dropping his ripped shirt from her clenched fists and running her hands over his abs. Her hands on his bare skin were good. So damn good. But he should have known it was going to get even better, because a split second later, his fierce little kitten leaned up to nip at his chest. His muscles twitched beneath her teeth as her tongue came out to lave the small bite.

"I've never wanted anyone like this," she whispered against his chest as she pressed one naughty kiss after another across his skin while her hands moved lower to cup and cradle his cloth-covered erection in her open palm.

He sucked in a breath between his teeth as she closed her palm around him, first tentatively, growing bolder as she felt him thicken even further inside her warm clasp. Gritting his teeth against the intense pleasure of her caresses, he made himself remind her, "Slow and easy, so that I don't hurt you."

Her gaze flew to his. "You would never hurt me."

Her trust in him landed straight in the center of his chest, in a place he'd thought was closed off for the foreseeable future. It was the same place that had reacted when she'd fallen asleep on his lap, when she'd appeared shy and fresh-faced in the kitchen, when she'd been laughing with the boy and girl who loved her music.

He didn't know how she was doing it, how she was managing to get in under his skin, his bones, all the way down to a heart that knew better. He should have been looking at her as Nico the pop star. He should have been reminding himself that she was going to move on after tonight and forget about him amid her world of flashbulbs and adoring fans.

She didn't need him. Not past this one night, in any case.

Marcus would never forgive himself if he ended the night needing her.

More than a little angry with himself for an ending that was starting to seem more inevitable by the second, he abruptly moved away from the bed to step out of his pants. He needed a few seconds of not touching her to get his brain to start functioning properly again.

Her eyes widened as she looked at him. "You're beautiful, Marcus."

He knew he had a good physique and plenty of women had looked at him like this before, but their admiration had never affected him so strongly. Maybe because no one had ever looked up at him with such wonder.

Or such trust.

Nicola couldn't do anything but stare.

His body, his muscles—his incredibly beautiful erection—made a mockery of any sculpture Rodin had ever made.

And even though she'd known he was big, without his clothes on he was huge, his muscles rippling as if he did manual labor for a living.

Somewhere in there, she realized he'd slid a condom on and was talking to her, saying, "Just because I've put this on doesn't mean we have to do anything that you're not ready for."

She'd loved following his lead tonight, but not if it meant he was going to leave out of some strange sense of honor because he wasn't sure she "was ready" to be with a man like him. She didn't like how he was still standing beside the bed, his hands in fists as if he was trying his best not to touch her again.

Nicola didn't wait another second—couldn't risk waiting for him to change his mind—before moving off the bed to jump into his arms, her arms around his neck, her legs around his waist. He moved between her thighs and her name rushed from his lips on a whoosh of air. Loosening her arms a little bit, she let gravity help her sink down onto him. She was so wet, so aroused, that despite his girth she easily took him in those first couple of inches.

Unfortunately, he felt the exact moment her body cried out at the wonderful intrusion.

"No, Nicola, not like this. Not yet."

But his body was saying the exact opposite of his words as his hands came around to cup her bottom and his hips started moving in a slow motion guaranteed to ease more of him inside of her. She gasped and her head fell back as she locked her ankles tighter together behind his hips to try to pull him in closer, deeper.

"Am I hurting you?"

His raw, rough words reverberated against her neck, his teeth scraping against her pulse point before she could answer.

She wanted to tell him no, he wasn't hurting her, because she knew that was what he wanted to hear. But she'd promised to tell him the truth tonight. She lifted her head to look into his eyes.

"A little. But it's a good pain. I want more of it. More of you."

Before he could tell her they needed to stop, she pressed her mouth to his and kissed him, her tongue wild against his, the little bit of pain rebounding back into shocking pleasure.

Soon, she was lying on the bed beneath him again, sweat dripping down from his chest onto hers as he worked to keep himself still above her. Their mouths came apart and she looked up at him, marveling yet again at how gorgeous he was, his muscular, tanned chest impossibly beautiful, his arms strong, his hips narrow.

"Slower," he rasped out. "We need to go slower."

Maybe they did, maybe that would be a better way for her body to accustom itself to him, but she wanted the exact opposite. She was beyond ready for fast and crazy. She wanted to know what it would be like for Marcus to lose control with her…and to know that she was the one who had done that to him.

She wanted to make him forget everything—everything except how much he needed her, wanted her, had to have her.

Because that was how she felt about him.

And she didn't want to be the only one who needed, wanted, craved like that.

"I don't want slow," she told him. "I just want you. All of you."

She bucked her hips up hard into his, forcing him to give her more, and she couldn't hold in her gasp at the shocking fullness of his body entering hers. Or the fact that with every inch he moved deeper, she felt like he was owning not just her body, but a piece of her soul that she'd never known was available to anyone.

"There's no going back now."

"I don't want to go back," she whispered.

But that didn't mean she wasn't scared knowing just how thoroughly he was going to possess her. A possession that wouldn't just be physical, despite the rules they'd set up for their one night together.

She twined her arms even tighter around his neck. "I like you, Marcus. I like you so much."

He bent his head, kissed her softly before saying, "I like you, too."

And then he was rearing up over her, her hands sliding from around his neck to the front of his chest as he braced his weight on his knees and gripped her hips to position himself between her thighs. She gasped as he pulled out and then filled her in one smooth stroke.

His eyes were dangerously dark. "You like that, too, don't you?"

"Mmm." She couldn't answer, couldn't get her lips to form the words for how much she liked it, but her body was doing a fine job of answering him, rocking beneath the long, hard thrusts of his pelvis into hers.

"Just like that," he urged her. "Squeeze me tight just like that."

As if he held the controls to her body, she felt her sex clench at his encouragement, and both of them groaned as the sensations built, multiplied, extended out to a place of nearly impossible pleasure. She could feel another climax building, growing, taking her over cell by cell.

"Oh, God, Marcus. Come with me. Please. I need you here."

Her frantic words, her unplanned plea, must have been magic, because in an instant, all of the control that he'd work so hard to hold on to was gone.

He pounded into her with no regard for hurting her, without a thought to whether she could withstand the force of his lovemaking.

And, oh, how she loved the way the oncoming orgasm hit her so hard it knocked all of the remaining breath from her lungs.

How she loved to be in the middle of the hurricane with him as he spun them both higher and tighter, his big body controlling hers so beautifully. So perfectly.

Sounds echoed through the large bedroom, his praise for how beautiful she was, how perfect, along with her moans, gasps, yes, even screams of pleasure. And even when she expected her climax to end—it couldn't go on forever like this, could it?—Marcus continued to rock with her, his hand moving between her legs, rubbing circles of pleasure.

"Give me one more," he urged her, and she was wondering how he knew there was a little bit left inside of her still when she felt it wash over her, another wave of pleasure, less intense this time, but still so good she had to reach for him and pull his head down again so that she could kiss him.

Their kiss was lazier now, slower in the aftermath of all that passion and intense need, and she loved the way his tongue stroked against hers.

A little while later, he shifted them so that he was on his back and she was lying half on the bed, half sprawled across him. Somewhere in there she felt him shift to remove the condom, but thankfully he was reaching for her and pulling her back against him a handful of seconds later, her head on his chest, with the rest of her body curled over and around his very hard muscles.

Nicola couldn't remember the last time she felt this tired…or this good. And yet, if she slept now, knowing it was all over in the morning, her dreams would be unsettled. Upset despite how amazing her night with Marcus had been.

And the truth was, had she been more awake, more lucid, she never would have asked, "How about two nights instead of one?"

The perfect way they fit together, the way he pulled her closer and stroked his hand over her hair, was her answer. No longer needing to stay awake, Nicola let herself relax all the way into sleep.

Holy hell.

Marcus stared at the ceiling, the bright lights of downtown San Francisco shining in through the sheer curtains on the windows.

He'd always loved sex, but what had just happened with Nicola tonight…it was way beyond good sex.

His mind wasn't just blown, his body was, too.

And now, she wanted another night.

Of course, he did, too. How could he not want a repeat of the most spectacular sex of his life, with what had to be the most beautiful, most responsive woman he'd ever had the pleasure of making love to?

But that was just the problem.

It should have just been sex.

It should have been mindless screwing.

It should have been nothing but pleasure, nothing but checking off one orgasm after another.

Nicola shifted against him, her soft curves already arousing him again when he should have been long past the point of no return, at least for a good thirty minutes or so.

Maybe if he wasn't thirty-six years old; maybe if he hadn't been screwed over by a woman he'd thought he was going to marry; maybe if he hadn't just been party to lovemaking so extraordinary it made his groin throb with renewed need… maybe then he could have told himself the lie he wanted to believe.

But he knew better than to even try.

Because the undeniable truth was that the night he'd just spent with Nicola had been more than he'd bargained for.

He'd meant it when he said he liked her. A whole hell of a lot more than he was comfortable with. Somehow all the visions of her with those kids at the elevator, his memory of the way she'd slept on his lap and then had been so sweetly nervous in his brother's kitchen, combined with the sex goddess she'd been tonight in bed, made her seem like his version of the perfect woman.

If one night could take him this far, then where on earth would he be after two?

Eleven

Nicola was having the most marvelous dream. She was in a deliciously cozy bed, cuddled into a hard, heated wall of muscle. With that warmth wrapped all around her, she felt so safe—safe enough to let loose her innate sensuality as a large male hand found its way over her breasts, down her stomach, to the V between her legs. It was pure instinct to arch into that arousing touch, to moan her pleasure, to widen her thighs and press into sure fingers now touching her.

Her lower belly clenched once, twice, with pleasure, and then—*oh, yes, right there!*—those fingers were moving lower still to slide through her slick wetness, to tease her mercilessly before pushing inside of her.

She felt it coming then, an orgasm so big it felt like it was starting at the tips of her toes and would end at the pads of her fingers. Her breath was coming out in gasps and through her fluttering eyelids she could almost see the dream cloud parting.

No! She didn't want to wake up, didn't want to lose the thread of one of the most amazing dreams she'd ever had before she—

Ring! Buzz! Ring! Buzz! Ring!

The loud sound of a cell phone jumping on a tabletop was almost immediately joined by the harsh ringing of the hotel's phone on the bedside table, barely three feet from Nicola's head.

Oh, shit! She bolted upright in the bed, her heart pounding as the word *shit, shit, shit!* played on repeat in her head.

How could she have forgotten about her video shoot?

She was a heartbeat away from throwing the covers off and running into the bathroom to fling herself into the world's quickest shower when she realized the large hand on her thigh wasn't a dream.

As the final vestiges of sleep cleared and everything came flooding back to her, she found her heart beating hard for a reason that had nothing to do with being late for work.

She was still throbbing between her legs with

almost-realized pleasure as she reached for the sheet and pulled it up over her naked body. She knew it didn't really make sense for her to do that after last night. Maybe it was how flustered she felt waking up so abruptly. Maybe it was that Marcus looked impossibly gorgeous, his skin tanned and dark against the snowy white sheets.

Or maybe it was simply that she wasn't used to waking up in bed with a man's hand between her thighs.

"I'm really late for my video shoot. I can't believe I forgot to set the alarm."

She'd made it a point to be early for everything, especially since the debacle with Kenny when her reputation as a wild party girl had blown up around her.

At her blurted words, Marcus's hand slid from her thigh and she immediately missed the warmth of his touch. He shifted on the bed to sit up, as well, only he wasn't at all concerned about his nudity.

He was big and hard and for a moment her brain forgot all about business. All she could think was how good it would feel to climb up over him, to sink down onto him and take him inside her body. A body that was more than ready to make love again.

And she probably would have done just that had he not said, "It's my fault. I kept you up too late last night, even though I knew you needed to work today."

God, why did their mornings always have to be so awkward? It didn't help that her phones wouldn't stop ringing.

"I'm sorry," she said, "I need to get that real quick just to let them know I'm on my way."

She grabbed the phone closest to her and said, "Hi. Sorry." She had her face in her hands as she said, "I overslept. I'll be there really soon."

She hung up. "That was Lori. She sounds really worried about—"

Her words fell away as she noticed that Marcus wasn't in the bed anymore, that he was standing on the opposite side of the room and had already put on his pants. She was the one who should have been dressed already and heading out the door, but from the look on his face, he was clearly planning to beat her to it. She could also clearly see from his suddenly stiff body language to the regret on his face that he wanted nothing more than to walk away from her, from the incredible night they'd spent together.

Of course, right then, she had to remember

FREE Merchandise is 'in the Cards' for you!

Dear Reader,

We're giving away FREE MERCHANDISE!

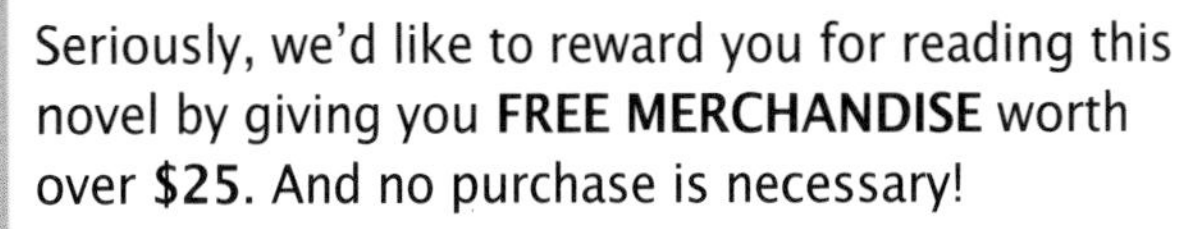

Seriously, we'd like to reward you for reading this novel by giving you **FREE MERCHANDISE** worth over **$25**. And no purchase is necessary!

You see the Jack of Hearts sticker above? Paste that sticker in the box on the Free Merchandise Voucher inside. Return the Voucher promptly...and we'll send you valuable Free Merchandise!

Thanks again for reading one of our novels—and enjoy your Free Merchandise with our compliments!

Pam Powers

Pam Powers

P.S. Look inside to see what Free Merchandise is **"in the cards"** for you!

FM-ROM-13

We'd like to send you two free books to introduce you to the Romance Collection. These books are worth over $15, but they are yours to keep absolutely FREE! We'll even send you 2 wonderful surprise gifts. You can't lose!

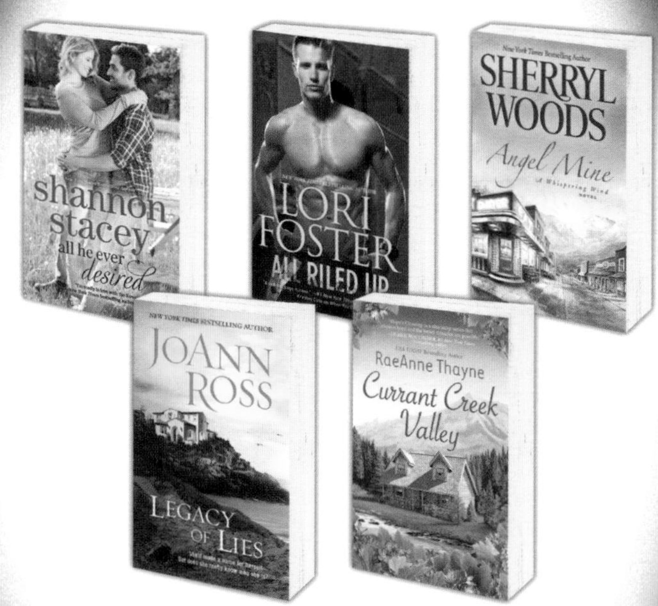

REMEMBER: Your Free Merchandise, consisting of **2 Free Books** and **2 Free Gifts**, is worth over $25.00! No purchase is necessary, so please send for your Free Merchandise today.

We'll also send you two wonderful FREE GIFTS (worth about $10), in addition to your 2 Free Books from the Romance Collection!

YOUR FREE MERCHANDISE INCLUDES...

2 FREE Books from the Romance Collection

AND 2 FREE Mystery Gifts

FREE MERCHANDISE VOUCHER

Please send my Free Merchandise, consisting of **2 Free Books** and **2 Free Mystery Gifts**. I understand that I am under no obligation to buy anything, as explained on the back of this card.

194/394 MDL F44P

Please Print

FIRST NAME

LAST NAME

ADDRESS

APT.# CITY

STATE/PROV. ZIP/POSTAL CODE

Offer limited to one per household and not applicable to series that subscriber is currently receiving.

Your Privacy—The Harlequin® Reader Service is committed to protecting your privacy. Our Privacy Policy is available online at www.ReaderService.com or upon request from the Harlequin Reader Service. We make a portion of our mailing list available to reputable third parties that offer products we believe may interest you. If you prefer that we not exchange your name with third parties, or if you wish to clarify or modify your communication preferences, please visit us at www.ReaderService.com/consumerschoice or write to us at Harlequin Reader Service Preference Service, P.O. Box 9062, Buffalo, NY 14269. Include your complete name and address.

NO PURCHASE NECESSARY!

▼ Detach card and mail today. No stamp needed. ▼

© 2013 HARLEQUIN ENTERPRISES LIMITED. ® and ™ are trademarks owned and used by the trademark owner and/or its licensee. Printed in the U.S.A.

FM-ROM-13

HARLEQUIN® READER SERVICE—Here's How It Works:

Accepting your 2 free books and 2 free gifts (gifts valued at approximately $10.00) places you under no obligation to buy anything. You may keep the books and gifts and return the shipping statement marked "cancel." If you do not cancel, about a month later we'll send you 4 additional books and bill you just $6.24 each in the U.S. or $6.74 each in Canada. That is a savings of at least 22% off the cover price. It's quite a bargain! Shipping and handling is just 50¢ per book in the U.S. and 75¢ per book in Canada.* You may cancel at any time, but if you choose to continue, every month we'll send you 4 more books, which you may either purchase at the discount price or return to us and cancel your subscription.

*Terms and prices subject to change without notice. Prices do not include applicable taxes. Sales tax applicable in N.Y. Canadian residents will be charged applicable taxes. Offer not valid in Quebec. Books received may not be as shown. All orders subject to credit approval. Credit or debit balances in a customer's account(s) may be offset by any other outstanding balance owed by or to the customer. Please allow 4 to 6 weeks for delivery. Offer available while quantities last.

If offer card is missing write to: Harlequin Reader Service, P.O. Box 1867, Buffalo, NY 14240-1867 or visit www.ReaderService.com

NO POSTAGE
NECESSARY
IF MAILED
IN THE
UNITED STATES

BUSINESS REPLY MAIL
FIRST-CLASS MAIL PERMIT NO. 717 BUFFALO, NY
POSTAGE WILL BE PAID BY ADDRESSEE

HARLEQUIN READER SERVICE
PO BOX 1341
BUFFALO NY 14240-8571

what she'd asked him before falling asleep in his arms. *"How about two nights instead of one?"*

Nicola's first reaction was to cringe, to feel like a pathetic idiot for having asked for more time with him in a perfect repeat of the morning after their first night together. She pulled the sheet off the bed to cover herself as she stood to face the man who had brought her more pleasure than she'd even known was possible.

Only, instead of letting him leave before she embarrassed herself any further, something hit her. Everything she'd ever wanted, she'd gone for.

Despite how hard it was, how potentially mortifying, despite the huge potential hit to her pride, she knew deep inside that she and Marcus had shared something special. Not just the sex, but those sweet moments of connection, too.

She wasn't willing just to let it all end. And she certainly wasn't willing to let herself be pleasured and left like this.

Which was why she refused to let the nervous pace of her heartbeat keep her from moving across the room to him. His eyes darkened as she came closer, the muscles in his rigid jaw jumping as the sheet slipped farther down on her chest.

She knew she could drop the sheet and get

what she wanted, that his reaction to her naked curves was almost guaranteed. And it was tempting, so tempting, to be consumed by his flames of desire all over again that she almost did just that.

Only, something held her back—that voice in her head that said she wanted his decision to spend another night with her to be more than just the fact that he wanted her body beneath his again.

Not, of course, that she could see any possible future beyond the next few days with Marcus. He was all wrong for her—a businessman who was surely in the market for a wife and kids in the very near future. And she was all wrong for him—a pop star who was on a plane more days than she wasn't.

And yet, there was emotion there between them. Even in the club that first night, something special had pulsed between them amid the loud music and strangers. Good or bad, the artist in her simply couldn't help but want to uncover more of it, just as she dove headfirst into the emotions of every song she'd ever written.

When she was standing barely a foot from him, she said, "I loved last night." She made herself hold his dark, incredibly intense gaze. "I loved everything about being with you." Nicola moved closer before he could respond and reached up to feather her fingertips over the very sexy stubble that covered his jaw. Just that small touch had her feeling as if electricity was coursing through her veins.

"I'm going to be in town for the rest of the week shooting a video for the next three days and then I have a concert on Saturday night. But between Thursday night and Saturday afternoon I'm mostly free."

She wanted to press herself against him, wanted to put her lips on his. But she needed to finish what she'd started first, needed to make sure that she got more than just a couple extra stolen kisses out of Marcus.

Reminding herself that direct had always been her best option, whether in business or songwriting—and hoping that it would be the same now, with the most beautiful man she'd ever known standing before her—she said, "I'd like to spend more time with you, Marcus. No strings for either of us. Just more of this."

She went up on her toes and softly pressed her lips to his, knowing she'd done everything she could, that she'd been completely honest with him.

Now all she could do was wait for him either to agree…or say goodbye.

* * *

Marcus's mind was made up.

This thing he was doing with Nicola—hell, it wasn't even a one-night stand anymore, since technically they'd spanned it out over two nights already—couldn't go anywhere.

Yes, physically they were perfect together. He wasn't going to lie to himself and say that he'd ever had as powerful a physical connection with any other woman in twenty years. What had happened last night with Nicola went so far beyond any response he'd ever had to a woman that he was still reeling from it. And the truth was that if every phone in the penthouse hadn't started ringing this morning, he would still be between her legs.

It was nearly impossible to try to force his brain—and body—to get beyond that physical perfection, especially when she was standing there in front of him, sunlight streaming in through the sheer curtains to outline her curves beneath the sheet she had loosely wrapped around her naked body.

But he already knew that a few more days with her would be too dangerous, too potent…and he didn't want to break her heart. Not when he knew just how sweet she was, how innocent.

He didn't understand why she looked at him with such trust in her eyes, and such hope. Maybe it was because he was a novelty to her, because his clean-cut business persona was a change from all the young, hip stars and other famous people she surely hung out with most of the time. But given that things hadn't worked out with Jill, who he'd thought wanted the same things out of life he did, there was no doubt in his mind that a relationship definitely wouldn't work out with a young pop star who would quickly tire of him and want to get back to her normal glitzy life.

A smart man would get out before he got burned. And until Jill, Marcus had always prided himself on being smart, on making the right decisions, even if they weren't easy ones. He thought he knew what he wanted—what he needed.

Nicola watched him carefully as the thoughts pinged around inside his head. He'd learned to read her well enough after two nights and two mornings together and he could see that she was nervous about his response. After all, on Saturday morning when she'd asked him for another night, he hadn't let temptation sway him. Not until he'd seen her again at the dance studio and realized that one hot night of sex with her was inevitable, as inevitable as the fact that it could never go beyond that.

Her phones all started ringing again and he knew it was his cue to say goodbye.

But instead of the words he planned on saying, the words he knew he should be saying to end it with her once and for all, somehow he found himself reaching out to put a hand on her lower back to drag her closer.

She felt so small compared to him, and yet he knew just how strong she was. Strong enough to dance and sing and make love for hours without needing a break.

She released a long, pent-up breath as he slid his other hand through her soft hair to cup her skull. He lowered his mouth to hers to take the kiss he'd wanted for hours as she'd slept so peacefully, sweetly spooned into him in her big bed. She wound her arms around his neck and sighed against his lips as the soft pressure of their lips quickly raged into an out-of-control dance of tongues and teeth and moans.

Yes, the end was inevitable, Marcus thought as he drank in Nicola's passion, her innate sensuality. But everything that came before that end promised to be so incredible, so mind-blowing, that even though he shouldn't let himself justify what they were doing as "just one more night together," he couldn't turn away from it, couldn't walk away from her.

Not yet.

He lifted his mouth from hers, but didn't let go of her. "I've got to head back to Napa to take care of some things, but—" he had to stop to press a kiss to her forehead, which had begun to furrow the moment he'd said he was leaving "—I'll come back Thursday night."

Her smile was brighter than the sun and just looking at all that happiness—happiness he was responsible for—suddenly made him feel like he could do anything, take on any challenge, if it meant making Nicola that happy.

Still, he knew he had to reiterate, "No strings."

He thought her smile might have dimmed a little bit, but when she said, "I'm definitely not looking for a relationship," he decided it must have been his imagination.

Even as he wondered why she wasn't game for anything more serious, he gladly told her, "Good. I'll keep your key and come straight here when I'm done taking care of business." He pressed one more soft kiss to her lips before saying, "You'd better get ready to go shoot that video."

As she reluctantly left his arms, neither of

them realized he was standing on the sheet until it slipped all the way off her body.

Obviously surprised by her sudden nudity, she instinctively tried to cover herself with her hands. Marcus knew they didn't have time to fool around, that her video shoot was likely hemorrhaging money every minute she wasn't there, but he wanted her to understand something.

"While we're together, I want your body to be as much mine as it is yours."

She was already blushing, but at his words, the flush spread from her cheeks to her chest and over the swell of her breasts. For a long moment, she stood just as she was, trying to hide her nakedness from him. And then, on a deep, brave breath, she slowly lowered her hands to her sides, and said, "I want that, too."

Knowing he was teetering on the sharp edge of control, he said, "Go take your shower."

For a moment, it looked as if she would try to argue with him. But even though every last cell in his body wanted to grab her, throw her on the bed and take her until she was hoarse from screaming climaxes, he respected her career enough to, instead, turn from her to reach for his shirt.

He heard her padding across the plush carpeting to the bathroom and forced himself to push away the taste of her sweet mouth still lingering on his lips.

"Marcus?"

He steeled himself to hold on to his control for a few more seconds before turning to look at her over his shoulder. She was impossibly beautiful, standing in the shower stall, her hand on the knob as she prepared to turn it on.

"I don't know if I can wait for Thursday night."

The water came on a moment later, and his brain was instantly reduced to speechless mush as he watched her tilt her head back so that the water poured over her breasts, her stomach, the soft, slick valley between her thighs.

He needed her one more time before he left. It wouldn't take long, would barely take thirty seconds he was so damned ready to take her.

Seconds later his clothes were off and he was putting on a condom and climbing into the shower stall with her.

"Tease," he growled.

She nodded, smiling as she wrapped her hands around his neck and lifted herself so that she could wrap her legs around his waist.

"You love it."

"I shouldn't," he admitted in a rough voice as he moved them so that her back was braced against the tiled wall and he could use his hands to cup her breasts, swallowing her gasp of pleasure, "but I do."

Everything she'd done since he'd met her in the club had teased his senses to the point where his control had shattered more than once with her.

Somewhere in the back of his brain, a voice told him she had to be sore from the way he'd taken her the night before, but his body was too far ahead of that thought to be stopped now. Running one hand down from her breasts to the curls between her thighs, he found her slick and ready for him.

"Nicola, I can't wait. I'm sorry." He could hear his voice as if from a great distance, a man pleading for forgiveness, but not being able to stop himself from taking what he needed, even if she couldn't possibly be ready to take him yet.

But then she was saying, "I can't wait, either," and it was as if the *Go* switch had been flipped on, a bright green that blinded him, that made it impossible for him to do anything less than take her.

Her body welcomed his as if she'd been made to surround him. She was in such good shape and so strong as she held on to him that he didn't need to hold her up at all, leaving his hands free to cover her breasts as his hips drove into hers. His mouth devoured hers and she devoured him right back until she dropped her head back against the tile on a gasp of pleasure that echoed against the walls of the shower.

"Oh, yes, please, just like that," she urged him.

Needing to get closer, needing to be as deep within her slick heat as he could, Marcus gripped her hips in his hands and took her as hard as he'd wanted to last night, hard enough that hopefully he could make it through three entire days without having to show up at her video shoot and drag her off into an empty room to take her.

She sobbed his name as she came, and God, how he loved the way she climaxed with her entire body, every muscle tightening as she rode it out before going completely loose.

He wanted to be completely lucid for her orgasm, didn't want to miss one second of her release, but he just didn't have that kind of control around her, and he had to take her mouth again in another bruising kiss as he found his own release. Just as it had the night before, his orgasm seemed to set off another set of sparks within her body, strong enough that she was whimpering against his lips, silently begging him to help her get over the second peak.

Marcus slid his hand from her hips to her pelvis. Her eyes flew open as her body instantly responded to the direct sensual contact of his rough fingertips on the center of her arousal.

He lifted his mouth from hers, knowing just what she needed, remembering so clearly how beautifully she'd responded the night before.

"Again," he urged her as he manipulated her between her legs. "Come for me again, Nicola."

Just as he'd hoped, his gentle command had her eyes closing, her breath hitching in her chest and her body giving itself over to another hit of pleasure.

He'd seen so much beauty at his winery in Napa, a hundred sunrises and sunsets over the vines that were each more beautiful than the next. But he would give up every sunrise, every last sunset, for the chance to watch Nicola's skin flush, to be right there with her as ecstasy took her over.

He moved both hands back beneath her hips as her muscles went lax and her arms and legs began to slip from around him.

"I've got you," he said against her ear as he sat on the built-in seat in the corner and cradled her in his arms.

"I'm really late." She lifted her head then, and

smiled up at him. "You're a bad influence on me." She reached for the shampoo bottle before she could see the surprise on his face.

Marcus had spent a lifetime trying to set a good example for first his siblings, and then his employees. And now a pop star actually thought he was a bad influence? Not, of course, that he could argue with her, considering he'd just made her incredibly late to shoot her video. If his sister Lori knew he was the one responsible for it, she'd kill him. The least he could do was make sure he didn't delay her any further.

He reached for the shampoo and began to lather up her soft hair.

"I can do that myself," she protested halfheartedly.

"Let me have the pleasure of taking care of you."

She nodded, saying, "Okay," before she relaxed into his hands.

Sixty very efficient seconds later, her hair was clean and conditioned and he was just finishing washing the suds from the bar of soap off her beautiful skin. Another minute later he'd dried her off with a plush towel.

With a soft kiss on her full lips, he said, "Go knock their socks off."

But she didn't move out of his arms. And she suddenly looked really uncomfortable. "This thing we're doing—I know this sounds really horrible, but I just wanted to be sure that we're both going to be really careful to keep it just between us."

He nodded, surprised that she felt she needed to confirm that. "Of course it's just between us."

"Good." She smiled up at him a little uncertainly. "Great!"

She gave him one last smile and then she was moving faster than he'd ever seen a woman get dressed and out the door, leaving him alone in her huge penthouse suite, wondering just how in hell he was going to keep from completely losing his mind over her.

Or if he already had.

Twelve

Even though Nicola had never bailed on a meeting or been late to a venue for a show or interview, she knew better than to think her previous track record would matter even a little bit today.

People believed what they wanted to believe about her. And she was pretty darn sure that everyone was automatically assuming she'd been partying too hard last night to show up for her own video shoot. So, while she was tempted to burst onto the set full of apologies, she knew better. She had to be completely in control of herself from the first second she stepped onto the set.

"Hi, everyone," she said in an easy voice. "Sorry about the delay. I had some important business to take care of this morning."

She didn't bother to take stock of everyone's response, not when she was very much afraid she'd end up blushing as she remembered the details of the very "important business."

The passion Marcus had shared with her simply blew her away, so much so that she'd even forgotten to be wary about trusting him. He had a key to her hotel room, which meant that he could snoop through her things to his heart's content if he wanted to. But even though she'd vowed never to trust a man again, knew there was the potential that maybe she was being stupid and naive again, she just couldn't imagine Marcus rifling through her things.

In any case, she wouldn't have the head space to process what she was doing with Marcus until the video was in the bag, so she forcefully pushed him out of her head. As much as she could, anyway, considering she still felt the imprint of him all over her body. His big hands, his mouth on hers, his huge shaft plunging in and—

"Nico, perfect timing!"

Lori's enthusiastic greeting yanked Nicola out of her forbidden thoughts. "I'm really sorry I'm so late," she said in a quiet voice meant only for her choreographer.

Marcus's sister waved away her apology. "Everyone had so much to set up, I swear they just finished. As soon as you're done with wardrobe and makeup, we'll warm up, okay?"

Nicola loved the way Lori didn't make a big deal out of things. So many people she'd worked with over the years would have held this over her head, would have tried to insinuate that she was a total flake and that they expected nothing less.

"Sounds great. Thanks."

She was turning away to go check in with the director when she felt Lori's hand on her arm. "I know we're in a hurry here, but real quick, I want to apologize for running out on dinner with you and Marcus last night."

Nicola didn't want to admit she hadn't given Lori another thought after she'd left. Feeling terrible about that, she asked, "Is everything okay?"

Lori shrugged. "It'll all work out one way or another, I suppose" was her cryptic response. "I wouldn't have left if I didn't know you were in totally safe hands with my big brother. Did he take good care of you and get you back to your hotel all right?"

Nicola had never had to work quite so hard to school her face into a completely blank expression. Her breath got caught in her throat as she opened her mouth to try to answer, and she needed to clear her throat a couple of times before responding.

"Yes. He was great."

So ridiculously, stupendously great that she had almost bailed on her video shoot altogether just for the chance to spend the entire day in his arms.

The director walked over just then, fortunately, and saved her from blushing any more than she already was. Glad for the chance to focus on business rather than the swirling emotions she felt over what had happened with Marcus, she spent the next three days working as hard as she ever had in her life.

Everyone might have begun the day thinking she was a flaky pop star…but by the end, she had outlasted them all.

Three days later...

She'd outlasted them, all right. But at what price?

After dragging herself into the elevator up to the penthouse, Nicola barely had the strength left to lift her hand high enough to slip her key into the reader beside her door.

She stood with her head against the wall and closed her eyes. Just another thirty seconds and then she could collapse and not move for another twenty-four hours.

The lock clicked and she shifted her weight to the door to push it open. She barely caught a flash of Marcus sitting at the dining table behind his laptop before he was pushing it away and coming toward her.

"Nicola." He grabbed her just before she dropped. "Jesus, what did they do to you at that video shoot?"

"It's not them. It's my stupid pride," she said, even though she knew it wouldn't make any sense. And then, oh, God, it felt so good to be held by him that she lost her train of thought altogether as she let him carry her over to the couch.

She closed her eyes against his chest and finally gave in to utter and complete exhaustion.

Nicola woke up disoriented but not uncomfortable in Marcus's arms. He was so sweet that he'd tucked cushions beneath her torso and her feet while she'd slept like the dead. She loved being with him like this, so warm and safe. No one had ever made her feel this comfortable, like she didn't have one single thing left to prove. She didn't have to be "on" with him, or perform to impress. She could just be herself. Nicola, rather than the world-famous Nico.

"What time is it?" Her eyes felt gritty and every muscle in her body hurt from dancing and performing at one hundred and ten percent for three days straight.

"Late."

Feeling terrible that she'd asked for this extra night with him, only to have him stuck beneath her on yet another couch while she snored, she said, "I'm always falling asleep on you."

He laughed softly. "I'm starting to wonder if I should take it as a hint?"

Relieved that he wasn't upset with her for being a big tease, she said, "I'll make it up to you. I promise."

She leaned forward to press her mouth to his, her tongue stroking against his for a split second, before he pulled back way too soon.

"You're tired. Tell me about your video first."

She'd much rather kiss him than talk about her crazy day, but when he began to massage one of her feet, she couldn't do anything but groan at how much it hurt…and how good it felt at the same time. His hands on her were so gentle and yet firm, exactly as he'd been when he was making love to her.

At some point, she realized he'd asked her a question about something, but it took her longer than it should have to remember what.

"The shoot went well," she told him, not sure how much he really wanted to know. He was probably just being polite, probably thought she was one of those stars who just liked to talk about herself when the truth was that she'd rather do anything but.

"Lori called right before you got back. She couldn't stop talking about how amazing you are."

Nicola's stomach clenched, hardly able to bear the praise. "I didn't tell her about us, I swear." Whatever *us* was.

"I know you didn't. My sister has been excited about working with you from the start. She told me she's never seen anyone as focused and hard-working as you. I'm not at all surprised to hear it."

Nicola was already feeling overly warm from the soft stroke of his hand moving up to her calf as he began to work out the knots in the muscle, but at the praise, her blush turned into a full-body flush.

"Most people are surprised." The slightly bitter comment left her lips before she could hold it back. At his questioning look, she explained, "My image isn't exactly a brainiac workaholic." She knew she must be tired to be talking so openly to Marcus about this kind of stuff.

He frowned. "Your image?"

Even though she knew she should drop the whole conversation, she said instead, "Come on, you have to know all about public images, considering one of your brothers is a big movie star."

"How do you know about that?"

"Don't worry," she said in a snottier voice than perhaps she should have. "I didn't go snooping online about you." He raised an eyebrow as she explained, "Lori told me that Smith Sullivan is your brother." Nicola cocked her head to the side and looked carefully at Marcus. "Maybe if I had been looking for the family resemblance I would have linked the three of you together."

"If you'd known I was Lori and Smith's brother, you wouldn't have left the club with me."

It was a statement, not a question. "You're right," she agreed, as blunt as he had been. "I wouldn't have left with you." She paused a beat before adding, "And if you'd known I was the infamous Nico you wouldn't have left with me, either."

His dark eyes flashed with something she couldn't read at her use of the word *infamous,* but before he could respond, she realized, "Hey, that was Smith's house we went to that first night, wasn't it?"

Marcus simply nodded and asked, "Why are you infamous?"

"You really don't know?"

God, she wished she didn't find that so hard to believe. But even though he hadn't known who she was that first night, he'd had plenty of time to do his research since finding out she was Nico.

"I haven't gone snooping online about you, either."

Ouch. It wasn't particularly fun to have her own sarcastic words thrown back at her. She winced and said, "Sorry. I was out of line with that comment."

"Yeah, you were," he agreed as he moved his hand up from her calf to her thigh to begin massaging that large, tight muscle, "but I'm sure you have to deal with that kind of stuff from people every day, don't you?"

She found it really difficult to believe that he didn't know anything about her story. Then again, he wasn't exactly her target audience, so why would he?

"I do," she confirmed, "but it's a necessary evil, just like my image. I've always figured that as long as I'm able to play my music for people, the trade-off is worth it."

"What *is* your image, Nicola?"

Shoot, she was hoping they could get off this whole topic before she accidentally told him more than she wanted him to know about herself and her past. Sure, he could find out anything he wanted to know online in seconds, but a big part of her—a really naive part, probably—couldn't quite picture him sitting down at his computer and scrolling through online pictures and stories in *People* magazine.

But now that he'd asked her a direct question, and was clearly interested in the answer, she couldn't quite find a way to deflect it. "My image is pretty obvious," she said with a crooked grin she didn't quite feel. "Sexy." She licked her lips, before forcing out the word. "Wild."

"I can see sexy," he said. "But wild?" He frowned, looked around the nearly dark, very quiet suite. "It didn't exactly look like you were having crazy parties up here in your big empty penthouse before we met."

She shrugged. "People believe what's easiest for them to believe."

"Sure they do," he agreed, "but only when there's a reason for them to believe it."

She hated talking about this, especially to Marcus, but she'd promised him she'd be honest. "I haven't always made the best decisions."

She could feel his eyes, warm and dark, on her as she studied her knee.

"Everyone makes bad decisions at some point in their lives."

She looked up at him. "Have you?"

His mouth tightened. "Not too long ago, actually."

She couldn't help but be somewhat comforted by that. "Unfortunately, I made mine in front of the world. Thus the wild image."

"Couldn't you change that, if you really wanted to? If you let people see who you really are?"

Nicola had actually asked herself that question many, many times during the past year, every time her stylist brought her skimpier and skimpier outfits made from the barest strips of fabric. If she were talking to her manager and record label and publicist, it seemed she couldn't. None of them were blind to the fact that her career had absolutely exploded after Kenny had betrayed her. She'd ended up on the cover of multiple magazines, had suddenly been hot property for late-night talk shows. Her popularity hadn't waned since. In fact, she'd only gotten bigger.

"I don't know," she said, and then, "Maybe." Another shrug. "My career has never been better. Maybe wild isn't necessarily a bad thing."

"No, wild isn't necessarily a bad thing," he agreed. "But it isn't you, is it, Nicola?"

How, she wondered a little helplessly, did he already know her so well? When their bodies were coming together, when he'd been pulling every ounce of pleasure from her, had he also been reaching into her heart to find the truth she'd been hiding from everyone else?

When she didn't answer his question, he continued to hammer her in his gentle way. "I've only heard one song so far, but it was great. Seems to me you're talented enough to let your songs speak for themselves."

All of this was hitting way too close to home. For a relationship that was just supposed to be about sex, it sure felt like Marcus was going a whole heck of a lot deeper. Like into a *real* relationship.

Simultaneously wanting to deflect his attention from her—and deciding it wasn't fair for him to be the one asking all the questions—she said, "Enough about me. During our breaks, Lori told me a little bit about your winery. How did you get started with that?"

Instead of answering her question, he said, "My sister likes to talk, doesn't she?"

She grinned. "You're her hero." Her smile slipped as she softly said, "She told me that you basically raised her and her twin, along with a couple of your brothers who are just a bit older than she is."

Lori had almost been offhand about the fact that her father had died when she was two, leaving her mother with eight kids to raise on her own. Nicola had immediately wondered how much of the burden had fallen on Marcus's shoulders. Looking at him—knowing after only two nights with him how steady, how strong, he was—she felt that she already knew the answer.

Marcus shifted her weight so that he could better reach her other foot. She groaned with pleasure as he began to press into the sensitive skin.

"Too hard?"

"No, it's just perfect."

The air sizzled after the word *perfect,* taking her right back to those moments when he'd been pounding into her and she'd been begging for more, for harder, for deeper. She knew he'd been afraid of hurting her.

But, oh, what little pain there'd been that first time had been so worth it.

"My father was a big backyard gardener," he said as he began to work his way from her foot to her calf. "My first memories are of digging in the dirt beside him as he planted tomatoes and strawberries."

Her insides went all gooey at the thought of Marcus as a toddler, jamming his shovel in the dirt. She tried to tell herself that she was just reacting like that because she loved babies, but she knew it was Marcus himself that had her melting. Of course, the fact that he was getting closer and closer to her thigh, nearer to the part of her body that was throbbing in anticipation of his touch, was definitely contributing to her overall meltability.

"I've always admired people who have a green thumb." She looked at her own. "I'm afraid mine are the black thumbs of death. Plants run screaming when they see me coming."

She loved his grin as he said, "I don't think my thumbs are any greener than yours. It's really just math and science."

He made it all sound so easy, like he didn't have anything to do with it, but she didn't believe him. "That's like saying songs are just combinations of notes and words." She shook her head. "They are, but I've always thought what makes a song really special is some indefinable magic that's either there or it isn't. I'll bet your grapevines are like that." She smiled a small smile. "And that you're the magic that makes them grow so well."

"I've never thought of it like that," he said slowly. "As magic."

She was waiting for him to discount what she'd said, to go back to his whole quantifiable math and science thing. Instead, his eyes were intense, filled with that hunger that had her blood racing.

"You know, I think you might be onto something."

In an instant, the magic that had existed between them from that first moment in the club leaped back to life as if some sex fairy had just flown over with her wand.

Thirteen

"Put your arms above your head."

She swallowed hard at his low-pitched command. After taking a shallow breath that didn't even come close to filling her lungs, she leaned into the pillow behind her back and slowly did as he asked.

Once her hands and arms were out of the way, he reached for the zipper of the loose sweater Lori had loaned her at the end of their very long day. "Do you remember what we agreed on this morning?" he asked her as he slowly drew the zipper down.

"Yes," she said, the sound more a breath than a word. "I remember."

"Good," he said, and then, "Tell me."

Oh, God, that breathing thing was getting harder

by the second, especially with his hands brushing over her breasts as he pulled the sweater open.

"While we're together—" She couldn't bring herself to repeat what he'd said.

"Go on, I'm listening."

She took a shaky breath. She knew she didn't have to say it, but something inside her wanted to, wanted to please him. "My body is as much yours as it is mine."

His eyes flared with approval…and so much desire it took what was left of her breath away. "Take your sweater and tank top off and then lie back with your hands above your head again."

Apart from the massage, he hadn't even really touched her yet, and she was already soaked between her thighs from nothing more than his sexy commands. Perhaps she shouldn't still be surprised at her reaction to his gentle dominance, to the fact that her body clearly *loved* it, but she was.

"Have you ever been spanked, Nicola?"

Her eyes flew to his as his shocking question yanked her from her musings. "Spanked?"

Her pulse began to flutter even more wildly at the thought of being laid out over his lap, bared to him from the waist down, his big hand coming down over her skin.

"No." She shook her head. "Of course not."

His mouth curved up at the corners at her reaction. But instead of saying anything more about spanking, he said, “What did I ask you to do?”

She suddenly realized that she hadn’t yet taken off her sweater or tank top. She was torn for a split second between leaving them on and risking a spanking—a flood of arousal shot through her at the shocking thought—or doing as he asked.

Fear of the unknown—and of her own surprising desires—had her moving quickly to do as he asked.

When she was naked from the waist up, she lay back against the pillow and started to lift her arms. But even though Marcus was more than a little familiar with her breasts by now, she was still shy about baring herself to a man like this.

“You’re doing beautifully.”

His sweet words combined with the warmth in his eyes had her finally lifting her arms all the way up.

She expected him to touch, to fondle, to taste. Instead, he simply looked at her, for so long that her breasts ached terribly for him and the V between her legs was throbbing and damp. And then, he surprised her by picking up her sweater and tying it around her wrists.

"Try to move your hands so I can see how tight that is."

His voice was husky, rich with desire. She moved her arms and found the binding to be soft against her skin, and yet, she knew she'd have to work quite hard if she wanted to be set free.

Last Friday night she would have sworn she would never let herself be put in a position like this. She should be pulling free. But she didn't want to, did she?

As if he were privy to the silent questions she was asking herself, Marcus said, "Tell me what you need, Nicola. Tell me what you want."

He put his hands on her waist, his tanned skin dark against her pale belly. She shivered at how small she was compared to him, at the knowledge that he could do anything he wanted to her right now, that she was completely helpless against his strength. Those thoughts shouldn't have made her more aroused. But, shockingly, they did.

"If you won't tell me, I'll just have to guess," he said before leaning over her bare torso. His hair tickled the underside of her chin as he pressed his mouth to her shoulder for just long enough that she was seared with his heat before he sat back.

She wasn't used to voicing her sexual needs, but they were strong enough that she forgot all about keeping her hands above her head. She started to reach for him before remembering her hands were bound.

By Marcus.

Obviously seeing the flare of desire in her eyes, he said, “That’s right. You’re all mine to play with right now, aren’t you?”

Seriously, for all that she portrayed a sex bomb for the world, she was a feminist. Girl power was her thing. She should be freaking out right now.

Not practically coming at the thought of being *all his to play with.*

“This isn’t—” She didn’t know how to tell him what she was feeling, but somehow she knew it was important that she did. “I shouldn’t be feeling like this.”

“Tell me what you’re feeling.”

His low voice that rumbled over her, through her, made her want to give up all her secrets, all her desires that she hadn’t even known were there, waiting to be uncovered this whole time.

“This isn’t me. I don’t like being bossed around.”

She swore he almost smiled and strangely, instead of being angered by it, instead of feeling like he was laughing at her, it made her feel like maybe she wasn’t so weird after all to be liking these things he was saying—and doing—to her.

"Am I bossing you around?"

She was about to say yes when she realized it wasn't precisely true. "You tell me to do things," she whispered, unable to look at him now, feeling more shy than she ever had before. "I shouldn't do them." She could feel how hot her face was. "I shouldn't like doing them."

His fingers slid beneath her chin and gently tipped her face back up to his. "I love watching you respond to me. I love watching the most beautiful woman I've ever seen tremble with desire in front of me. I love hearing you beg me to touch you, to kiss you, to take you."

Everything he'd just said, the rough quality of his voice as he said it, had her shivering with lust. But still, she felt she should try one last protest, one last bid for sanity. "But I'm the one who usually tells people what to do."

"Have you thought that maybe this is the break you've been waiting for?" he said softly. "That this is the chance to let someone take care of you for a few hours, instead of having to take care of everything yourself?"

Her brain felt fuzzy with desire, but even so, what he was saying made sense.

"Touch me now, Marcus. Kiss me." She paused, gathering up all her courage. "Take me."

The next thing she knew, her shorts and panties were off, and she was laid out flat with Marcus over her, his large body pressing hers into the cushions. He made sure her bound hands remained over her head with one of his hands while the other moved between her legs at the exact moment that he covered her breast with his mouth.

She arched into his touch, their conversation about how much he liked telling her what to do and how much she liked doing it—not to mention the massage before that—more than enough foreplay to prime her for even the slightest touch.

"Give me more, Nicola," he urged her, his words hot as he feathered kisses across her chest so that he could take her other nipple into his mouth. "Give it all to me."

Her inner muscles clenched so tightly on his fingers in response that she actually cried out at the pleasure-pain as she climaxed beneath him. His thumb made delicious circles of pleasure over her and she pressed her hips into his hand again and again as her orgasm continued to shake through her.

Almost incoherent with exhaustion from the way the climax had wrung out her system, she was only vaguely aware of Marcus unwrapping the sweater from around her wrists and moving to remove his clothes. Through half-closed lids she watched him go to the bathroom and then return with a condom on. Her arms weren't bound anymore, but she simply didn't have the strength to move them.

And then he was kneeling in front of the couch and shifting her so that her back and shoulders were braced against the cushions, but her hips were hanging off the edge. Before she could take her next breath, his hands gripped her bottom and he surged into her.

She curled her fingers into the couch, needing to hold on to something as he took her body, made her irrevocably his, owned her as nothing but music ever had. And even as exhausted as she was from the video shoot, from the massage, from the mind-splitting orgasm she'd just had, the feel of him inside of her had her pulling from her final well of energy.

Needing to feel his hard muscles beneath her fingertips, she reached for him. Winding her arms around his neck, she pulled herself up so that her breasts were rubbing against the dark hairs on his chest. Her mouth found his, greedy for his kisses—kisses she'd dreamed of for three long days, even as she'd tried to convince herself that she was too busy to think of him.

He kissed her back just as hungrily, as if he couldn't get enough of her, and then he was groaning against her lips, and she could feel him grow even bigger, filling her so completely she had to fight for breath.

When he broke their kiss and threw his head back, coming with a loud roar that excited her so much, with the sound of his pleasure still reverberating in the room, Nicola was pitched over the edge yet one more time.

Straight into Marcus's waiting arms.

Fourteen

Marcus was getting too used to waking up with Nicola curled up in his arms. When he was making love with her and she was coming at him with all her hunger and passion, he almost forgot how small she was. But as he spooned her body in the big bed, he was reminded all over again.

His erection stirred against her hips as she shifted in her sleep and rubbed against him. She was holding one of his hands over her breasts and he had to dig deep for a control that had been missing since practically the moment he'd met her. He would not take her before she even woke up, damn it.

He tightened his hold on her, pulled her closer into him, even as he forced himself to face the insanity of what he was doing.

He shouldn't have spent another night with

Nicola. Hell, even one night on Smith's couch while she slept on his lap had been too much. And he definitely shouldn't be looking forward to an entire day with her, shouldn't feel like a kid in a candy store at the chance to see the way her skin glowed in the sunlight, to wait with held breath for her to laugh again and fill his soul with her joy and beauty.

And he sure as hell shouldn't be dreading saying goodbye to her when she got on her next plane to another town, another show.

He was so focused on steeling himself against everything he shouldn't be feeling for her that he was caught off guard by the slow slide of her tongue against one of his fingers, and then another, and another.

Jesus, was she really going to lick her way up each finger, one at a time?

Holy hell, she was.

Thank God he'd put some condoms close enough to the bed for him to easily grab one. Hating to take his hands from her for any longer than he absolutely needed to, he broke the wrapper open with his teeth and quickly slid it down his throbbing shaft.

There were no words between them as he put his hands on her thighs and shifted her hips so that he could take her. Nicola's breath left her lungs in a hard whoosh as he bottomed out inside of her and gripped her hips to pull her back tightly against his chest.

"Marcus," she whispered, her voice catching on his name as pleasure took her over.

This was what he'd miss most, he realized as he slid his hand over her breasts and felt her heart beating strong and fast. Not just her incredible body, not just her passion, not just the way she was always ready for him to take her like this… but how pure, how sweet, she was.

The unexpected flood of emotions for Nicola had him losing hold of the shreds of control he still held. Knowing he barely had thirty seconds left before he exploded, he slid his hand down from her breasts. She gasped as his fingers moved between her thighs to slip and slide over her wetness and then she was pushing back into him in wild jerky movements that told him it was safe to come, because she was already there.

Together, Nicola helped him greet the day with more pleasure than he'd ever known. And as her climax drew his out, he could no longer deny the truth: she now held a piece of his heart.

Whether he wanted her to or not.

* * *

Nicola looked at Marcus over the small round table by the window where they'd just devoured pancakes and sausages and a huge bowl of fruit. How was it, she wondered, that eating breakfast together could feel as intimate as making love?

Probably, she told herself, it was simply that she hadn't shared a leisurely morning-after like this with a man in a very long time. Ever, really, considering Kenny had always been too hungover to wake up much before noon.

Although Marcus worked in the wine industry, she couldn't picture him drunk. It was just one more thing about him that made her feel safe.

Suddenly wanting him to know how much she appreciated him, how much she was enjoying their stolen, secret hours together, she said, "I know how much you must have to do at your winery." She reached for his hand across the table, thrill bumps moving up her arms when he threaded his fingers through hers. "Thank you for spending this time with me."

"There's nowhere else I'd rather be," he said, and then, "What do you normally do on your days off?"

She bit her lip. "I don't know. I haven't had many since I started singing." Especially this past six months after her heart—well, her pride, actually—had been broken, it had been easier to focus all her attention on her music and her career.

"It's the same with me. Like you said, the vines demand a lot of attention."

For all the obvious ways that they were different, Nicola was surprised to realize they weren't at opposite poles on all fronts.

She grinned at him. "Aren't we sad? Two workaholics who can't figure out what to do with a beautiful day off."

He pulled her onto his lap. "I can think of a good half dozen things."

She giggled as he nibbled on her neck, ridiculously tempted to spend the entire day in bed with him. Especially when he was being playful like this. She turned her face to meet his as he lifted his mouth to hers and sank into the sweetest kiss anyone had ever given her.

"How about I take you to one of my favorite places?" he offered.

Marcus had struck her, from the first, as a very private person. His offer meant even more to her because of that.

"I'd love that." She hated having to remind

him, "The thing is, most places I go get pretty crazy."

"I know. My brother Smith has the same problem. Our family has learned to work around it pretty well over the years. So, don't worry, I think the spot I have in mind will be perfect." He brushed his finger across her lower lip, sending shivers through her. "It's very remote."

Her voice was barely more than a breath as she said, "Remote is good." Images of those half dozen things they could do to each other somewhere remote had her blood running even hotter than it already was.

She was about to press her lips against his when he murmured, "If I kiss you again, we might never leave the hotel."

"Okay."

A split second later, his hands were in her hair and he was pulling her mouth down to his. Starved for each other, she moved herself so that she could straddle him in the chair. He was big and hard between her legs and it was pure instinct for her to rock against him as they made out.

It was the first time she'd been in control of their lovemaking, and just as much as she'd loved obeying each of his sensual commands, she loved this, too, loved knowing that she was driving him crazy with her mouth, with her hands on his chest as she ran them beneath the long-sleeved shirt he'd put on after their shower. An incredibly sensual shower that should have kept her sated at least until the sun went down.

Only, her need, her desire, for Marcus knew no rational bounds. Fortunately, she thought with a smile, he seemed to feel the same way.

She broke their kiss and said, "I'll be right back."

Slipping off his lap, before he could catch her, she went to get a condom. When she returned, she was pleased to note the surprise—and desire—light his eyes at the fact that she'd stripped out of her clothes.

Still shy with her nakedness, it was the pleasure in Marcus's eyes as she moved toward him that made her bold. He reached for her as she came closer, but instead of getting back on his lap, she slowly dropped to her knees between his.

"Nicola?"

His voice was raw, almost hoarse, as he said her name and her hands trembled as much with desire as uncertainty as she went to unzip his pants.

He took her hands in his. "You don't have to do this."

She met his gaze head-on. "I want to." And she did, wanting it so much it shocked her.

His low groan at her honest response had her nipples peaking. Praying that he wouldn't be disappointed with her technique—or lack thereof—with his help, she managed to pull his pants open and his boxers down to reveal…

Oh, God. He was beautiful, but so big. Bigger than her brain had computed, even though she'd seen him, felt him inside of her, more than once already.

She reached out to touch him, to stroke her fingertips down the soft skin covering such incredibly hard heat.

"Jesus, that feels good."

Nicola was so focused on exploring Marcus, she barely heard him as she wrapped her hand around him. He bucked up into her fist and her mouth actually watered. Without thinking, she bent forward and licked him. On a loud groan, his fingers grasped her hair. She knew he could have taken control of things, could have turned the tables on her and held her there while he took his pleasure in her mouth, but even though she was realizing a part of her would be pleased by that dominance, this time around she was glad that he was letting her take things entirely at her own pace.

His skin was clean and salty all at the same time and she realized one taste wasn't nearly enough. A moment later, she was running her tongue up him like he was the most delicious Popsicle she'd ever tasted, but even that wasn't enough. She wanted him inside her mouth. All of him.

But before she could open her mouth wide to swallow him down, Marcus finally took control and lifted her up from her knees to straddle him again.

"I wasn't done," she protested.

At that he pulled her mouth down to his and kissed her hard. She was so lost to his kiss she was surprised to realize he'd put on the condom until he pushed into her, so hard and fast she gasped against his lips.

He stilled inside her, asking, "Nicola?" and she realized he was still worried about hurting her.

She replied first by rocking her hips closer to his, then by saying, "It's perfect. Absolutely perfect."

And as they both found the peak and jumped off together one more time, it really was.

* * *

When they were about to step out of her hotel room a short while later, she steeled herself to deal with what needed to be dealt with.

"Why don't you go down first and I'll meet you by the side entrance?" She lifted her baseball cap and big sunglasses out of her bag. "I'll be wearing these and an oversize shirt."

Fifteen minutes ago she'd been warm and safe in his arms. Now she was coldly strategizing how to get out of the hotel without being seen together. And she hated it, hated being able to see the contrast so clearly.

"I don't like doing things this way, Nicola."

"I don't, either, but—" She sighed, shook her head. "What do you think about Smith's life?"

"He's done well for himself. I'm proud of him."

"Yes, but do you envy him? Have you ever wished you could be on TV and have women asking for your autograph?"

"Hell, no."

She'd known that would be his response. "I know you hate having to hide like this, but you'd hate what would happen to your life if we did it the other way even more."

Marcus stared at her for several tense moments. "I'll meet you downstairs."

She watched him leave, the door closing a little too hard behind him, and she had to swallow past the lump in her throat. She hated that he was upset, but she knew she had to stand firm with him about not letting anyone know about their relationship.

Not because she had any more fear that he might be using her like her ex had. Marcus clearly had zero interest in fame or bright lights. And she was pretty sure he didn't need the money that selling their story of "sinful nights" would bring in.

Unfortunately, her fears were of an altogether different sort now.

She was very much afraid that she was going to make the mistake of falling in love with him if she wasn't super careful about keeping a big, thick wall up around her heart.

The thing was, Nicola would have claimed him as her boyfriend in front of the world in a heartbeat if she thought their relationship had any chance of working out. But she knew better than to believe in that fantasy. She and Marcus were having great sex. Lots of it. Of course they would connect during all that intimate skin-to-skin contact, with all the hours they were spending together.

But the fact was that on Monday she would

go back to her life and he would go back to his. The last thing she needed was visual reminders of their time together or interviewers asking her what had happened to the gorgeous businessman she'd been seeing.

Yes, she wanted to protect Marcus from the circus his life would become if he were linked with her.

But she needed to protect herself, too…and remember to prepare her heart for their inevitable goodbye on Monday morning.

Fifteen

Marcus had spent a lifetime being fair. After breaking up at least a thousand fights between his brothers and sisters, he'd always assumed he was skilled at seeing all sides of a problem and analyzing it without getting emotionally involved on either side.

So then, what was his problem where Nicola was concerned? She didn't deserve his anger, his frustration, over needing to sneak around. It wasn't her fault that she was famous. She'd given him the chance to walk away from the complications of fame on Monday night and he hadn't taken it.

He needed to get over himself, and fast, before Nicola drew into herself any more and disappeared completely on him long before they ever said goodbye. He could feel her closing herself off more with every mile they covered in his car as they crossed over the Golden Gate Bridge, heading north into Marin. And the fact was, he hated losing his connection to her even more than he'd hated having to be in goddamned stealth mode leaving her hotel room to go pick her up at the VIP side entrance.

He reached for her hand and threaded his fingers through hers. "I'm sorry."

Her eyes were big, surprised, as she turned her beautiful face to his. "Marcus?"

"I know how hard fame can be on people. Heck, I've seen it firsthand with you in the hotel lobby. Will you forgive me for being an ass?"

He was glad, so damn glad, to see her full lips curve up slightly at the corners. "There's nothing to forgive."

He lifted her hand to his lips, pressed a kiss to the palm. "There is. I won't do it again."

He kept her hand on his lap, pulling her closer to him. They were too far apart in his car. She belonged on his lap, curled up against his chest, where he could stroke her hair, where he could keep her safe, where she could relax and let go of the stress of her high-pressure life for a little while.

"That night in the club," she said softly, "you

didn't sign up for this. I'm the one who needs to apologize for not being up-front with you from the start. I should have apologized a long time ago for letting you believe I was just any girl."

"You could never be *just any girl.* And it has nothing to do with the fact that you're famous." His hand tightened on hers. "You're very special, Nicola. Very, very special."

Didn't he realize he couldn't say things like that to her if he didn't want her to fall head over heels for him? Lord knew the spectacular sex was bad enough.

Now he was telling her how special she was....

Worried he was going to say something else even sweeter—and knowing damn well the wall she was trying to build around her heart didn't have a chance of holding out against much more—she decided talking about his family seemed like safe ground.

"Speaking of special," she said, "I'd love to hear about your siblings. Even with just three kids in our family it was really loud and crazy in the house I grew up in."

"Loud and crazy is dead on," he agreed, lighting up the way he did every time he talked about his family.

One day he was going to be the most spectacular father. Husband, too. She tried to ignore the pangs of longing in her chest at those unbidden thoughts, along with the shot of jealousy that hit her over the lucky woman who would share those things with him. But somehow, even knowing she was being ridiculous to feel those things for a man she'd only known a handful of days didn't make her feel any differently.

"Lori said she's a twin. Are she and her sister really similar?" Marcus laughed at that for long enough that she said, "I'm taking that to be a no."

Still grinning, he said, "Their nicknames are Naughty and Nice."

"I take it Lori's Naughty?" she easily guessed.

"You bet she is. And Nice, aka Sophie, is a quiet, mild-mannered librarian."

"Do they get along?"

"Sure," he agreed, "except for when they don't."

"It must have been ugly when Lori and Sophie started dating."

"They've started dating?"

He looked so serious that she almost believed him for a second. Laughing, she said, "How many potential boyfriends have you had to beat up?"

"Enough that they should still be celibate."

Still laughing, she said, "Tell me about your brothers."

A few minutes later, her brain was reeling as she tried to put together the fact that there was a firefighter, a pro baseball player, a movie star, a photographer and a whiz with cars all in one family.

"You Sullivan boys must have kept your mother busy growing up."

"We still do."

She put together what she'd learned about his family, his love for his siblings and his father's untimely death, and said, "It must have been so hard for you to have so much responsibility thrust on you, just a kid who had no choice but to step into his father's shoes to take care of his brothers and sisters."

She caught his expression too late to take her words back. He'd looked so open when he'd been talking to her about his siblings. His eyes weren't completely shuttered yet, but he couldn't hide the pain her words had brought to the surface.

"I'm sorry," she said softly, squeezing his hand with hers. "That was thoughtless of me. I'm just sorry you had to deal with so much, so young."

"No, you're right. I did feel like I needed to

step into my father's shoes. And I wanted to. I wanted to help."

Remembering how kind his mother had been to her on the phone that first night when Nicola had called her up from out of the blue to ask if she would be safe with Marcus, she had to ask, "How did your mother deal with it all?"

"She was always there for us. Looking back, I can see the way she put the rest of her life on hold to just focus completely on her kids. She didn't date, didn't even think about it as far as I know. And I can never remember a time when she wasn't right there with a hug or Band-Aid or to help with homework or applaud a home run."

"She really sounds amazing," Nicola said, and then thinking how she would have felt in his mother's shoes if she'd lost the man she loved and had a family with, asked, "Did she cry a lot?"

"I'm sure she did, but I never saw it."

She squeezed his hand tighter, knowing she had no right to ask him the same question, but needing to, anyway. "Did you cry?"

Marcus was silent for a moment. "Do you remember telling me how you're willing to put up with the pressures of fame if it means you can play your music for people?" When she nodded, he said, "Making sure my family is happy has been worth any trade-off."

"You're the one who's special," she told him as her heart broke for him, for all that he'd held inside for so long, and all that he'd had to be for so many people. She knew it was why he was the spectacular man he was today…and yet she wished that it had all been easier for him. "I love how close you are to your family. I don't know many other people who feel that way."

"Family is important to you, too, isn't it?"

"Very." She'd already told him how much she loved children. Now she found herself saying, "I've always wanted a big family of my own. A family like yours, with lots of brothers and sisters who all fight and love in equal measure."

"How are you planning to balance your career with having children?"

Nicola shrugged. "I've always figured if I want something bad enough I'll figure out a way to make it work."

"What else do you want?"

She gave him a wide smile. "This day with you."

She leaned over and kissed him hard and fast before letting him get back to the business of driving them to their secret destination.

* * *

Marcus pulled off the freeway onto a side road and the terrain grew wilder. After so many days and months spent in windowless studios and concert halls, it was thrilling to be out in nature. She turned on the radio until she found a song she liked, then gave in to the urge to roll down her window and stick her head out of it into the sun and wind like a happy dog as she sang along to the catchy Bangles song about walking like an Egyptian.

Marcus never let go of her hand the entire time, and as she felt pure joy move through her, she worked to drink it in, to savor the incredible taste of it.

They hit a bump in the road and Marcus pulled her back inside, her rear hitting the leather seat with a thump, followed by a burst of laughter she couldn't possibly contain. When Marcus started laughing along with her, her entire soul was swept up in the joy on his face.

As a Whitesnake song came on next, she said, "I love oldies stations like this."

"Oldies are songs from the fifties, not the eighties," Marcus argued.

Oops, she thought, realizing too late that she'd just inadvertently pointed out the difference in their ages. "You're right," she said cheerfully before turning off the radio.

A few moments later he was pulling into the parking lot of a really tiny little store.

"I'll be right back."

He returned with a large insulated bag slung over his shoulder. She wanted to ask what was inside, but he looked so much like a little boy with a happy secret that she decided to let him keep it. She'd seen him serious. Intense. Sensual, of course. And caring. But this playfulness was another wonderful layer.

It wasn't long until he pulled off onto a really rough, really narrow dirt track that required all of his concentration to get them to the bottom in one piece.

She'd guessed that they were heading out toward the coast, but that didn't lessen her surprise when he helped her out of the car, slung the heavy bag over his shoulder and said, "Close your eyes."

After Kenny she'd been afraid of ever trusting anyone again. But trusting Marcus was as natural as breathing. She took a deep breath, closed her eyes and was surprised to feel him lifting her off the ground.

Her eyes flew open and she found him smiling down at her.

"You don't need to carry me," she made herself say, even though the truth was that she was glad to be back in his arms, to feel his heart beating steadily against her.

"I can't have you tripping on any branches," he said against her ear. "Close your eyes again."

She shivered at his gentle command, even as a devil on her shoulder asked, "What if I don't want to?"

The look he gave her was so hungry, so full of sensual intent, that her lips actually tingled, though he hadn't kissed them. "Do you really want to find out?"

Her brain screamed, *Yes,* even as fear of the erotic repercussions he'd mentioned the night before had her closing her eyes just as he'd asked her to.

He chuckled as she wrapped her arms around his neck and snuggled in closer to him. All of her senses came to life as he carried her surely and steadily down the narrow path between the tall pines. She could hear the birds calling to one another from the treetops. She could feel the light breeze brushing over her skin, cooling her where Marcus touched her and made her hot.

"The air smells so good."

He kissed her forehead in response and, with

her eyes still closed, she tilted her face up to his, moved her hands to the back of his head and pulled his face down to hers to kiss him.

Giving her one last kiss, he said, "If you aren't careful, you'll never see anything but trees."

His low voice, rough with desire, had her more than a little tempted to do just that. But then he was moving again and she let herself be taken to the place he'd chosen just for her. For both of them.

The air around them changed from pine needles to salt spray as he stopped walking and slowly put her down, her back to his front.

"Go ahead. Open your eyes."

She had spent plenty of time on Malibu beaches these past years that she'd been working down in Los Angeles…but she wasn't prepared for the incredible sight that awaited her.

The blue-green water was so vibrant her brain could hardly believe it was real, that it hadn't been painted just for them. And the way the surf crashed on the tall, craggy rocks that rose up on either side of the fine, white sand of the beach reminded her of the parts of New Zealand she'd managed to see during her tour stops there.

"Marcus," she said with wonder, "this is beautiful."

His arms tightened around her and he nuzzled her. "I'm glad you think so."

She'd been given expensive bouquets, fancy dinners, even jewels, but only Marcus would think to give her the simple joy of a day at the beach.

She had to turn into his arms, had to tell him how she felt with more than words. She kissed him softly, slowly, then said, "Thank you for the best day I've ever had."

The sun was right above them and it was barely noon, but she already knew nothing could touch the joy she felt from being all alone with Marcus in one of the most beautiful settings in the world.

He looked down at her, his eyes dark with the need she knew had to be reflected in her own. "Are you hungry yet?"

She was, but not for food. Just for him. For the chance to savor every one of these precious hours with the man who was stealing her heart one beat at a time.

She shook her head and kicked off her ballet flats. "Ahh." She sighed with pleasure at the warm sand squishing between her toes. "It feels so good."

Marcus had sat down on a nearby rock to take off his shoes and socks and roll up his pants, and she was surprised when he pulled her down onto his lap and kissed her. Just as abruptly, he put her back down on shaky legs and grasped her hand in his to begin walking down the long stretch of completely empty beach.

"You like doing that, don't you?"

"Yes, I like kissing you."

"No," she said, "lifting me off my feet. Carrying me around. Pulling me down to kiss you whenever you get the urge." She turned to him with a mock glare. "I think it goes hand in hand with the telling me what to do stuff."

He didn't let go of her hand as he lifted his to run the back of one knuckle down her cheek. "You like it, too."

His sure words, the flat-out statement that she enjoyed being his plaything for him to move and command however he liked, should have upset her.

But they both knew that it didn't.

Suddenly feeling like she was on a boat that had lost its anchor and was drifting slowly but surely out into the middle of the ocean, she blurted the one question she hadn't been able to figure out the answer to in the time they'd been together.

"How did a gorgeous, successful, great guy

like you get to thirty-six without a wife and kids?" Quickly realizing she'd come at it all wrong when he went stiff beside her, she added, "I mean, considering how good you are in bed, I would expect women in wedding gowns to be knocking on your door all the time."

That earned her a small smile. "Exactly how good am I?"

"Now you're just fishing for compliments." She laughed, then added, "Really freaking good."

The surf crashed bigger and higher than it had before and she made a move to run, but Marcus wouldn't let her get away from the cold water that came up almost to her knees, bared in her short jean skirt.

"That's cold!" she protested.

"I like seeing you all wet."

"You have a dirty mind," she told him, but the breathiness in her voice gave away the fact that she did, too.

"You're right," he said, that dark, hungry look pinning her where she stood in the sand, causing her breath to catch in her throat. "So here's what my dirty mind wants, Nicola. Take off your clothes."

She looked up and down the empty beach. "Are you crazy?"

"Only when I'm with you." He raised an eyebrow. "I'm waiting."

Oh, God, she could hardly breathe at the thought of stripping down here for Marcus.

"If someone comes—" she began, before realizing, "No one is going to come to this beach, are they?"

"No," he confirmed. "It's completely ours today."

She had spent enough time with really wealthy people—worth a heck of a lot more than a pop star like her—to know keeping a huge stretch of coast completely private was entirely possible.

She was about to reach for the hem of her tank top when she realized what he'd done. She'd asked him a personal question and, instead of answering it, he'd thrown her off by using her own body—and the endless desire she had for him—against her.

She smoothed her hands down on her hips. "I'll make you a deal."

"A deal?"

She lifted her chin and said, "Yes," glad to catch the hint of smile playing around the edges of his lips at her defiant response.

"You have a beautiful backside, Nicola. I've

been looking forward to seeing it bent up over my knees."

Shockingly, he wasn't the only one.

Trying to push the senselessly erotic vision out of her head, she said, "Don't keep changing the subject," in her toughest voice.

She was rewarded with the sweet sound of his laughter. "Such a fierce little kitten." He caught her fists before she could knock them into his chest. "Go ahead. Make me a deal."

"I'll take my clothes off if you'll answer my question about why you're not married yet, or even in a relationship."

The laughter left his eyes so quickly she almost cried out at the loss. And yet, even though she knew this was supposed to be no-strings, even though she knew she shouldn't be straying away from the safe zone where only their bodies were involved, she knew it was already too late.

Her heart was in.

Way in.

She wanted to know more about Marcus. Needed to understand how he'd come to be the man he was.

"My girlfriend cheated on me," he told her in a hard voice. "I caught her the same day I went to that club."

She'd known things had gone badly with his ex from comments he'd made before, but couldn't stop her eyes from widening.

"*She* cheated on *you?*"

"I've never screwed around on a woman."

"No," she said quickly, "I know you would never do something like that. I just can't understand what woman in her right mind would cheat on you. You must be so angry with her."

"I was," he admitted, "but then I realized that she actually did us both a big favor."

"How?"

"We weren't right for each other and catching her in bed with another man saved me a lot of wasted time."

Even though she knew the answer might kill her, she had to ask. "Did you love her?"

He paused, the silence stretching on between them, before he finally admitted, "I thought I did."

Ouch. It shouldn't have hurt to think of Marcus being in love with someone else, but it did. A lot. Which was why it took her longer than it should have to realize he hadn't actually said he loved his ex.

"Wait, you thought you did? So is that a yes or no?"

He frowned, shook his head. "No. I only loved the person I wanted her to be. But that wasn't who she really was."

"I know exactly how that is," she said before she could catch herself.

"You do?"

Six months fell away in the span of two simple words from the sweetest man she'd ever known, and she knew if she talked about Kenny she'd probably end up crying all over him and making a complete idiot of herself.

"I do."

He tipped his hand beneath her chin and made her face him. "Whoever he was, whatever he did to hurt you, he was the world's biggest idiot."

The tears she'd been hoping she wouldn't cry spilled out. "I was the bigger idiot for believing his lies."

"No, Nicola," he said as he gently wiped away her tears with the pads of his thumbs. "You could never be anything but bright and beautiful and absolutely perfect just the way you are."

His mouth covered hers a moment later and then he was making her forget everything but how good it felt to be in his arms…everything but the fact that she was so incredibly glad she'd been there at the nightclub to help him over his bad breakup, a little bit, at least.

"Help me take my clothes off," she murmured against his lips.

His eyes glittered as he covered her hands with his and they pulled off her T-shirt together. Her bra came off next and he tossed both up onto the dry sand. Her jean skirt and panties came off just as quickly and then she was standing before him, completely naked.

And senselessly aroused.

Sixteen

"Do you have any idea how beautiful you are?"

The biggest, most trusting eyes in the world looked up at him. "Only when you're looking at me like this."

Marcus put his hands on her hips and pulled her against him as his mouth covered hers without any restraint at all. Nicola kissed him back just as passionately, her hands grasping at his clothes. Only breaking their kiss long enough to pull his shirt over his head, they were right back at it as they got his pants and boxers off.

His mouth still on hers, he lifted her into his arms again and walked into the surf.

A wave crashed up onto them and Nicola gasped at the cold. "Are you crazy?"

"When you're with me like this," he answered, "I think I must be."

She attacked him with her lips, planting kisses all over his face, his neck, his shoulders. He'd never been with someone so unrestrained, so ready to give in to her joy...and so willing to share it with him. The hours he'd spent with Nicola had been happier than any he could remember before her.

Yes, he'd been telling her the truth when he said he didn't regret any of the trade-offs he'd had to make on his family's behalf. But he was glad he didn't have to make any of those trade-offs now so that he could put Nicola—and his feelings for her—first for a few days.

"I want so badly to make love to you out here," she told him as she licked at his earlobe, "but we don't have any protection."

Marcus had to forcefully push aside the urge to be inside of her without anything between them. If this were more than a few crazy days together they could get tested and—

No. He needed to stay focused on the here and now, on the fact that Nicola had already given him more pleasure in a handful of days than any man should rightfully expect to have in one lifetime. She'd made it clear to him that she didn't want a relationship.

Just as clear as he'd made it to her, in fact.

That was when he showed her what he was holding. "I planned ahead."

She shook her head on a surprised laugh. "How the heck did you get this out of your pocket and unwrapped without my noticing?" Without waiting for his answer, she grabbed the condom from him. "Never mind. Just put me down so that I can do the honors."

Not sure he'd survive having her hot little hands on him, he warned her, "Don't even think about teasing me," as he put her back on her feet in the surf.

She blinked at him, all sexy innocence and pure wicked intent. "How else am I going to know if you're ever going to make good on all those spanking threats?"

"Oh, I'll make good on them, all right," he told her, tempted to take care of her sweet round ass right then and there, but then her tongue was coming out to lick at her upper lip as she focused her attention on his erection.

"You're the beautiful one," she murmured as she dropped to her knees before he saw it coming and put her mouth over him, so hot and wet and perfect.

Jesus, he couldn't believe he was out in the ocean with the most beautiful woman on the planet giving him a blow job in the swirling surf. This wasn't him, wasn't what his life was like, wasn't any part of his plans.

Forget his plans, he thought as he slid his hands into her hair and decided to take what she was so happily giving him. He tightened his hold on her hair as she suctioned him with her cheeks and tongue. All the while, even as the pleasure of her mouth nearly took him over the edge, he watched her carefully to make sure he wasn't hurting her. Fortunately, he could tell from the sexy little sounds she was making that she loved giving up her sensual control to him.

Waiting until he was a split second from losing it, he dragged himself out of her mouth.

"Put the condom on me, Nicola."

Her gaze was fuzzy as she blinked up at him, but she obeyed him with shaking hands.

Gritting his teeth against the sweet tug of her hands on his rock-hard shaft, he marveled at the way she completely gave up her body to him when they were making love. He wanted to be as good as the trust she gave him, wanted her to know she'd made the right decision in trusting him.

"Come here." He waited for her to take his hands and stand up before he said, "Wrap yourself around me." She jumped up to wrap her toned limbs tightly around him and he couldn't hold back his confession. "I love holding you like this."

"You can't possibly love it as much as I do," she said against his lips as he started walking deeper into the cold water.

"Oh, God," she gasped as the surf pushed over her bottom, "it's so cold." Her big eyes flicked up to his. "You're going to have to work really hard to keep me warm."

"That's the plan," he said, and then as he moved between her legs, "How's this working?"

"Mmm, pretty good. But—" she held out one arm "—I still have goose bumps." He pressed first one kiss, and then half a dozen, up her arm. "You're only making me shiver more," she said in a husky voice, and he lifted his mouth from her soft skin.

"Maybe this, then?"

Their eyes held as he took her in one hard stroke.

"Oh." Her eyelids fluttered at the pleasure of coming together. "Yes. Just like th—" Her words broke off on a gasp of pleasure as he angled his hips to stroke over the most sensitive parts inside her.

Being with Nicola like this was as natural, as

unstoppable, as the tides. There was no ebb and flow to his desire for her, only a constant crashing of need and want that kept dragging him deeper under her spell.

Her eyes glittered with emotion as she looked up at him and he could feel the dangerous pull of more than just bodies coming together in that moment as she held on to him, the sun illuminating her stunning beauty, the golden hue of her smooth skin.

For all his sensual demands, Marcus knew damn well who was really in charge. Nicola had owned him from that first moment in the club when she'd looked into his eyes and claimed him.

She'd had his body from the first, but he'd been so sure his heart—his soul—were safe. That no woman could possibly touch him.

So then, why did being with her like this touch him as nothing ever had before?

And when, he had to helplessly wonder as their bodies took more pleasure from each other than he'd ever known, had hot sex with his beautiful pop star turned into making love, even out on a beach beneath a sun that felt like it was shining just for them?

Seventeen

Laughing together as they put on their clothes over wet skin, they walked hand in hand up the beach to sit on the soft sand and plunder the contents of the bag Marcus had put together at the small Point Reyes corner store.

Nicola loved being with Marcus like this, sharing a meal and sitting together, their legs touching as they ate and kissed between bites. She was frankly amazed to find that their picnic was in some ways even more intimate—and scary—than making love in the ocean had been.

When he'd been holding her, driving her insane with his kisses and caresses, she'd been so close, barely another kiss away from spilling what had been growing deep within her heart. But now, she had a feeling it might not take more than one of his beautiful smiles to send her all the way over the edge, way past no-strings to turning into one of those girls she'd teased him about earlier, wearing the wedding dress and knocking on his door, begging him to keep her forever.

Somehow, despite the fact that she was having the best day of her life, despite how sweet he'd been when he was telling her that her ex hadn't deserved her, she needed to remember to keep a firm hold on her heart at all times.

"So," she asked as she tore another chunk of bread off and dipped it in the red-pepper hummus, "how do you know about this place?"

"This was my father's favorite beach." She followed his gaze down the beach to a pretty cottage perched on the rocks. "His best friend from college owned that house and this stretch of sand." A shadow passed over his face as he said, "Joe died a few years ago. He left my mother this place in his will, told her his best memories had been of all of us playing on the beach when we were kids. And that he hoped our grandkids would play here one day, too."

Nicola had to move closer to Marcus, had to take his hands in hers and hold them over her heart as though she could give hers up for his if it meant she could take away all of the pain he'd had to deal with at such a terribly young age.

"Tell me about your father. What was his name?"

"Jack." He smiled. "He was great. There was never a day when we didn't know how much he loved us, how glad he was to have us all. Even when a bunch of us were fighting and yelling and calling one another names, he would sit back and let us work it out until we reached the point of no return."

"What did he do then?"

She was pleased to hear him chuckle softly. "He'd walk into the room and say, 'It's over.'"

"That's it?"

He shot her a crooked grin. "He walked softly but carried a big stick."

"Sounds a lot like you."

"I used to think so."

She cocked her head to the side. "What do you mean? You don't think you're going to be a great father?"

"I used to think that. I'm pretty much over the whole wife and kids thing right now."

There was absolutely no reason for his statement to hurt her. But the fact that the pop star he'd been sleeping with could never possibly be under consideration for that role made her feel—for the very first time since she'd met him—cheap.

The sudden pain that slashed in past her breastbone made her careless enough to call him on what he'd just said. "So, just because some bitch you were dating cheated on you, you're giving up on having a family?"

His eyes flashed a warning that she decided to ignore. What the hell, the hole she was digging was already so big she could pretty much bury herself in it. Why stop now? Especially if she was never going to see him again come Monday morning. She might as well try to help…even if Marcus really didn't want her to.

Yes, she decided, it was a purely altruistic thing she was doing by pointing this out to him. It wasn't at all that he'd hurt her and she wanted him to pay for it.

"All I'm asking is if it's occurred to you that maybe you chose a totally worthless woman to date so that you wouldn't have to face actually marrying her and starting a family? So that you wouldn't have to risk losing a woman you loved, the mother of your children, like your mother lost your father? You're using your ex as the reason to hide from love." She shrugged, tried to act nonchalant. "Heck, that's probably why you chose me, too. Because it's easier to sleep with a totally inappropriate singer there is absolutely no chance of having a future with."

The silence was thick, almost cold, after she finished her point-by-point analysis of his life. Suddenly, she realized she'd never seen Marcus look at her like this before.

He was angry.

Angry with her for having told him what she thought.

"What about you?" His eyes were narrowed, his jaw tight. "You could have anyone, Nicola. So why did you date a worthless liar that you probably knew would end up hurting you? Is it the same reason you think you need to fill some sex-kitten image? The same reason you hide behind your body and your pretty face rather than letting people see how smart you are? And isn't that why you chose me, too, because I'm fun for a couple of nights, but we both know you'd never consider sticking it out with a boring old guy in a suit in a million years?"

She hadn't expected him to come back at her with that, with any of it, and she tried to take her hands from his, but he held them fast.

"You have no right to say those things to me."

"Don't throw stones if your own damned house can't take it, kitten."

Oh, God, she hated hearing him use that endearment now, when he was angry with her.

"Seems to me you're the expert on hiding," he told her in a low, hard voice. "Hiding from the press. Hiding how smart and talented you really are. Even in the bedroom, the last place in the world you should have been trying to hide yourself from your lover, I have to push every one of your buttons to get you to drop your walls for a split second."

She understood that she'd upset him with what she'd said, so much that he was actively trying to push her away. But that knowledge did nothing to douse her pain. If anything, it only made it worse.

Because she'd stupidly trusted him not to hurt her.

She yanked her hands from his grip and got to her feet in the sand. "Fine! You don't want me to hide anymore, then how about I stop right now?"

He stood up, too, facing her. "I dare you to try."

As the gauntlet crashed down between them, she blurted, "How about I face up to the fact that I'm still the world's biggest idiot for believing that we could actually do this with no strings? How about I tell you that I knew better than to start falling in love with a guy who would never want me for anything more than a few days of hot sex?" Her breath was coming too fast and her vision was blurring with tears as she yelled, "How's that for smart?"

She had to turn away from him, couldn't bear to let him see her cry. Not now that everything was ruined and her dream of the perfect day had been crushed.

And not after she'd actually gone and confessed her stupid feelings to him in the perfect way to make sure that he would never, ever return them.

Not, she knew, that he would have, anyway.

His mother had promised Nicola that she'd be safe with her son. But Mrs. Sullivan had been wrong.

"I need to go," Nicola told him in a tight voice that she willed not to break. "My crew is going to be expecting me at the venue for rehearsal soon. I can't be late again."

She headed toward the path between the pine trees that would take her back to his car. In the surf when he'd been holding her in his arms, despite how cold the water swirling around them had been, she'd felt so warm.

But now, even with the warm sun beating down on her back, she'd never felt colder.

* * *

It wasn't just the shock of knowing how deep her emotions for him ran that had Marcus reeling. It was the fact that here he'd been going on about her needing to treat herself as more than a sex kitten when that's the way he'd been treating her all along. Like she was a piece of ass that was good enough to take again and again…but when she actually turned that big brain—and heart—on his life, to analyze the decisions he'd made, he'd lost it on her.

Throwing everything into the picnic bag, he moved quickly through the trees to find her waiting in his car. Her back was straight, her hands were on her lap and she was staring straight ahead as he got in behind the wheel.

"I'm sorry."

He wanted to reach for her hand, but he knew how she'd react, that the last thing she wanted was for him to touch her. The irony wasn't lost on him that the very thing she didn't want was now what he needed most—to reconnect with her even in that one small way.

"I'm sorry, too."

Marcus was surprised to hear her say those words to him. He'd been planning to say so much more, needed to let her know how wrong he'd been to hurt her like that, that he hadn't realized what a sensitive topic his father's death was for him.

But when her eyes met his, flat and empty, he knew he was too late.

"I shouldn't have pressured you for these extra days together," she said softly, regret puncturing every word.

He thought he saw the shimmer of tears in her eyes, but when he looked again they were clear. And still so flat his gut clenched at the memory of the passion—the joy—that had been there just minutes before.

"You were right to want to end things after that first night." Her mouth moved up at the corners, into something no one would ever call a smile. "Lesson learned. One-night stands should stick to the number in their name."

Marcus had always been the steady Sullivan, the one who knew what to do in any situation. However, from the first moment with Nicola, he'd been completely out of his depth. More so now than ever before. Even though he'd known all along that their relationship was going to end in the very near future, he hated the thought of it ending this way.

"You've never been a pop star to me, Nicola. You've always just been you. A woman I wanted and liked from the start. If I've ever treated you like you were nothing more than a sex object, I'm truly sorry."

She was silent for several very long seconds. Finally, she said, "It's nice of you to say that."

He waited for more, waited for her to tell him she thought he was more than just some guy in a suit who knew how to make her scream with pleasure when she came, but she simply pulled her cell phone out of her bag and looked at the time.

"How long will it take to get to the Warfield?"

Suddenly, he felt like he was bending over backward to try to get her to listen to his apologies, but she wasn't willing to bend at all.

Hadn't he spent two straight years bending over for Jill, doing whatever he could to make her happy? Look how that had turned out. If he'd been too boring, too emotionless, for Jill, then surely one day soon, even if he and Nicola found a way to patch things up today, she would surely end up bored with him, too...and eventually he'd have the extreme nonpleasure of walking in on her doing some exciting guy with piercings and a goatee, knowing he'd been a fool one more time.

After all, they led completely different lives. He was up early to tend to the vines, to test the latest vintages, to meet with restaurant owners and wine sellers. She was either up late on stages and in recording studios, or attending parties like the ones in Hollywood that Smith went to so often.

He worked to remind himself yet again that they had nothing in common…even if, damn it, a part of him couldn't help but still feel that they had everything in common that really mattered.

"The Warfield is about an hour away."

"I hope there's no traffic. If you know any shortcuts, I'd appreciate you taking them."

How had it come to this so quickly? From making love in the ocean to sitting in his car while Nicola spoke to him like he was a stranger?

But his pride wouldn't let him beg her again for forgiveness. He'd tried. She'd pushed him away.

They were done.

"Don't worry," he told her in a voice that was just as distant as hers had been, "I'll make sure you're there on time."

Eighteen

Thank God she'd done a thousand shows like this one, Nicola thought as she went through the motions of sound-checking and joking around with her band the following evening. She might have been smiling, laughing, but she felt hollow. Empty.

And really, really sad.

The things Marcus had said to her kept repeating over and over in her head, so loudly that she'd actually forgotten the lyrics to one of her songs during rehearsal and had to stop in the middle, apologize to her band with a joke, pretend she didn't see the way they looked at her, at one another, with questions in their eyes.

One slip. She was only ever one slip away from people assuming late nights and drugs and wild parties.

Of course, she wasn't exactly helping herself by playing into the wild image with her videos, the clothes she wore onstage, the fact that she let herself be photographed with people whose wild images were earned, not simply imagined.

It was as much as Marcus had said to her out on the beach, when they were angrily throwing words at each other.

She knew that was a large part of why she'd been so angry. Maybe if she could have taken one breath, and then another, she could have let herself admit to him—to both of them—that she was tired of the sexy-girl image. That she'd been wondering more and more why she was bothering with it. And that she wanted to let her songs stand for themselves.

Just the power of her music—sink or swim—without the silent promise of sex to sell them to the world.

But she hadn't taken that breath, had she?

Instead, she'd barreled headlong into the stupidest, most idiotic confession of her life.

She'd told him she was falling in love with him.

No.

She'd *yelled* it at him.

Of course, he'd said nothing about love. Not there on the beach…and not later in his car.

She sat in her dressing room, which her tour manager had set up per her usual specifications, making the space as comfortable and cozy as possible, and stared into the large mirror with the strip of lights shining down above it. They were way too bright, highlighting all the parts of her soul she didn't want to have to see.

To his credit, Marcus had come back to the car and immediately apologized. But she'd been too afraid to hear what he was sorry for, terrified that he was going to say, *I'm sorry you're in love with me. I never meant for that to happen.*

She turned away from the mirror, unable to look herself in the eye any longer.

Heartbreak was supposed to be perfect for writing songs. She should be picking up her guitar and writing a masterpiece, channeling the Joni Mitchell inside herself and singing about blue boys and bright red devils she couldn't live without.

But she couldn't do that. Not tonight, anyway. Not when it was all too raw. Not when she still felt so stupid, so painfully foolish to have lost her heart so quickly, so completely, to a man she had known from the start would never be a good match for her.

One night was all they ever should have shared.

But as she sat in her dressing room feeling sorry for herself, it was as if the guitar, the mirror, were both staring at her from opposite sides of the room and calling her coward.

They were right.

She was being a coward.

And she'd been one for too long.

Finally, Nicola took that breath she should have taken out on the beach. And then another and another until she felt strong enough to make the right decision.

Ignoring the skimpy, shiny outfits her stylist had laid out for her to wear onstage, clothes designed to dance in and provoke, she moved off her chair, picked up her guitar and turned to face herself in the mirror.

The woman who stared back didn't look like a pop star in full makeup and shimmering skin-tight silk and spandex. For the first time ever, Nico looked like Nicola, a young, pretty, twenty-something girl in a jean skirt and T-shirt who had written some songs she wanted to play for people.

Finally, Nicola was able to find a small smile.

Sink or swim, tonight was the night she'd take that first step toward her new future.

And even though she wouldn't have Marcus by her side, at least she'd always know she had him to thank for helping to give her a push in the right direction.

He didn't love her, but he'd always been clear about respecting her.

Tonight, she'd respect herself, too.

Holding her guitar to her body as if it were a lover—knowing it was the only lover she would have for a long time to come—Nicola stepped out into the hallway and went to find her band leader to discuss the change of plans.

Marcus had told his sister that he couldn't come to Nicola's concert with her on Saturday night, that he had plans for the night that couldn't be broken. The last thing in the world he needed was to sit beside Lori watching Nicola onstage.

He'd gone back to his winery in Napa, back to his normal life where sweet, sexy pop stars had nothing to do with his world unless they walked into his winery with an entourage and demanded a personal tour. But he simply couldn't stay away. Couldn't possibly resist the chance to be in the same room as Nicola for a few more hours.

And so, not only had he flat-out lied to one of his siblings, but despite his story about being too busy to attend the concert, here he was standing outside the Warfield in San Francisco staring up at a sign that said Special Guest for One Night Only: NICO!

In his car at the beach, his pride had told him he was better off without her, that he needed to end things before she could end them later and break his heart.

Fuck his pride.

Because the memory of the way she'd gotten out of his car in front of the venue Friday afternoon had haunted him every second since.

"It was nice meeting you" was what she'd said.

What the hell was he supposed to say to that? That it was nice to have met her, too, like they were nothing more than a couple of business colleagues?

Even though he should have been gentle with her, even though his only goal should have been to try to get her to listen to his apologies, he'd growled her name instead.

Her eyes had flicked over him for a brief second, before she'd pulled out her cell phone and alerted her crew that she was out front. Moments later, she was disappearing through the doors, which were locked behind her to keep not only her fans from disturbing her during rehearsals… but to also create a barrier between her and the guy staring after her from behind the wheel of his car.

"Hey, man, you want a ticket to the show? Nico usually plays much bigger places and this one sold out in twenty minutes. Not gonna get the chance to see her this close anytime soon."

The scalper's words ripped at his already torn-apart gut as Marcus stared at the ticket. It was why he was here, wasn't it? To see Nicola one more time, to drink her in, even from a distance, because he already missed her like hell.

He'd been close to her, so close. And he'd taken her completely for granted, had been looking toward Monday as an inevitable end.

Marcus bought the ticket and was surprised to find the crowd was made up of not just kids, but college students and more than a few people his own age who had obviously come not as chaperones to young fans, but because they wanted to see Nicola play.

As he sat down, he heard a couple of teenagers discussing her.

"I heard that guy she was dating last year totally scammed her. You know, got her high and then took a bunch of pictures and sold them."

"He totally looked like a creep, didn't he?"

"Totally. I wonder why she even dated him? If I was as awesome as Nico, I'd hold out for the best-looking guy in the world who worshipped me."

Their conversation moved on to the guys they had crushes on who didn't know they existed and Marcus sat back to process what he'd just learned.

Out on the beach, she'd alluded to being hurt and betrayed by a former lover. And she'd already told him that she'd made some bad decisions that had landed her with a wild party-girl image.

Marcus knew it would be so easy to pull up the internet browser on his phone and find out the rest of the story, but he remembered how wary she'd been once he'd learned who she was, the way she'd assumed he'd done a Google search on her.

Whatever he learned about her past, he needed to learn from her directly.

That is, if she would ever talk to him again.

And why would she? he wondered as the lights dimmed and the crowd began to cheer. He might not be looking her up on the internet, but he was sitting here in the dark like a creepy stalker, waiting to watch her perform without her knowledge.

Had her ex done any worse?

Marcus knew he needed to get up out of his seat and leave. But he'd never had any self-control where Nicola was concerned…and he still didn't.

For all that he'd tried to keep their relationship to just sex, it hadn't been. Not even close. Her music was such a big part of who she was, and he needed to see it, needed to understand it, needed to know that part of her as well as he knew the contours of her beautiful body.

The stage lights went up slowly and everyone shot to their feet as Nicola walked onstage. Marcus's breath caught at how small she looked beneath the bright lights, but how she owned it—and everyone in the room—nonetheless.

He was surprised to see that she was wearing a T-shirt and skirt. From the pictures he remembered seeing of her when he'd flipped past the music cable stations with his remote, he'd assumed she'd be wearing one of her skimpy costumes, the outfits that were part and parcel of the sex-kitten image he'd ripped apart on the beach.

"Hi, everyone."

The two large screens on either side of the stage showed him her smile. She looked strong, but a little nervous at the same time. He thought he saw hints of sadness in her eyes, but there was excitement there, too.

What was she doing?

But then, suddenly, he knew, even before she said or did anything else. His beautiful girl was taking control.

"I'm so glad everyone could spend tonight with me. The Musicians for Literacy Foundation is really important to me."

A voice called out, "We love you, Nico!"

She laughed. "I love you, too."

The words fell so easily off her tongue and he knew she meant it. Her fans meant the world to her. She didn't take the opportunity to play her music for so many people lightly.

"I'm in the mood to play my guitar and piano tonight and take this acoustic for a while. Is that okay with you guys?" Five thousand voices cheered her and her smile lit up the dark room. "Awesome."

She reached out to take a guitar from a roadie and slipped it on over her shoulders. Marcus thought how right she looked like that.

He suddenly saw that he'd been wrong out on the beach. She hadn't been hiding all of herself, just one half of herself. Because she was both the sex goddess from her videos and this beautiful girl whose voice rang out pure and strong as she strummed her guitar and broke all of their hearts with the simple magic of her songs.

People sat back down in their seats. Not because they weren't thrilled with the music, but because they wanted to be able to listen more closely, to better hear every note and nuance of her performance. A performance that held them all spellbound.

Between songs, she was utterly disarming as she told the stories behind her inspiration for the lyrics and made everyone laugh. And then, when she sat down at the piano in the spotlight and began to play the song he'd heard at her video rehearsal—"All it took was one moment, one look in your eyes, one taste of your lips, to know that you were the one"—she held out her entire heart to her audience.

A heart for them to hold...or to crush.

And as he watched, as he listened, as his heart—and soul—drank her in amid a room full of strangers, Marcus knew himself to be the world's biggest fool.

The woman he'd accused of hiding was braver than anyone else he'd ever met.

A hell of a lot braver than he was.

If Marcus hadn't already faced the fact that he was head over heels in love with Nicola, he would have fallen right then...along with five thousand other people in the sold-out concert hall in San Francisco.

Nineteen

As the applause continued after her third and final encore, Nicola quickly moved down the hallway to her dressing room. She needed a few seconds to herself before she went out in the group area to say hello to the fans who had paid extra to the charity for the privilege of a picture and a chat with her.

Her crew had been with her long enough to understand this need, and although they smiled at her and gave her the thumbs-up, they let her pass without conversation.

She closed the door behind her and leaned against it, finally letting out the breath she felt like she'd been holding for two hours.

She'd done it, had actually stood up on the stage the entire night with just her guitar and piano and voice to lead her through. God, it had been incredible—although, she was surprised to realize, a part of her missed the lights and flash and dancing.

All or nothing, that's how it had always felt like things needed to be. Had she been wrong the whole time? And, if so, could she possibly figure out how to walk the line between flash and heart without losing her fan base and giving up the career she'd worked so hard to build?

"Nico." A knock came at the door. It was Jimmy, the bodyguard who usually worked her shows.

She took a breath and opened the door with a smile. "Hi."

He was frowning. "I'm really sorry to bother you."

"Is something wrong?"

"I just wanted to let you know there's a guy outside who doesn't seem to want to take no for an answer about coming back here to meet you."

Her gut clenched a split second before her heart followed suit. "He's probably just a college kid who drank too much," she said, even though she already knew better.

"Nope," Jimmy confirmed. "He's an older guy. Different from the usual type trying to convince me that he knows you. Looks like a business-man."

Oh, God, Marcus was out there. Did he know she'd been looking for him in the crowd the entire night? That every man with broad shoulders had stopped her cold, but none of them were ever him? Finally, she'd convinced herself that he wasn't there. But now it turned out he'd seen her show and he wanted to come backstage to see her.

Only, having just given every last piece of her shattered soul over to the crowd, in this state, she knew exactly what she'd do the second she saw him. She'd beg him to take her back. Even just for one hour, if he'd have her that long. And when morning came, she'd hate herself for not being able to hold on to her pride where he was concerned.

She shook her head, started to say, "I can't—"

Jimmy nodded. "Don't worry. I won't let him back here. I just wanted to make sure you didn't leave alone tonight, just in case he decides to wait around in the shadows outside for you. I'll take you back to your hotel."

She nodded. "Okay." She tried to smile her thanks, but she couldn't manage it. "I appreciate you letting me know about the situation."

His smile was gentle. "You were great out there tonight. Blew us all away."

Tears prickled too close to her eyelids. "Thanks. I'm glad you liked the show." She gestured toward the dressing room. "I just need a few seconds and then I'll come out and do the meet-and-greet."

"I'll let them know you're on your way."

She closed the door again with a soft click, holding her hand over her heart. Just thinking about Marcus out by the stage door had it beating so fast, too fast. He was so close....

No. She needed to stop thinking of him, needed to get on with her job.

She didn't dare look in the mirror, didn't want to see her own haunted eyes, as she grabbed a water bottle and headed out to say hello to her fans. Tonight was about them, about their generosity to a very deserving charity. Nicola wasn't going to let a stupidly broken heart get in the way of that truth.

Thirty minutes later, her cheeks hurt from smiling so hard, but she wanted to hug each and every one of her fans, because for a little while she'd almost felt normal, like she had before Marcus had come into her life and held her so gently.

Before he'd kissed her, touched her.

Before he'd shown her something far more

beautiful—and, ultimately, far more painful—than she ever could have imagined.

Before love.

"Oh, my God, you were amazing!" Lori pushed through the throngs of people surrounding Nicola to throw her arms around her.

She was glad to see Lori, of course she was, but the link to Marcus was way too close for comfort and Nicola had to work even harder than she already was to school her expression into a smile.

"Thanks," she said, wondering if Lori knew her brother was there. "I had a lot of fun out there tonight."

"I wish Marcus had been able to come. You would have a new biggest fan."

Nicola barely held on to her smile. If he were any other guy, maybe she would have let herself confide to Lori how she'd completely lost her heart. Girl talk was just what she needed, someone to drink too many glasses of wine with while they trash-talked men.

Instead, she said, "I've really enjoyed spending time with you this week."

Marcus's sister grinned at her. "You're not leaving until Monday, right?" At Nicola's nod, Lori said, "Once a month, the whole clan gets together for Sunday lunch at my mother's house.

Please come and hang out with us. You already know Marcus, but I know how much everyone else would like to meet you after I've spent the past week talking their ears off about how amazing you are."

"Wow, that's really nice," Nicola said, not wanting to be a bitch and ruin their budding friendship by turning down Lori's friendly offer, "but I can't intrude on a family event."

Misunderstanding Nicola's hesitation, Lori said, "We all get the fame thing with Smith. I promise everyone will be totally normal. Besides," she said with an obvious matchmaking gleam in her eyes, "I can't help but hope you'll meet one of my brothers and the two of you will fall in love. Have I told you about Gabe? He's a firefighter and my friends are always telling me how hot he is."

Everything was spiraling out of control so quickly that Nicola could barely force out a joke. "Who could possibly resist a firefighter?"

Lori hugged her again. "I'll text you the address. I know you're busy, so I'll let the rest of your adoring fans have some time with you. See you tomorrow!"

Maybe, Nicola thought as a group of excited young girls squealed at meeting her, this lunch was for the best. She'd already been brave enough to start changing her image, had taken that first step tonight to stop hiding behind her sex-kitten exterior.

But not letting Marcus see her backstage just now hadn't been very brave.

Tomorrow at Sunday brunch she'd face him one more time. She'd prove to both of them that she could handle it, that she was big enough, strong enough, to stop hiding, and clear up any lingering hurt feelings. That would leave both of them free to move on with their lives, the few days they'd spent together in each other's arms nothing but a distant memory.

Still, Nicola knew she wouldn't sleep much that night. How could she when her brain would be busy looking at her relationship with Marcus from every possible angle, even though she already knew the final answer?

Ending it was the best thing for both of them. Yes, they could have done it in a cleaner, nicer way, but at least they weren't fooling themselves into thinking they could actually have a relationship.

He would be so much happier without her.

And she'd eventually learn how to deal with being miserable without him.

Twenty

Marcus had a hell of a night. After driving back up to his winery in Napa after the concert, he'd sat on the porch and stared out into the darkness until the sun came up. It was the first time since he'd moved to the wine country and built his home surrounded by vines and mountains and oak trees that he wasn't able to take in the beauty. Even when things had been going bad with Jill, he'd still been able to appreciate the magnificent setting for his house.

This morning it had all been lost on him. And there hadn't been any point in trying to sleep, not when visions of Nicola continued to haunt him.

All night long, he'd asked himself the same question: How could he fix the mistakes he'd made with her? Everything he'd done to hurt her, to push her away, to keep her at arm's length, to guard his heart, came at him as the moon shifted to let the sun take its place.

That first morning in Smith's kitchen, when she'd asked him for another night and he'd hurt her by telling her no, that it had been a huge mistake to leave the club with her at all.

The night when he'd found out who she was, and had been not only angry with her for keeping her famous identity from him and making them use the private entrance, but he'd also decided both those things gave him license to selfishly force her body past the point of no return.

The way he'd made her work like hell the next morning to have extra time with him, when a real man would have owned up to his feelings and saved her the pain of another possible rejection.

The hurt in her eyes out on the beach when she'd yelled at him about being stupid enough to fall in love with him…and he didn't have the guts to admit he was falling in love with her, too.

Marcus's entire body grew tight and tense as he made himself own up to each and every one of his mistakes.

He walked for miles over his land, from which he'd built a thriving business, but no matter how far he walked, the vines that stretched out over the hills held no beauty for him. Not after he'd held the most beautiful woman in the world in his arms…and had been too stupid to realize he needed to do anything and everything in his power to convince her to let him love her the way she should be loved.

Thank God Nicola's bodyguard hadn't let him in to see her last night, had firmly told him, "Sorry, man, she's busy. You're not getting in to see her." Marcus hadn't been rational and would definitely have made things worse.

Unfortunately, after a long night of thinking, he still hadn't come up with a plan that had any chance of working. Not when he knew he couldn't heal what was broken between them with flowers or jewelry.

He didn't have the will to do more than put on clean jeans and a T-shirt for his mother's Sunday lunch, even though he knew someone was bound to comment on the fact that he clearly wasn't at the top of his game. That was the thing about family—they were always there with you to celebrate the good stuff…and to point out when you were screwing up. And if Lori knew what had gone down with Nicola, she would kick his ass so hard he'd feel the imprint of her foot for the next decade.

* * *

Marcus opened his mother's front door and walked inside. The ranch-style house had been barely big enough to fit all eight kids when they were growing up. He'd shared a room with Smith and Chase, while Ryan, Zach and Gabe had shared another, and then later, the twins had shared a third. Close quarters had led to plenty of fights over the years, but also the kind of family memories he wouldn't give back for all the space in the world.

He *knew* who each member of his family was, and they knew him. He had the money to buy his mother a mansion in the fancy part of town, but she wouldn't let any of them do that. Marcus thought he knew why, that it had less to do with the actual charms of the house itself, or the great neighborhood...but with the fact that her memories of her husband were here. And she couldn't bear to leave Jack Sullivan behind.

Smith walked into the room with a couple of beers in his hand. "Hey, you look like shit."

"Nice to see you, too," Marcus replied. The closest in age of all the siblings, the two of them had spent plenty of time talking with their fists as kids. "Didn't know you'd be in town."

Smith handed him a beer. "We have to reshoot

a couple of city scenes this week. Figured I'd get here a day early and see everyone." He raised an eyebrow. "I was pretty surprised by your text earlier this week. So, Jill's not in the picture anymore, I take it? Otherwise, you wouldn't be needing my place."

"Right, she's gone."

Smith grinned. "Good." His grin widened. "So tell me about the new girl. After two years with the ice queen, I hope her replacement was seriously hot. Just as long as you changed the sheets when you were done."

There was no reason for Marcus to want to knock a couple of Smith's teeth out of his movie-star face. His brother couldn't know he was inadvertently slamming Nicola.

"There were no sheets to change" was all he was going to say about it.

Before his brother came at him with more questions, he headed for the backyard, where in good weather the large table was always set up for brunch. Smith's voice came at him again before he could make it to the French doors.

"We've got a special guest outside. Lori said you've already met Nico. Gorgeous girl, isn't she?"

Holy hell. The beer bottle slipped in Marcus's

grip and he had to fumble to keep from dropping it.

Marcus was torn between walking over to the table where Nicola was surrounded by his siblings and dragging her off to lock her in the nearest bedroom to do whatever it took to make her listen to him—or turning on his heel and getting the hell out of there.

He knew he needed to see her again, knew he needed to get down on his knees before her and grovel…but could he do those things in front of his entire family?

Marcus hadn't made it any farther than the threshold between the living room and the patio when his mother made a beeline for him.

Her arms were warm as she hugged him and her voice was soft as she said, "She's lovely."

He didn't have time to school his expression into anything but surprise.

His mother's smile was soft and understanding. "I'm glad to be able to have more than a few minutes to talk with Nicola today. That impromptu phone call the other night was much too short for me to get to know her."

Oh, no. How could he have forgotten about that call to his mother the night they'd left the club?

At his dumbfounded silence, his mother continued, "I'll have to admit that I was surprised when she arrived with Lori rather than you." She raised an eyebrow. "And I'm even more surprised that no one, not even your sister who's been working with her, seems to know about you two."

No one was better at getting information out of her kids than his mother. Among her specialties were questions that subtly pinned you in place, then forced you to spill your guts when you'd sworn to keep your silence on a subject forever.

"We're not actually together right now." It wasn't hot out but he was sweating. "I blew it."

His mother watched him carefully before her mouth curved up into a smile. "I've hoped for this for so many years, waited for someone to finally come along whom you could love more than your family, someone who would turn you inside out and toss you off your path." His mother looked positively gleeful in the face of his misery. "Someone just like Nicola for you to blow it with."

Dumbfounded, Marcus could only watch his mother walk away with a smile on her face as Lori yelled out, "Marcus, you're here!"

Finally, he got his feet working again and headed toward the group out in the middle of the backyard.

A half dozen voices came at him, but all Marcus could see was that Gabe was sitting way too close to Nicola. He knew his youngest brother's type. Nicola was exactly the kind of woman Gabe and the other guys at the fire station liked to take home for the night.

"Gabe," he said, "you're needed in the kitchen."

His brother looked doubtful. Gabe was notorious for leaving the kitchen looking like a tornado had hit it. Fortunately, he shifted his seat back and started to get up, but before he did, he leaned over to say something in Nicola's ear. She laughed and Marcus's hands started to curl into fists.

Hell, he'd practically raised Gabe from a baby. He shouldn't want to kill him now just because he'd made Nicola laugh, and had looked at her a little too long, with a little too much interest.

Fortunately, before Marcus could leap across the yard to flatten his youngest brother, Chloe walked over to say hello with a hug. "I feel like I haven't seen you in forever."

Chase was a step behind his fiancée. "We're thinking about coming up to Napa for a visit sometime soon," Chase told him, pulling Chloe close.

The two of them had fallen in love at his winery and Marcus had been amazed to watch his brother fall head over heels for a woman he'd just met. Marcus hadn't really been able to understand how something so big could happen so fast.

But now he understood perfectly.

"Come anytime. The guesthouse is always yours. It's been too long."

He meant what he said, but he could hear how stilted his words were even to his own ears.

Zach was on his cell phone on the other side of the yard, Ryan was at the grill flipping burgers and Sophie and Lori were on opposite sides of the table again. They'd been at odds with each other for months.

Marcus had always been the one to break up the twins' fights, to force the two of them to sit down and actually talk to each other. If this were a normal Sunday brunch, he would have dragged them off by their ponytails and done just that.

But he couldn't focus on anything but Nicola today, could barely remember how to put one foot in front of the other or speak without sounding like a complete fool. Now that he'd let himself look at her, he couldn't pull his gaze away. She looked so beautiful, so right, sitting in the backyard he'd grown up in.

"Hi."

She blinked at him, clearly wary. "Hi, Marcus. It's nice to see you again."

God, he hated the way she sounded so distant. Just the way she had when she'd told him she was glad to have met him, then walked out of his life.

Not picking up on the strained atmosphere between them at all, Lori cheerfully explained to everyone, "Marcus came by to visit our rehearsal at the dance studio on Monday." She patted Gabe's open seat. "Come sit down."

Marcus didn't know how he'd manage to sit that close to Nicola without touching her, without pulling her onto his lap where she belonged. But he couldn't just keep standing there with his entire family looking at him like he'd lost his mind.

He felt as if he were moving in slow motion as he came around the table. Nicola's eyes widened as he approached and he couldn't look away from her. He sat down, and when his thigh brushed against her, she jumped out of her seat.

"I'm going to go see if your mother needs help with anything in the kitchen."

Lori beamed after her as Nicola hurried off. "Isn't she sweet? I think she and Gabe are really hitting it off."

Smith shook his head. "I don't think so, Lori."

Lori frowned. "What do you mean? They were

totally flirting earlier and now she's using Mom as an excuse to go spend more time with him in the kitchen."

"Marcus, you got any theories on why she left in such a hurry?"

He took a long swig from his beer. It was either that or tackle Smith across the table. Or go inside and pound the hell out of Gabe for flirting with his woman.

Hell, he'd happily take on every last one of his brothers right now if it meant he could work through some of the frustration coursing through him at being this close to Nicola but not actually being in any position to tell her how he felt, how sorry he was for ruining everything.

Clearly, Smith had put two and two together. And it didn't seem that he liked the idea of Marcus hooking up with Nicola much at all.

Smith could go fuck himself.

Fortunately, Lori was still clueless. He didn't think Chase and Chloe had linked him with Nicola yet, but they still looked worried about him.

Only Sophie was safe to talk to right now. "How's the new project going at work, Nice?"

She made a face. "Don't call me that in front

of our guest. It's embarrassing. I have a name, you know."

"What's that again?" Zach teased as he came and sat down, shoving his phone into his pocket. "I kind of remember it starts with a letter toward the end of the alphabet."

She punched Zach in the arm before answering Marcus's question about her latest research project at the San Francisco City Library.

"Remind me again why I thought it would be a good idea to get a grant to pull together a bibliography of the greatest love stories of all time." She sighed. "I thought it was going to be so romantic."

Clearly surprised, Chloe said, "How can love stories not be romantic?"

"Well, most of the famous love stories are completely tragic, for one."

"Oh, you mean like Romeo and Juliet?"

Sophie nodded. "At this point, I've pretty much decided never to fall in love. Not if death and betrayal are what's waiting at the end of the rainbow."

Marcus was a week too late for Sophie's epiphany. Especially because he had a bad feeling that every second that passed without being able to properly talk with Nicola pushed them one step closer to being another one of those love stories gone tragically wrong.

Just as he'd known she would, Lori argued with her twin more for the sake of arguing than because she wanted to be right about this particular issue.

"You're the one who's tragic," Lori said, and then, "Trust you to ignore all the really great love stories, like *Pride and Prejudice*."

Sophie scowled at her sister. "As far as I can tell, the way things ended in that story was nothing but blind luck." She turned her scowl into a smile for Chase and Chloe. "Like the two of you. I still can't believe you met on the side of the road in Napa and now you're getting married. It's so beautiful."

"Hear that?" Chase said to his fiancée, clearly bemused. "Our relationship is nothing but blind luck."

"If the worst day of my life turning into my best is blind luck, I'll take it," Chloe said softly.

They all knew about her previous marriage, how bad it had been, that her ex had hit her and she'd had to run. Marcus knew that, by comparison, he had nothing to complain about.

Still, he'd clearly been messed up enough about

what had happened with Jill to completely blow a great thing with Nicola.

Sophie sighed wistfully as Chase kissed his fiancée. "What about you, Marcus? Do you have anything new going on lately?"

Nicola walked out into the backyard with a large tray of cut vegetables and dip just as Sophie asked Marcus what was new in his life. Thank God she was wearing flats; otherwise, she surely would have tripped over her heels and the food would have scattered all over the neatly mowed lawn. She somehow managed to keep moving toward the table.

"I've been spending some time in the city the past week."

"Really? Why didn't you come by the library, then?"

Right then, Marcus turned his gaze from Sophie to her and what Nicola read in them had panic bubbling up even higher inside her. Oh, God, he wasn't going to say anything, was he?

She shook her head at him, as a silent signal that she prayed he'd understand.

We're done, remember? Done!

He hadn't wanted to tell anyone about her while they were together. He had been just as on board with hiding their temporary relationship from everyone this week as she had been. There was no reason to blow everything up now, just because it was uncomfortable having to be in the same place for a few hours after their no-strings fling had ended badly.

Finally, he said, "I had some unexpected things to take care of in San Francisco."

"I'll bet you did," Smith muttered, shooting a look at Nicola.

Smith had been perfectly nice—had actually been flirting outrageously with her—until Marcus had arrived. Since then, every time she looked up he was frowning at her.

Oh, no. He couldn't have figured out that she was the woman Marcus had brought to his house that night, could he?

Up until now, she'd thought the only one who knew about the two of them was Marcus's mother. Nicola had been stupendously nervous when she'd finally met Mary. Fortunately, his mother was as fantastic in person as she had been on the phone. And, amazingly, she didn't allude to Marcus or their obvious affair in any way. Instead, she simply said, "It's lovely to finally meet you, Nicola," then welcomed her into the house as if she were part of the family.

But now, as Nicola chewed on the fact that Smith might have figured it out, she could feel her face flaming as she put down the platter. "There's more to bring out from the kitchen," she said, wanting nothing more than to escape again.

Unfortunately, Lori said, "No way. You're our guest. You need to come sit down. I'll help Mom."

Nicola's heartbeat was wild—borderline frantic—as she eyed her empty seat beside Marcus, knowing it would look strange if she took a different chair. The problem was, she was so afraid she'd give herself away by accident, so worried she'd lose control and touch him…or, worse yet, give in to the desperate urge to kiss him in front of his entire family.

They were all being so nice to her right now, but if they knew that she'd had a fling with the brother they all loved and respected so much, the oldest brother who had done everything for them, they'd never forgive her for tramping her way into his life.

And they'd never forgive her for hurting him.

"Scoot, gorgeous," Ryan said to her as he brought over a steaming platter of burgers and hot dogs.

Before she could go take her seat, Marcus growled, "Watch it, Ryan."

His brother frowned at him, clearly without the first clue what the problem was. But Nicola instantly realized Marcus didn't like his pro baseball player brother flirting with her or calling her *gorgeous*.

She would have had a harder time wrapping her head around all of these good-looking men in one family if she'd been able to focus on anything but Marcus. Technically, her brain told her that Zach was the best-looking of them all, with Smith not far behind, while the rest of them were still jaw-dropping. But to her, it didn't matter how perfect their features were.

Marcus outshone them all and she could hardly tear her eyes away from him, even though she knew it was a dead giveaway to her feelings.

Thankfully, their mother appeared just then, along with Lori and Gabe. The three of them put the rest of the food on the table, and for a few moments everyone was focused on filling their plates.

Everyone except Marcus…and her.

"What can I get for you?"

It was the first thing he'd said to her today apart from the quick "Hi" right when he'd walked in. And even though he was only asking her if she preferred hamburgers or hot dogs, her body—and heart—reacted as if he'd just said the most sensual, intimate words in the world.

How she was going to miss the warmth of his low, slightly rough voice as he held her, as he stroked her hair.

As he made love to her.

Her skin felt hot, her insides turning to goo beside him. "A hot dog. Thank you."

But he didn't reach for the food. Instead, he caught her hand beneath the tablecloth.

For a long moment—way too long if she wanted to keep their relationship a secret for much longer—she was lost in his eyes, in the sweet caress of his thumb across her palm.

It took every ounce of the strength she had left for her to mouth, *"No."* Marcus deserved a great life, damn it, not the circus he'd get from being with her.

She reinforced the short word by pulling her hand from his and reaching for some of the food. She hoped no one noticed that she couldn't stop her hand from trembling.

Once everyone had a full plate and was starting to dig in, Marcus's mother said, "We're so glad you could join us today, Nicola." If anyone thought it strange that their mother hadn't called her Nico, they were too polite to say anything about it. "I hope everyone has been on their best behavior while I was inside."

"Everyone has been great." Realizing she was mumbling, she made herself sit up straighter and smile at Mary. "I don't get to see my family as much as I'd like to. I miss Sunday lunches like this."

As Mary asked her about her family and she had them laughing with stories about the pranks she and her twin brothers would play on one another when they were kids, Nicola was almost able to relax.

The problem was, she was palpably aware of the fact that neither Marcus nor Smith were laughing along with the rest of them. It didn't take long for everyone to realize something was up.

"Marcus?" Lori asked. "You're not eating and you look kind of, well, not so good." She scrunched up her nose. "In fact, I can't think of the last time you didn't shave. Are you feeling okay?"

"No," Marcus replied, "I'm not okay."

Six faces—Chloe and all the siblings apart from Smith—went slack with shock. Clearly, this was the first time their overly capable big brother had ever admitted to having a problem in front of them.

Nicola was glad she hadn't had more than a couple of bites of her hot dog, because it would have come back up all over the pretty tablecloth. He couldn't be about to do what it looked like he was going to do, was he?

Okay, yes, the two of them had a few more things to say to each other. But not in front of his whole family.

Marcus had just turned to face her and was obviously about to say something when Smith abruptly stood up.

"There's something I need to show you in the garage, Marcus."

"We're in the middle of lunch," Mary protested, but there wasn't any heat behind her words. In fact, she sounded strangely pleased with the turn events had taken.

"Sorry, this can't wait." Smith stood up and headed for the house. "Marcus needs to see it right now."

For a moment, Nicola didn't think Marcus was going to follow. But then, on a muttered curse, he threw his napkin down and shoved his chair back.

Nicola expected his mother to look upset at the way her meal was falling to pieces. Instead, she simply raised her eyebrows at her other sons and said in a mild voice, "Go ahead. I know you boys are dying to see it, too."

A few moments later, Nicola found herself sitting alone with the women.

"Sullivan men." Mary smiled at her. "They're really something else, aren't they?"

The understanding in Mary's eyes nearly broke Nicola, and no matter what else went on here today, she needed Marcus's mother to know. "You have a beautiful family."

"I know, honey. I'm so glad you're here with us today."

And, amazingly, even though this lunch had been a struggle from the very first moment she'd walked in the door, Nicola realized she was glad she was here, too.

Because she hadn't just fallen in love with Marcus...she'd fallen for his entire family while she was at it.

Twenty-One

"What the hell is going on with you guys?" Gabe asked as he and Zach walked into the garage, with Chase and Ryan following closely behind.

"Marcus has been doing our pretty young guest."

Marcus grabbed a handful of Smith's shirt. "Watch it, asshole! Talk like that about her again and I'll make sure you can only do horror films from now on."

"Whoa," Gabe said, moving to put himself between his brothers. "Hold on a second."

Marcus was on the verge of letting Smith go when he said, "What the hell are you doing with someone like her? Isn't she a little young and slutty for you?"

A split second later, Marcus was throwing the

first punch. The two of them each got a couple of good slams in before Zach and Gabe worked together to pull them off each other.

"You don't know the first goddamned thing about her."

"And you're telling me that you do? Beyond how wild she is in bed, that is."

"I warned you," Marcus growled.

Smith held up his hands and took a step back. "Look, I'm not trying to piss you off. I'm just trying to talk some sense into you."

"Hold up," Zach said. "Somebody give me the CliffsNotes version of what the hell is going on."

All eyes turned to Marcus and he bit out the words, "Nicola and I met after the engagement party last weekend. I didn't know who she was at first."

Gabe whistled low and long. "Trust old man Sullivan not to recognize a huge pop star. So, when did you figure it out?"

"When Lori invited me to the dance studio on Monday for their rehearsal." He ran his hand over his face. "I thought Nicola was one of the dancers."

"You're an idiot."

Zach was right. He was an idiot. What the hell was he doing in the garage with his brothers when

Nicola was outside in the yard with his mother and sisters? He'd vowed that the next time he saw her he'd fix everything. Instead, all he'd done was make everything worse.

"I've got to go talk to her," he said, but Smith grabbed his arm. Hard.

"Do you have any idea what it will be like to date her?"

"I don't give a crap about her fame."

"That's easy to say now," Smith said, "but what about the fiftieth time you guys try to go out? You'll think you're having a private conversation about grapes or songs or whatever the hell you two talk about and someone will snap a shot that looks like you're fighting. The next thing you know, the headline will be that you couldn't hack it, that you were too different from the start. They'll even throw in some quote from an anonymous friend saying Nicola always knew you were wrong together. You'll want to trust her when she says it isn't true, that she didn't say that to anyone, but you'll start wondering if she actually did."

It was the most Smith had ever said to any of them about the trials of fame, but Marcus didn't give a crap right now about how hard life could be for his hugely famous brother. All he cared about was the woman he'd hurt by being careless with her heart.

"I know you think you're helping, but this is between me and Nicola, not you guys, and not the rest of the goddamned world."

But Smith wouldn't stay out of his face. "Listen to me, I get it, she's probably great in the sack."

Marcus came at him again, but Smith held his ground, despite the fact that Marcus's hands were around his throat.

"But for a guy like you who likes his expensive wine, his peace and quiet out there in the grapevines, all that fame crap will drive you crazy. Fast." Smith frowned. "What I don't get is how the hell no pictures of you two have surfaced yet."

Marcus abruptly dropped his hands from Smith's throat. Hopefully he'd left one hell of a bruise.

"We've been careful," he said between his teeth.

"You two are skulking around in corners? See, it's already messed up." Smith gestured to his brothers. "We all get that Jill turned out to be a cold bitch and Nico is a hot rebound—a damned great rebound, bro—but her life is way too messy for a straight-ahead guy like you."

Ryan nodded. "Hate to say it, but he's right,

Marcus. The press will drive you insane. Even playing baseball, they're in my face way too often."

Surprisingly, Chase nodded. "She seems great—much sweeter, more innocent-looking than I thought she'd be after some of things I've heard about her." He pinned Marcus with his steady gaze. "But it doesn't help that she looks like she's barely graduated high school. Everyone is going to think you're nothing but a dirty old man."

Only Gabe broke in to say, "Hold up a sec. Are you in love with Nico?"

"Her name is Nicola," Marcus shot at his youngest brother.

And Gabe wasn't the one who needed to know that he was in love with Nicola. None of his brothers were the ones who needed to hear those words.

The one person who needed to know exactly how he felt about her was sitting out in his mother's backyard thinking he didn't love her back.

All because he'd been too much of a coward to own up to his feelings.

"Get out of my way," he growled to his five younger brothers.

No one said another word. They just parted ranks to let him through.

"Jesus," Zach swore as Marcus left the rest of them standing in the garage with their mouths open. "I can't believe the six of us were in here talking like a bunch of girls about love and relationships."

"At least I tried to talk sense into him," Smith said as they followed him out in single file. He shrugged. "But since he's clearly a basket case over her, we might as well get a good seat for the show."

"Nicola, I can't keep doing this."

She looked up from the conversation Marcus had interrupted between the women with extreme alarm on her pretty face.

Marcus knew she didn't want him to out their relationship in front of his entire family, but he couldn't keep pretending he didn't know her. He couldn't keep acting like he didn't love her. And he sure as hell couldn't stand to listen to Smith talk about her so dismissively, like she was nothing more than a hot piece of ass.

Marcus wanted everyone to see her the way he did—as a smart, focused, brilliant artist and businesswoman.

So what if he didn't fit into her world and she didn't fit into his?

How could he give her up?

She was shaking her head, her eyes desperate as she silently begged him to stop talking. But he couldn't stop now, knew he had to get it all out before another second passed where she didn't think he loved her.

He moved to her, pulled her up out of her seat.

"No, Marcus."

She looked wildly around at his family, who were now all assembled in their seats at the table, their faces pressed up to the invisible glass. Hell, knowing them, they probably all wished they had bowls of popcorn to munch from. But he didn't care. Nothing mattered now but Nicola.

And the fact that he was going to lose her if he didn't do something quick.

"Don't," she begged him. "Please don't."

Maybe if he'd gotten five minutes of sleep, he would have been able to see how serious she was, that his declaration was the last thing she wanted right now. But in that moment, all Marcus knew was how right it felt to touch her, to be close to her.

"I love you."

She backed away from him and would have

stumbled on a tree root in the grass if he hadn't been gripping her hands in his.

"Please don't do this. Not here. Not now." Her words were barely a whisper, but the backyard was so deadly silent, with not even a bird chirping or a breeze to sound through the trees, that everyone heard her plea loud and clear.

"I should have told you before. I was a fool to let you go, to let you believe I didn't love you."

Nicola was trying to pull her hands from his and clearly wanted nothing more than to escape. But he couldn't let her go, not without making her face what was between them.

Marcus knew there were a million different ways he could have done this better, but right now there was nothing left for him to do but pull her against him and kiss her…in front of his whole family.

Her body was stiff against his, her mouth tight and closed. But then, their connection took over despite the fact that she clearly wanted to fight him, and the passion neither of them had ever been able to hold back from each other came crashing through. They kissed each other like it had been years since their mouths had touched instead of two days.

Abruptly, Nicola shoved at his chest, knocking him away from her. Both of her hands were clamped over her mouth and her eyes were wide with horror.

Nicola turned in the general direction of his family. "I'm sorry I ruined your lunch," she said in a broken voice, then turned and ran toward the house.

Marcus had never put his heart out on the line to anyone like that before, only to have it returned diced into tiny little pieces. His pride told him to let Nicola go, that he hadn't needed her before and he didn't need her now.

At least this time he knew enough to tell his pride to go straight to hell.

A split second later, Marcus Sullivan was chasing down the pop star who had stolen his heart.

"Wait a minute," Lori said in the wake of Marcus's departure. "What just happened here?"

Her twin snorted. "Seriously, are you still the only one who's completely clueless? Can't you pay attention to anyone's life but your own for three seconds?"

Before Lori could turn around and jump down her twin's throat, Zach said, "Looked to me like Marcus just completely blew it." He shook his head, looking less than impressed. "Man, that was messy."

"It might not end up being quite so funny when it happens to you," his mother told him with a pointed arch of one eyebrow.

"No chance," Ryan said. "The rest of us are perfectly content to leave love out of it."

Knowing it would irk his siblings, Chase said, "Not all of us," then planted a big wet kiss on Chloe's lips. She laughed and kissed him back.

"I just don't understand," Lori said. "When did Marcus and Jill break up?"

Speaking as if she were addressing a two-year-old, Sophie told Lori, "I guess he finally dumped her and now he's in love with Nico—"

"He says her name is really Nicola," Smith interrupted, and Sophie shot him a death glare for cutting her off.

"As I was saying, the only problem is that *she* doesn't seem to be in love with *him*."

Gabe's radio went off suddenly, a loud shrill noise that couldn't be missed, along with a quick burst of information about the situation that they all listened in on as he turned the volume up. As a firefighter in San Francisco, everyone in the family had heard calls like this many times over the years as Gabe was frequently called away from family events to a fire in progress in the city.

He was already standing and pushing away from the table before the fire dispatcher stopped speaking. "Sorry to eat and run, especially when we've just gotten to the good stuff."

Mary stood, too, and gave him a hug and kiss. "After all these years, I should be used to watching you leave on a call." She reluctantly let him out of her arms. "Be safe, honey."

"Don't worry," Gabe replied. "Nothing's going to happen to your favorite son."

"He's right," Smith joked. "I'm going to stay here and be just fine."

Everyone laughed but Lori. As soon as Gabe left, she said, "I can't help feeling responsible for everything with Marcus and Nico. I mean, Nicola." Her usually bright smile was completely nonexistent. "I mean, I'm the one who introduced them and then left them to have dinner alone." She bit her lip. "Or whatever else it was they ended up doing."

"Don't feel bad, Naughty. Evidently he met her before you introduced them."

Lori looked at Chase with huge eyes. "No way. He had no idea who she was when I introduced them and she—" Her words fell away. "Oh, my

God, Marcus must have been the guy she was telling me about that day at the studio. And then they both tried to act like they didn't know each other. No wonder he was so weird that afternoon and she kept forgetting the steps that she'd known all morning."

Everyone leaned in closer. "What did she say to you about him?" Sophie asked.

Suddenly, Lori seemed to realize that she was spilling Nicola's secrets. "I shouldn't tell you guys."

Ryan and Smith grinned at each other, both of them knowing how close they were to getting more dirt on their—until now—perfect older brother. "We've already seen the worst of it, Lori," Ryan said, followed by Smith with, "Maybe we can help him if we know more."

Seeing right through her sons, Mary said, "Smith, Ryan, I think we've already seen and heard enough about their private business."

"Mom's right," Lori said. "Besides, all she said was that she met some guy on Friday night and then she fell asleep on his lap before they'd even kissed."

Zach laughed out loud. "Poor sap couldn't even keep her awake."

Mary shushed her kids. "Enough. We're not

going to sit here gossiping about your brother when there are tables that need clearing and plates that need washing."

After everyone hopped to attention, Chloe and Chase hung back with each other for a few moments. "Your mother is so sweet that sometimes I forget she raised eight children on her own and knows perfectly well how to handle all of you," Chloe commented with great affection in her voice.

"She didn't do it alone. Marcus helped her more than any of us." He twined his fingers through hers and pulled her close to him beneath the shade of a large oak tree. Postengagement, the spark between them only burned brighter and brighter every day. "My brother sacrificed a ton for us. He deserves a happy ending."

Chloe tilted her face to look into his eyes. "I couldn't agree with you more. Marcus is amazing. But you know what? I'm betting he'll get his happily ever after. Really, really soon."

He looked at her in clear surprise. "How can you say that after what went down here today?"

"Women's intuition." Her eyes sparkled as she informed him, "Nicola is in love with Marcus."

Before he could ask how she knew, Chloe pressed a soft kiss to his lips, then said, "A woman in love always recognizes the signs of another woman in love. Like Lori said, suddenly it all makes sense—the way they couldn't take their eyes off each other during lunch, the way he jumped all over Gabe for making her laugh and Ryan for calling her gorgeous. I guarantee Nico is head over heels for your brother, whether she wants to be or not."

"Good thing Sullivan men are so persuasive, isn't it?"

Chloe wound her arms around Chase's neck as he pulled her closer.

"Yes," she said as she brought her mouth to his. "It's a very good thing."

Twenty-Two

Marcus came flying out of the house, only to stop short when he saw Nicola standing beside Lori's car. Nicola knew that if she were smart, she'd keep running away from Marcus, away from everything that hurt so damn bad.

But she'd come here today to face him down one last time, hadn't she? Only to panic in front of his entire family.

"Lori picked me up from the hotel and brought me here. I guess I'll need to call a cab."

"Don't leave." Marcus approached her slowly, cautiously. "Please don't leave."

She could still taste the sweetness of his kiss as she licked her lips. "I shouldn't have run like that." She swallowed hard, made herself say, "Not when I know we need to talk."

She saw relief mix with wariness on his face

as he came closer. "I'm sorry if I embarrassed you back there."

"It's okay." And it was, because she understood the desperation he'd felt. How could she not, when she felt it, too?

"No, Nicola. You deserve better. So much better." He reached out a hand to her. "Give me another chance. Please."

She wanted so badly to take his hand, to give him that chance.

But she couldn't. Not when she knew it would only end up hurting them both.

"Marcus." Her throat caught on his name. "Is there somewhere we can go that's more private than this?"

He nodded, his jaw tight as he dropped the hand she hadn't taken. He led them down the sidewalk to a short path that cut between houses. A small children's playground that looked like it hadn't been used in a decade sat forlornly beneath the old oak trees.

"We used to come here and play when we were kids."

Her heart ached for the child Marcus had once been…and for how short his childhood had been. Fourteen years old was far too young to have to shoulder the responsibilities he had taken on.

"Your family is amazing." She sat on a cracked bench. "I'm so glad I got to meet them all. There was so much love in your mother's backyard."

He didn't move to sit beside her, but went to his knees in the dirt before her. She let him take her hands, utterly unable to push him away one more time. Not with her hands, anyway.

"Did you mean what you said on the beach? Were you really falling in love with me?"

She met his eyes, read his pain in them, his surprising fear that she might not actually love him. She shouldn't admit that she still did.

But she had to.

"Yes," she said softly. "I love you."

"Thank God."

"No," she said quickly, "I've done a lot of thinking since last night." She swallowed hard, shook her head, tried to fight back the tears that were right there, waiting to fall. "I can guess why Smith wanted to talk to you in the garage. He was warning you about me, about what it would be like to date me, for real, out in the open, wasn't he?"

The look on his face gave her the answer even though he said, "What you and I are doing is none of Smith's business."

"No, but I'll bet everything he said to you about the circus of lives like ours is true."

"I've always liked the circus."

She wanted to throw her arms around him, wanted to kiss him for saying he would give up everything for her. But she knew she'd never forgive herself for being so selfish. And, ultimately, he'd never forgive her, either.

He'd already given up so much for his family. She couldn't let him give up even more for her.

"I cheated last night," she confessed. "I looked you up online. I read all about Sullivan Winery. I saw how magnificently you've done with it and what an important role you play in your community. You deserve to have a wife who can support you in all that you do, one who can be an equal partner in it all. Not someone who's on a different plane every week to another state, another country, another hemisphere. It didn't take me more than five minutes with your family to see that you're not like Smith or Lori or even Ryan. You're not about the party. You don't need everyone to want to take your picture. You don't need to use your charm and charisma to try to impress people. Who you are at your core is what's impressive, Marcus, and you don't need a big stage or a crowd to know your own worth."

He opened his mouth to interrupt and she put her hand over his lips before he could say something that would break her resolve.

"See, the thing is, I know my life is crazy and a circus and even though it sometimes drives me nuts that I can't go out like a normal person to get a coffee or go see a movie, I still love it. I don't just want to sing for a little while. I want to be around twenty years from now, still writing and playing songs that millions of people will want to listen to."

"You will."

"Thank you for believing in me so much," she told him. "Despite the words we threw at each other yesterday on the beach, you've never treated me like a dumb pop star. You've respected me and now I need to respect you just as much. It's just another reason why I can't do this to you, why I can't ask you to be a part of my world."

"Shouldn't that be my decision, kitten?" he asked, taking her hands in his.

The endearment nearly broke her, enough that she admitted, "Do you know the craziest thing about all of this? I wanted to be the one to heal all of your heartache. But instead—" She had to stop, try to take the breath that was lodged in her throat. "Instead, I was the one who made it all so much worse. I'm so sorry for that, Marcus. So much sorrier than you'll ever know."

She made herself slip her hands from his and stand up. "We can't see each other anymore. If you could take me back to my hotel now, I'd appreciate it."

Somehow, someway, she thought as she turned her back on him to walk away, she was going to keep from sobbing until she was alone.

And then, long after he was gone, she would have to find a way to stop.

Marcus moved behind her and put his hand on the small of her back. Just as he had that first night.

"Everything you said to me out on the beach about choosing the wrong woman to date before meeting you because it was easier than really loving and risking everything was right."

Surprised, she turned to look him in the eye as he continued. "I always thought it was my family who needed me. But I've finally realized that I needed them just as much. I needed them to hold on to when everything was so scary and difficult and uncertain, when the man I loved most in the world was suddenly gone one day. But when I met you, I realized I'd finally found someone I was willing to let go of them for."

"No, Marcus," she said, shaking her head. "You shouldn't ever have to let go of your family. You have enough love in your heart for all of them and the family of your own you'll probably have soon." She made herself choke out the words. "I know you're going to find someone perfect for you. Perfect for your life."

"I already have."

The tears she'd vowed not to let loose began to fall. "Please, don't make this any harder than it already is. Not when you and I both know no matter how much we want this to work, that it never will." She looked up at him through her tears. "I'll never regret being with you. Not when they were the most beautiful moments of my life." She took a deep breath that shook through her. "I changed my plane to leave tonight instead of tomorrow morning. I should go back to the hotel to pack up my things."

She turned to walk back to his mother's house when his voice stopped her in her tracks one more time.

"We both know you don't want this. We both know one kiss, one touch, is all it would take for me to change your mind."

Gone was the man who'd been pleading with her to listen, to see things from his side. In his place was the dominant lover who had thrilled her so much, who made her shiver with desire and shared the most incredible pleasures with her.

"You're right, Marcus," she agreed, making herself turn to face him again. "I'm powerless against your kisses. I can't resist the way you touch me." She looked into his eyes and admitted everything, purposefully gave him a fully loaded arsenal of ammo to use against her. "I can't fight the hunger in your eyes when you look at me or my reaction to it. But is that what you want? For me to be nothing but a warm, willing body that can't resist coming for you?"

Dominance turned to anger in a heartbeat, and then he was moving fast, his hands on her shoulders, his mouth punishing hers as he took everything he wanted, everything she wished she could give him, but couldn't.

As he'd just pointed out, Nicola knew it was pointless to try to fight his kiss. Even in front of his family she'd been lost to her need for him. Even when he was furious with her for trying to leave when he wanted her to stay, even when she should be furious right back at him for finally treating her like the sex object he said she didn't need to be anymore, all she could feel was his heart beating against hers...along with her love for him beating just as strong, even as he used her weakness for him against her.

But just when she thought he was going to rip off her clothes and take her right there, up against the old metal slide, he pushed her away and held her out at arm's length.

"This isn't over between us. Not even close."

She let herself take one last long look at him. "It has to be over."

And this time when she made a move to walk away, he let her go.

Only, even after he took her back to her hotel, even hours later when she was settled beneath a blanket in first class and the plane was flying away from San Francisco, she knew better.

Marcus Sullivan was a man who decided exactly what he wanted and then went out and took it. And for some crazy reason, he seemed to want her.

As she fell into an uneasy sleep on the plane, even as she told herself she didn't want him to fight for her, her dreams of Marcus—full of his kisses and caresses, his hungry eyes and his sweet words of love—wouldn't let her hide from the truth.

Twenty-Three

It had been fifteen days, six hours and twenty-three minutes since she'd last seen—or heard—from Marcus.

She'd been wrong. He didn't want her.

Nicola knew she should be glad about it, happy that she wasn't going to have to keep resisting him. But she was a long, long way from happy... about as far as she could be, actually.

Her manager walked into her office, waving a fax. "*Billboard* just let me know that 'One Moment' debuted at number one on the pop charts! And—wait for it, you're going to really freak out when you hear this—your entire tour just sold out in two hours! We're going to need to add dates. A ton of dates. You won't be seeing your house for a good year and a half if we're lucky!"

This was everything Nicola had ever wanted.

The huge smash hit. The big, international sold-out tour. But even as she and Jane hugged and high-fived and Jane started talking a mile a minute about how brilliant Nicola had been to shoot another last-minute video for "One Moment"—just her and her piano on an otherwise empty stage—and insist that the record label release the acoustic version, too, Nicola knew that she would have been so much happier if she could have shared this success with Marcus.

She could almost picture him telling her how proud he was, saying he'd known she could do this.

And that he loved her.

Without warning, one fat tear spilled down her cheek. Fortunately, her manager thought it was happy crying and after planting a kiss on both of Nicola's cheeks, she grabbed the phone that was ringing off the hook and spun out of the room to go wheel and deal them into a heck of a lot more money.

Nicola walked over to the window and pressed her hand against the glass, staring out at the busy Los Angeles streets below. Three weeks ago she'd been staring out at the streets of San Francisco.

She'd been in so many tall buildings. Had visited so many busy cities. The world was her oyster now more than ever. It wasn't that it didn't mean a damn thing without love—of course her success meant something. And yet, love made everything so much richer, so much sweeter. Yes, sex with Marcus had been mind-blowing, but just knowing his arms were waiting to hold her, that she could lay her cheek against the steady beat of his heart…well, that was the kind of happiness that lasted forever.

Unfortunately, none of that changed the fact that all the reasons she had to leave him were still true.

Still, as Nicola stood in the window, she silently cursed herself for not letting things with Marcus at least linger longer. Why couldn't she have let herself be happy with him for more than a handful of days?

Nicola turned away from the window with a sigh, knowing exactly why she'd forced herself to get on that plane and leave him for good.

No matter how hard they might have tried to hide their relationship from everyone around them, eventually they would have been caught. The circus would have pulled Marcus in and turned his perfectly ordered life inside out. She couldn't have lived with herself for hurting someone she loved like that, couldn't have stood hearing people question his judgment for getting involved with her.

And yet, a totally contrary part of her wished they hadn't been quite so good at hiding their relationship from the world, because at least if there had been pictures of the two of them on the internet, maybe they would have had to deal with each other in some small way…rather than being able to cut each other completely away.

She looked down at her watch and realized she'd now officially made it through fifteen days, six hours and thirty-four minutes without him. At some point, the day would come that she wouldn't be counting minutes and hours anymore.

And at some point, she'd stop hoping that she'd hear her name on his lips again, an out-of-the-blue "Nicola" that would have her looking up at his shockingly beautiful face, her heart racing with anticipation as she waited for him to issue another one of his sensual commands.

Damn it, setting everything up had taken much longer than he'd anticipated. Too long.

Marcus had never been big on watching TV or reading magazines, but for the past two weeks he'd been glued to them. Until he could be with Nicola again, he needed constant reassurance that the woman he loved was okay. He'd been ecstatic when her song had gone straight to number one and her tour had sold out immediately. She deserved all of that and more. So much more.

Lori had turned up on his doorstep a couple of nights ago with a plan to get them back together. She'd been beyond pleased when he informed her that he was already on it, and now while she drove him to the airport, they were listening to Nicola being interviewed on the radio.

"I'll be honest with you, Nico," the radio personality said, "when I first heard 'One Moment' it sounded just like any other great pop song that makes me want to dance. But then I saw your acoustic video and finally realized what heart there is behind the song. Tell us about that."

"I've always loved what I do," she replied, her voice washing through Marcus's veins like the first perfect cool glass of wine on a hot, dry day, "but I recently realized that I've only let people see one side of me."

"What made you decide to show us that other side of yourself, the heart-wrenching singer/songwriter that you've been hiding all this time?"

"A friend wasn't afraid to get in my face about it." She laughed and he could practically see her smile, her flashing eyes, even across the radio waves. "I'm afraid I didn't take the advice very well at first, but eventually I came around. And that's why I went to record the song again that way. I love the full production on my songs, I love dancing with my crew, but a stripped-down version of one of my songs was something I've been wanting to do for a very long time."

"So, Nico, what's next on your plate to conquer now that you've got the number-one single in the country and a sold-out tour?"

Marcus could feel Lori's eyes on him as they waited for Nicola's response.

"Love, I hope."

The interview over, Marcus turned off the radio just as Lori exclaimed, "God, Marcus, she's amazing, isn't she?"

"She is."

"How could you *not* have fallen in love with her?"

He shook his head, knowing his sister was speaking the complete and utter truth. "I never had a chance."

Lori covered his hand on the gearshift with her own. "I really hope your plan works out, big brother."

So did he.

Boise, Idaho

At the end of the first show on her tour in Boise, Nicola did her final encore, a version of "One Moment" that began with just her in the middle of stage, playing guitar and singing the acoustic version before kicking into overdrive with a flash of lights and smoke that had every band member coming back onstage…and her body being covered almost head to toe in shimmering sparkles of light.

Her crew had worked with her to retool her show practically every waking minute until opening night to incorporate her dance pop with her new acoustic segments. It had been utterly exhausting. And wonderfully thrilling.

Nicola had welcomed the work, had driven herself harder than anyone else, partly because it made her too tired to think about Marcus more than every other minute. If the reaction the crowd had given her all night was any indication, it had paid off. Big-time.

She was determined to enjoy herself at the postshow celebration tonight with everyone. Even though the most important person hadn't been out there in the audience, she'd still felt as if he were with her, cheering her on, loving her in a way no one else ever had.

But first, she needed to head over to the special meet-and-greet that took place backstage after every show so that she could give something to literacy foundations in each county she played in. Despite the fact that she was exhausted by the time the lights went down onstage and up for the audience, the cause was important enough to her to push through her tiredness for another hour each night.

She walked into the curtained-off area, where Katie, her tour manager, immediately led her over to the first group. Her skin prickled and heated up as she moved through the area, but even as she took a quick glance around the room to look for the only person on earth who had ever made her feel like that, she knew that there was no way Marcus could be in Idaho. She was simply keyed up from the show and her imagination was running away with her very tired mind.

From the corner of her eye, she could see Jimmy, her bodyguard, frowning and talking into his headset in a tense voice. Not sure what was happening, but trusting Jimmy to take care of it, she threw herself into chatting with her fans, smiling into their cameras, signing their CDs and iPod devices and concert T-shirts, never letting herself forget for one second that she was beyond lucky to be in her position.

She had just hugged a young girl goodbye when Katie came up to her with a frown. "Jimmy needs to talk to you."

That prickling feeling came back as her body-guard approached. "The man from San Francisco is back, isn't he?"

"Yes. The cops are on their way to come pick him up."

The cops? She almost laughed out loud at how absurd the whole thing had become. "He isn't a stalker," she said to Jimmy.

Her bodyguard looked seriously confused. "He isn't?"

"No, he isn't." She took a deep breath. "Where is he? Can you bring him in here?"

Jimmy frowned. "If he's some guy who's been forcing you to—"

She put her hand on his arm. "Please, I need to see him."

Not looking at all happy about it, Jimmy nod-ded. "I'll go get him."

Thirty seconds later, when Marcus walked in, closely followed by Jimmy, Nicola had the crazy thought that she'd been fantasizing about him so much, she'd conjured him out of thin air.

She needed to try to think straight, needed to give herself time to take a few deep breaths and forcefully slow her heartbeat down. She tried to prepare herself for the urge to leap into his arms, but nothing could have prepared her for the look in his eyes.

Pure love.

And something else that looked like...patience.

She knew he still wanted her—that much was blatantly clear, judging by the sparks that were flying around in the two feet of open air between them—but at the same time she felt as if he was silently saying, *I will wait for you to come around. However long it takes.*

She hadn't forgotten how handsome he was, but seeing him again after so many weeks apart stunned her with the force of his incredible male beauty all over again.

Instead of playing it cool, her hands moved over her heart and she completely forgot that Katie and Jimmy stood close by to make sure she was okay as she all but gasped out the words, "What are you doing here, Marcus?"

He didn't answer for several long moments as his eyes roved over her face. She was glad for the chance to do the same thing, to drink in the lines the sun had made around his eyes and mouth, to note that while he was still the most beautiful man she'd ever set eyes on, he looked as if he'd lost some weight since she'd last seen him.

Finally, he said, "There's a label designer in town that I've been thinking about using. This was a good chance for me to meet with them."

None of this felt real and she half wondered if she was so tired she was dreaming it.

"It was a great show, Nicola. Really incredible. I can't wait for the next one."

The next one?

And then, before she could get her brain or limbs to start working again, he was gone. All three of them watched him turn and leave.

A beat later, Katie turned to her and said, "You look really pale. Here, sit down."

Nicola was no fading flower and had never fainted in her life.

But tonight, she knew she'd better take the seat Katie was pushing against the backs of her knees. Either that or she was going to go running out of the venue, calling Marcus's name like a desperate woman.

She knew by heart the reasons a relationship with him would never work. Good reasons. So instead of running after him on shaky limbs, she forced herself to take a deep breath—and then another dozen when that didn't work—and tick through those reasons again.

Lord knew, if he was coming back to do this another night, she'd need every one of her walls up and in place to stay strong.

Still, she couldn't get it all to add up. Her lover had flown all the way up to Idaho to see her show and he hadn't just grabbed her in front of everyone and kissed her like he had at his mother's house?

Why hadn't he kissed her?

Salt Lake City, Utah

Nicola walked offstage after her concert in Salt Lake City the next night and knew she'd killed it. She'd taken each song and yanked every ounce of passion and guts and fun and joy from it. And it had all been for Marcus. She'd sung every love song for him, had moved her body across the stage for his eyes only.

Just like the previous night, as she greeted her fans she could feel him backstage even without seeing where he was. It took every ounce of concentration to give her all to her fans who had donated so generously to literacy when she knew she'd soon be talking to Marcus again, but she refused to give anything less than her best to everyone in the room.

And then, there he was again and Jimmy and Katie were looking between the two of them.

"Should I call Security, Nico?"

"No, Jimmy. I'm fine."

Better than fine, with Marcus standing in front of her again.

Katie asked, "Should we leave you alone for a few minutes?"

Oh, God, no. Alone was a bad idea.

Scratch that. It was a *terrible* idea.

Of course, all Nicola could do was nod. And say, "Please."

Marcus didn't wait for her to ask about how he'd spent his day in Salt Lake City. He simply said, "There's a great bottling factory near here. I think I'm going to use them for our next champagne release."

She'd given all of this some thought the night before—all day today, too—and made herself say, "You can't keep doing this."

He reached out to brush his hand across her forehead, where her hair was falling over one eye. "I'm having a good time doing this."

Her body instantly recognized her sweetly dominant lover as his hand lingered on her skin in a possessive way that had it heating up, top to bottom and everywhere in between. She couldn't resist turning her face into his palm for a split second, but then, knowing there were any number of eyes on her—and that each of them was wondering just what in hell was going on between her and the good-looking stranger in the expensive suit—she made herself draw back when all she really wanted to do was curl up against him as she once had.

Lowering her voice to make sure no one could possibly hear, she said, "Are you planning on following me around the globe?"

His grin would have stolen her heart if there had been any part of it he didn't already have.

"You're playing some of my favorite cities."

It was pure torture to imagine how glorious it would be to slip under the covers with Marcus late at night after her shows, in a tour bus or plane or hotel room.

"I won't forgive myself if your winery goes to hell without you there."

He raised an eyebrow. "I don't think my management team would take too kindly to hearing what you think of them."

"That's not what I mean!" she told him, too frustrated with the game he was playing—and how much she wanted him to keep playing it, despite knowing better—to keep her voice down.

"You were beautiful up there tonight, and so damn good you blew me away all over again."

The only way she could keep herself from blurting out how much she loved him, how much she missed him, was to say, "It's not just the fame, Marcus. It's not just how impossible our schedules are. I'm not good for you. If your community, your colleagues, knew about me..."

"I didn't cheat," he said, and just when she realized he meant he hadn't looked her up on the internet, he added, "But your fans talk. And they love you. They're on your side. Just like I am. And I love you, too. We were all young and stupid once. We've all done things we aren't proud of. We've all trusted people we shouldn't have trusted. Yes, people are probably going to believe something they read or saw. Lots of people, even. But I can guarantee you that anyone who actually meets you and gets to know you will fall as much in love with you as I have."

She could almost taste his kiss, was actually dying for it, when he said, "I promised you I wasn't going anywhere and I'm not. But this is your decision just as much as it's mine." He took her hand in his and brought it to his lips to press a kiss to her knuckles. "Good night, Nicola."

Denver, Colorado

"Don't tell me," she said when she and Marcus were the only two people left in the meet-and-greet the next night. "There's a winery in Colorado that you're thinking of acquiring."

"Actually, an old college friend lives nearby. I had a great day visiting with him and his family."

He grinned at her and she couldn't help but grin back. All day she'd been looking forward to seeing him.

And all day, she'd been having a harder and harder time convincing herself that being without him was the right thing. Marcus, she had started to realize, didn't seem to care much for what people thought of him. If he did, he wouldn't be buying the VIP charity meet-and-greet package every single night.

After only three nights of hanging out with her crew while she chatted with her fans, it was already like he was one of them, like he was supposed to be on tour with them. She was starting to suspect that was part of his plan…and she was more than a little amazed at the fact that he'd managed to pull this kind of schedule off in the first place.

Still, how long could he continue with it?

"Please tell me you're headed back to Napa, Marcus. Back to your real life."

"Actually, I'm on the board of a local charity event that's taking place tomorrow night, so yes, I'll need to head back for the next couple of nights."

Her stomach sank down to her kneecaps. "Good. I know how much it will mean to everyone to have you there."

She was surprised to feel his fingers beneath her chin, tilting her face back up to his. "Come with me, Nicola. I've got a plane chartered that leaves tonight. We could make it there by morning, spend the day at my winery, attend the event, and I'll easily have you back at your next venue in time for interviews and sound check."

"Marcus, I—"

His mouth was over hers before she could even figure out what she was going to say. His kiss was soft and sweet, but she felt as if her entire world had been upended by it.

"That's not fair," she protested in a breathless voice.

"I'm not playing fair anymore. I love you too much to stick to the rules."

And then his hands were in her hair and her arms were around his neck and she was kissing him like she'd been dreaming of kissing him for weeks. If it hadn't been for the many pairs of eyes burning a hole through them, she would have never stopped kissing him.

Forcing herself to pull away from his lips, she said, "How about I introduce you to my crew?" against his mouth.

"I think they've already got a pretty good idea who I am."

She was amazed to find herself laughing with him as they broke apart.

She'd been so careful to make sure she didn't give anyone—even the road crew she'd grown to trust over the years—any potential ammo to use against her that she'd basically been living like a nun for the past six months.

Now, she had to wonder if the reason she'd cared so much what everyone thought was because it was easier to use the press as an excuse, rather than risk getting hurt again.

But maybe, she was just starting to think, some things were worth the risk.

"I'm going to grab my things off the bus," she

suddenly told Katie, who was standing a few feet away. "Turns out I've got a plane to Napa Valley waiting."

Her tour manager looked between Nicola and Marcus, then nodded her approval. "Just as long as you have her back for her interview at noon in Dallas in two days."

Grinning, Nicola said, "You guys can work out the schedule while I go get my stuff." She was halfway out the door when she looked over her shoulder to see Katie and Marcus with their heads together going over the calendars on their phones.

But as she walked down the hall toward her tour bus, she knew that kissing Marcus in front of her crew had been the easy part.

He'd told her that her circus life didn't scare him.

Now he was actually showing her that he meant it.

Unfortunately, the bigger question remained: What would his world think of her? Would they welcome her with open arms the way she was sure her crew was already welcoming Marcus?

Or would her youth and bad reputation hurt Marcus in just the way she feared?

There were so many things that Nicola knew needed to be said between them as she boarded the private jet, but when Marcus wrapped his arms around her and strapped his seat belt over them both, she gave in to the warmth of his arms, curling into him the way she always had, with his heart beating against her ear, the feeling of being perfectly safe easing her into a deeper sleep than she'd had in weeks.

Finally, as Nicola fell asleep against his chest, Marcus let the breath he'd been holding go.

Nicola was back where she belonged. In his arms.

Now all he needed to do was convince her to stay.

This time, by any means necessary…

Twenty-Four

"My God, this is beautiful."

The sun was rising over the Sullivan Winery and the birds were just coming awake. Nicola laughed softly as a blue jay peeked its head up out of its nest to greet them. As they stood on his porch and looked out over the rolling grapevines, Marcus silently thanked his property for putting on its finest show for Nicola.

They'd both slept on the plane and even though it hadn't been a full night's rest, he felt more refreshed and alert than he had since Nicola had left San Francisco almost three weeks ago.

"This winery is where you came to heal, isn't it?"

No one had ever laid it out so clearly to him… or had hit it so directly on the head.

Pulling her closer, he told her, "The first time I

ever saw this land was on a high school field trip. It was crazy, but I swore I saw a man who looked like my father working the vines. As soon as I got my driver's license, I drove up here to look for him again."

"You weren't alone, were you?"

"Nope." He smiled at the woman he loved. "Most of my brothers and sisters crammed into the car with me. I didn't tell them about what I thought I'd seen, but I knew right then that one day this land would be mine. And that I'd make him proud."

He watched her swallow, saw her eyes glitter at his story. Her voice was raw, husky, as she asked, "How can you even think of leaving this for days and weeks on end?"

He knew what she was asking, that she didn't understand why he would want to be with her on the road.

"It's been twenty-two years since my father died and, until you, I never told anyone how hard it was on me to take his place in the family. I never wanted to admit it to myself. And no one dared push me up against the wall on it. I'm sure others saw it. They had to. But I managed to keep them all away."

She had turned to him and he didn't know if

she realized it, but she'd taken his hands and was holding them both over her heart.

"But not you, Nicola. You were shoving your way in from that first moment in the club, and no matter how hard I tried to push you away, you never let me keep you out."

"I'm annoying like that," she said in a soft voice. "Always pushing in where I don't belong."

"I love that you push, that you decide what you want and don't let anyone get in your way. No wonder your career is shooting through the stratosphere and they want you to come play shows in Timbuktu."

He was glad to see her smile at that, to see the dark shadow begin to slide from her pretty eyes.

"I didn't completely lose my youth, but there were big chunks of it that just disappeared." He shook his head, trying to put words to his feelings even as he finally registered what they were. "I don't regret spending so much time with my brothers and sisters to help my mother. They were worth it."

"So are you, Marcus."

He pressed a soft kiss to her lips and then said, "Do you know what my mother said to me that Sunday at lunch?"

"'What the hell are you thinking, getting involved with a girl like her?'" she guessed, but her mouth was quirking up on one side and he knew she was teasing.

"She told me she'd been waiting for me to find someone I could love more than I loved them."

"I told you before, in that old playground behind your mother's house, that I don't want to get in the way of your relationship with your family."

"Not in the way. You've shown me it's time to finally cut the strings, to let them live their lives. And that it's finally time for me to live mine. All this time, it was easier for me to focus on my brothers and sisters and helping my mother and running this winery than it was for me to focus on my own heart." He tugged her even closer. "You once told me people believe what's easiest to believe. Both you and I believed so strongly that we couldn't make this relationship work, that we were too different…didn't we?"

She nodded. "It's safer that way."

"I know it is, but I'm finally ready to believe in the thing that's hardest to believe instead." He smiled down at her. "I knew words would never convince you that we could make this work, that I'd need to show you, to prove it to you by pushing just as hard as you always pushed me."

"My crew thought you were crazy. Jimmy was

going to call the cops that first night, you know. The second time, too."

He grinned. "I know. But you're worth the risk, sweetheart. Any risk. Every risk. I'm going to enjoy joining you for as many of your tour dates as I possibly can, and I have a pretty good feeling that you're going to enjoy the peace and quiet of being here with me as often as you possibly can. I have no doubt that this land, the beauty here, will feed your soul the same way it's always fed mine."

"How do you always see the things in me that no one else ever does?"

"I met Nicola long before I ever met Nico," he reminded her. "Forget the stupid things I said to you on the beach. You've never hidden yourself from me."

"I don't know how. Even when I tried, I couldn't hide what you were making me feel." She paused. "Especially when you were telling me what you wanted me to do in the bedroom."

Ah, it was just the lead-in he'd been hoping for. "Three weeks ago, I played by the book. And you left." He pinned her with an unabashedly hungry gaze. "Today I'm not going to play fair. As far as I'm concerned, once you got on that plane with me, all rules were off."

Her pupils had dilated and her breathing was

already speeding up, both beautiful signs that she was becoming aroused…and that she wanted this as much as he did.

Knowing she'd greatly enjoy the anticipation, he told her, "I'm planning to use all the weapons in my arsenal to convince you that we belong together. I'm not afraid to play dirty this time, kitten."

She licked her lips. "I like dirty."

He grinned at her and it was a smile full of wicked promise. "I know you do. My sweet, sexy, smart, dirty girl." He swept her up in his arms and kicked open the front door to carry her into his bedroom. "I want you in my bed."

"I want to be there, too." She cupped his face in her hands and pulled his mouth down to hers.

Needing to concentrate on kissing her, not climbing the stairs, he stopped halfway up, sitting down on the stairs so that she was straddling him.

There was no way they were going to actually make it all the way upstairs to his bedroom.

Not this time, anyway.

"Lift your arms for me."

Heat flared in her eyes at the sensual command he'd given her that first night, and then again and again. She slowly brought her hands up and let him slide her long-sleeved T-shirt up her torso and over her head.

Her bra was wicked black-and-red lace with a sweet white bow in the middle.

"Until I met you, I always thought I had to be one or the other, the sexy pop princess or the sweet girl with the guitar. I want to be both, Marcus."

"I first started falling for the sex goddess in the leather dress with the impossibly high heels…and I knew I was a total goner when you fell asleep on my lap like a contented little kitten." He moved his hands to the small of her back, then around to cup her ass, and slid her closer. "I've always loved both sides of you." Without skipping a beat, he said, "I want you to stand up and take the rest of your clothes off."

Her eyes widened, but she quickly scooted off his lap and moved a step down to slip off her jeans and then her bra and panties.

He put his hands on her stomach, curving them up to cup her breasts. "Gorgeous."

She took a shaky breath that did fantastic things to her breasts in his hands.

"I think it's time for that spanking I've been promising you," he said as he brushed the pads of his thumbs over the beautifully aroused tips of her breasts. "A little punishment for taking so long to come around and see that we can make things work."

Her eyes glittered with arousal even as she made a soft protest. "What if I don't want to be spanked? What if I don't like it?"

Instead of answering her questions, he moved his hands from her chest and said, "Turn around, and hold on to the stair rail."

He could see her heartbeat pulsing through the soft skin on her neck as she paused and thought it over. Finally, she did as he bid.

Sweet Lord, her ass was a miracle, gorgeously heart-shaped as she flared it slightly for him before taunting him with a naughty look over her shoulder.

Moving his hand over her stomach, he held her torso in place as he ran his other hand over the swell of her hips.

"So pretty. So sweet." He pressed a kiss to the small of her back. "And all mine."

His hand came down a moment later, a swat on her behind that left a faint pink mark on her tanned flesh.

She didn't cry out, but he felt her nipples bead against his palm where he'd moved his left hand higher to cup her breasts again.

A moment later, he was marking her other cheek with the flat of his palm, and this time he couldn't miss her moan of pleasure, moans that only increased in volume as he made contact two more times.

But as erotic as the spanking—and her reaction to it—was, he'd have to continue their sexy game another time. Marcus didn't know how he'd managed to skip going down on her in their previous lovemaking sessions, but he needed to rectify that right this second.

"Let go of the rail, sit back against the steps and open your legs for me."

She was shaking with need as she did so, and after she was spread before him, he gladly gave in to the urge to run his lips across her breasts, to continue down her taut stomach, to dip his tongue into her belly button.

The first swipe of his tongue over her slippery, aroused flesh had her bucking into his mouth while her hands held on to his hair. He thrust two fingers into her and slick heat surrounded them, throbbing and pulsing around him.

He blew softly against her, making her hips move on his fingers as she tried desperately to find completion.

"I love you."

He backed up his words with the slow move of his fingers out, then back into her. He was half-way to insane at the thought of actually taking her soon.

Marcus pushed his fingers back inside at the same moment that he lowered his mouth between her thighs and covered her sex with his lips. He curled his fingers inside of her until she was gasping, arching, begging, crying out for more.

He loved the way she held on to him as she came apart against his tongue and fingers.

"Oh, my God, your tongue." She inhaled a shaky breath and looked at him with that wonder, with the trust, he knew he'd never grow tired of seeing. "And what was that spot you found with your fingers?"

He grinned at her reaction. "I'll show you again soon."

She licked her lips and said, "Yes, please," and a few seconds later he was carrying her the rest of the way up the stairs to lay her down in the center of his big bed. She moved to reach for him, but he shook his head.

"No. Just let me look at you. I can't believe I have the prettiest girl in the world in my bed."

She blushed, but this time she didn't try to hide any part of herself from him. Not her beautiful body...or the beauty that was inside all that luscious, creamy skin and mind-blowing curves.

He stripped off his clothes and put on a condom before moving over her. And then her arms were around his shoulders and her legs were wrapped tightly to his hips and he knew the rest of the naughty things he wanted to do to her would have to wait.

Because right now all he wanted to do was make love to the woman he'd waited a lifetime to find.

"Love me, Marcus," she whispered as their bodies came together.

And, oh, how he loved her.

Not just with his entire body, not only with every beat of his heart...but from the very depths of his soul.

The midday sun was coming in through Marcus's bedroom window as they sat naked on top of his covers eating the picnic lunch he'd pulled together from the sparse contents of his fridge.

Nicola had never felt so exhausted—or so happy—and with her stomach full of food and her body full of pleasure, she yawned and lay down in one of her favorite positions, her head on his lap and one of her hands in his. She never wanted to stop lying there looking up at his beautiful face.

But her long tour hours—and the three rounds of incredibly acrobatic sex they'd just had—had her yawning.

He smiled down at her. "You sure tire out quick for a young thing."

"Funny," she said on another huge yawn, "I was just about to say you have surprising stamina for an old man." She hummed a few bars of the Joni Mitchell hit "My Old Man," ending at the line about "keeping away my lonesome blues."

She loved hearing him laugh and hum along in a really off-tune voice.

Looking up into his eyes, she knew it was time to admit everything to him.

"I didn't push you away just because I was trying to save you from my circus life." When his hand didn't still on her hair and his leg muscles didn't tense up under her, she knew it was safe to say, "That was a big part of it, but I was also scared of trusting. Scared of falling. So hugely scared that I'd be hurt again. Only this time I knew it would be so much worse, because I loved you. That's why I ran that day after lunch at your mother's house, because I thought it would hurt less that way. But running only made everything hurt more."

"I missed you just as much," he told her. "Although, I can't help thinking that if you hadn't run, I wouldn't have gotten the chance to chase after you."

Just that quickly—as he made her burn up at the wicked thought of being chased through the vines and then caught in the most delicious way—Marcus erased any chance of recriminations, of making her feel guilty or selfish for what she'd done.

And as he shifted them so that his naked body was pressed against hers and his mouth was moving over hers, she forgot all about fear and gave in to the most natural emotion in the world.

Pure, sweet love.

Sitting in the back of a limo with Marcus that night as they drove through the wine country, Nicola wore a fantastic dress that managed to be classic and yet fun and flirty at the same time. The dark green velvet on the bodice hugged her breasts, while the sparkles sewn into the silk of the skirt drew attention even as the fabric molded to her hips and legs as she moved.

All day she'd been in heaven being with the

man she loved, but as the driver pulled up in front of the Napa Valley mansion where the charity event was being held, last-second panic gripped her.

"This is the big moment." She gripped his large hands with hers and squeezed them tightly. "Are you sure you're ready for this? For not being my secret boyfriend anymore?"

Instead of answering her with words, he put her hands over his heart, then leaned in to kiss her.

"As long as you're by my side, I'm ready for absolutely anything."

And as the limo door was opened for them and flashbulbs started going off, his kiss erased what remained of her worries…leaving sweet safety and boundless pleasure in its place.

Epilogue

Over the next two months, the weather cooled and the leaves turned color, falling from the trees throughout Northern California. Marcus racked up the miles on buses and planes as Nicola played dozens of dates on the first leg of her U.S. concert tour and he commuted back and forth between Napa Valley and whatever part of the country the woman he loved was in. For the first time since he'd purchased the winery ten years earlier, he left the bulk of the details of the crush to his staff. Ellen received an enormous promotion along with the matching salary to go along with her new duties.

It was early December when Nicola and Marcus walked into the San Francisco fire station. The entire fire crew was there, along with their families, to meet her.

Gabe shook his brother's hand, then hugged Nicola extra long and hard, knowing it would bug the crap out of his possessive older brother. Gabe didn't bother to hold back his grin as he said, "Thanks so much for agreeing to play this concert, Nicola."

"It's my pleasure," she said before turning to his brother. Going up on her toes, she pressed a kiss on Marcus's cheek. "You're scaring the kids with that scowl."

Marcus put his hand on her chin and turned her face to his for a real kiss that said *Mine* loud and clear to any man in the room who might have been confused as to which Sullivan brother she was with.

Gabe made sure his grin stayed in place, even though something inside his chest was pinching tight. Over the past months, he'd gotten used to seeing Chase, and now Marcus, as part of a couple. Their mother was beside herself with joy over her sons' relationships.

Jackie, the girl Gabe had been casually dating off and on for the past few months, was practically shaking with excitement at the thought of finally meeting Nicola. She'd been angling to be invited to Sunday lunch at his mother's house to meet not just Nicola, but Smith, too. The thing was, Gabe just couldn't see her around his family. She was too young, too eager. Sure, Nicola was young, too, but there was a reason she and Marcus fit so well together. Nicola was far more mature than other twenty-five-year-old girls.

Especially Jackie, Gabe thought as she started toward them, stars in her eyes.

Gabe knew he'd strung her along for too long. Quickly deciding that he'd break it off with her tonight, he wasn't looking forward to her tears. She was a crier, which was partly why he hadn't had the balls to make a clean break over these past weeks.

"How the hell did you end up with her again?" Gabe asked Marcus a couple of hours later as they stood to the side and watched Nicola charm the pants off the tightly packed crowd who had paid big bucks to see her do a short acoustic set in the fire station's parking lot. The money they'd bring in today with her help would go a long way to getting the new equipment that budget cuts were making hard to come by.

Rather than trying to take any credit for it, Marcus simply said, "I'm the luckiest bastard on the planet." He nodded his head in Jackie's direction, way up at the front of the group, clearly in awe of every little thing Nicola said or did. "What about her?"

Gabe shook his head. "Just a casual thing that's run its course."

Nicola had just finished her set when the station alarm rang and dispatch rang out over the station's loudspeakers, alerting them to an apartment fire.

Gabe and the rest of the crew immediately moved to put on their turnouts and headed out, their alarms blaring to clear the busy city traffic.

"Wow, that was intense and they're not even at the fire yet," Nicola said a few minutes later when she and Marcus were standing together in a corner of the station. "I don't know how your mother deals with this so well. I feel like a basket case right now."

"This is what Gabe does. He'll be fine," Marcus reassured her.

But fifteen minutes later, after they'd said their goodbyes to the volunteers who had set up the concert and were about to get into Marcus's car to head back up to Napa Valley, another station alarm went off.

"All units responding to 1280 Conrad Street, be advised, upgrading to third alarm."

Nicola looked at Marcus with huge eyes. "That's

the fire Gabe went to. It sounds like it's gotten worse, not better."

"My brother is a hell of a firefighter," Marcus told her. "He's not the kind of guy who'd ever do something dangerous or stupid."

Only, as they stood together while the siren continued to blare and dispatch repeated the call, both of them knew there were plenty of other reasons why firefighters got hurt in the line of duty.

And all they could do was hold on to each other and hope that Gabe would be all right.

* * * * *

#1 *New York Times* Bestselling Author

ROBYN CARR

Single dad and Thunder Point's deputy sheriff "Mac" McCain has worked hard to keep everyone safe and happy. Now he's found his own happiness with Gina James. The longtime friends have always shared the challenges and rewards of raising their adolescent daughters. With an unexpected romance growing between them, they're feeling like love-struck teenagers themselves.

But just when things are really taking off, their lives are suddenly thrown into chaos. When Mac's long-lost—and not missed—ex-wife shows up in town, drama takes on a whole new meaning. They're wondering if their new feelings for each other can withstand the pressure…but they are not going down without a fight.

Available wherever books are sold.

Be sure to connect with us at:

Harlequin.com/Newsletters

Facebook.com/HarlequinBooks

Twitter.com/HarlequinBooks

MRC1452R

New York Times bestselling author

BELLA ANDRE

introduces the third novel in her eight-book series The Sullivans!

How much is worth risking?

Gabe Sullivan risks his life every day as a firefighter in San Francisco, but he knows better than to risk giving his heart again. Especially not to the woman he saved from a deadly apartment fire…and can't stop thinking about.

On sale July 30 wherever books are sold!

Be sure to connect with us at:

Harlequin.com/Newsletters

Facebook.com/HarlequinBooks

Twitter.com/HarlequinBooks

MBA1558

#1 *New York Times* Bestselling Author

SUSAN WIGGS

Tess Delaney's history is filled with gaps: a father she never met and a mother who spent more time traveling than with her daughter. So Tess is shocked when she discovers the grandfather she never knew is in a coma. And that she has been named in his will to inherit half of Bella Vista, a hundred-acre apple orchard in the magical Sonoma town called Archangel.

The rest is willed to Isabel Johansen. A half sister she's never heard of.

Against the rich landscape of Bella Vista, Tess begins to discover a world filled with the simple pleasures of food and family, of the warm earth beneath her bare feet. A world where family comes first and the roots of history run deep.

Available wherever books are sold.

MSW1493R

REQUEST YOUR FREE BOOKS!

2 FREE NOVELS FROM THE ROMANCE COLLECTION PLUS 2 FREE GIFTS!

YES! Please send me 2 FREE novels from the Romance Collection and my 2 FREE gifts (gifts are worth about $10). After receiving them, if I don't wish to receive any more books, I can return the shipping statement marked "cancel." If I don't cancel, I will receive 4 brand-new novels every month and be billed just $6.24 per book in the U.S. or $6.74 per book in Canada. That's a savings of at least 22% off the cover price. It's quite a bargain! Shipping and handling is just 50¢ per book in the U.S. and 75¢ per book in Canada.* I understand that accepting the 2 free books and gifts places me under no obligation to buy anything. I can always return a shipment and cancel at any time. Even if I never buy another book, the two free books and gifts are mine to keep forever.

194/394 MDN F4XY

Name (PLEASE PRINT)

Address Apt. #

City State/Prov. Zip/Postal Code

Signature (if under 18, a parent or guardian must sign)

Mail to the **Harlequin® Reader Service:**
IN U.S.A.: P.O. Box 1867, Buffalo, NY 14240-1867
IN CANADA: P.O. Box 609, Fort Erie, Ontario L2A 5X3

Want to try two free books from another line?
Call 1-800-873-8635 or visit www.ReaderService.com.

* Terms and prices subject to change without notice. Prices do not include applicable taxes. Sales tax applicable in N.Y. Canadian residents will be charged applicable taxes. Offer not valid in Quebec. This offer is limited to one order per household. Not valid for current subscribers to the Romance Collection or the Romance/Suspense Collection. All orders subject to credit approval. Credit or debit balances in a customer's account(s) may be offset by any other outstanding balance owed by or to the customer. Please allow 4 to 6 weeks for delivery. Offer available while quantities last.

Your Privacy—The Harlequin® Reader Service is committed to protecting your privacy. Our Privacy Policy is available online at www.ReaderService.com or upon request from the Harlequin Reader Service.

We make a portion of our mailing list available to reputable third parties that offer products we believe may interest you. If you prefer that we not exchange your name with third parties, or if you wish to clarify or modify your communication preferences, please visit us at www.ReaderService.com/consumerschoice or write to us at Harlequin Reader Service Preference Service, P.O. Box 9062, Buffalo, NY 14269. Include your complete name and address.

ROM13R

$7.99 U.S./$9.99 CAN.

Limited time offer!

$1.00 OFF

From
New York Times bestselling author

BELLA ANDRE

comes the third book in her Sullivan series,
CAN'T HELP FALLING IN LOVE

Readers are introduced to Gabe Sullivan, a firefighter who risks his life every day. But when it comes to his heart, he knows better than to take that risk again...until he meets Megan Harris.

Available July 30, 2013, wherever books are sold!

www.Harlequin.com

$1.00 OFF **the purchase price of *CAN'T HELP FALLING IN LOVE* by Bella Andre**

Offer expires August 12, 2013.
Redeemable at participating retail outlets. Limit one coupon per purchase.
Valid in the U.S.A. and Canada only.

Canadian Retailers: Harlequin Enterprises Limited will pay the face value of this coupon plus 10.25¢ if submitted by customer for this product only. Any other use constitutes fraud. Coupon is nonassignable. Void if taxed, prohibited or restricted by law. Consumer must pay any government taxes. Void if copied. Nielsen Clearing House ("NCH") customers submit coupons and proof of sales to Harlequin Enterprises Limited, P.O. Box 3000, Saint John, NB E2L 4L3, Canada. Non-NCH retailer—for reimbursement submit coupons and proof of sales directly to Harlequin Enterprises Limited, Retail Marketing Department, 225 Duncan Mill Rd., Don Mills, Ontario M3B 3K9, Canada.

U.S. Retailers: Harlequin Enterprises Limited will pay the face value of this coupon plus 8¢ if submitted by customer for this product only. Any other use constitutes fraud. Coupon is nonassignable. Void if taxed, prohibited or restricted by law. Consumer must pay any government taxes. Void if copied. For reimbursement submit coupons and proof of sales directly to Harlequin Enterprises Limited, P.O. Box 880478, El Paso, TX 88588-0478, U.S.A. Cash value 1/100 cents.

® and TM are trademarks owned and used by the trademark owner and/or its licensee.

© 2013 Harlequin Enterprises Limited

MBA0713CPN